Rebel Alliances

Chris Reher

Chris Reher

Also by Chris Reher

The Catalyst

Only Human

Rebel Alliances

The Gods of Chenoweth

ACKNOWLEDGMENTS

Thank You to Malory Moutinho, Tracy Leach
and Bev Wiseman
Also to Donal, the loquacious Brit

Chris Reher

ONE

Approaching the clearing silently had not been especially difficult. No sentries in sight, no surveillance devices detectable by her data sleeve, no heat seekers randomly zigzagging among the towering vegetation.

Still, Captain Nova Whiteside moved cautiously, her physical senses as alert as those of her mechanical aides. She skirted the clearing where at least ten or twelve heavily armed people, most of them dressed in sweat-stained fatigues, guarded a small group of captives. The prisoners sat on the ground, arms bound behind their backs, unresponsive to their guards. There was a sullen silence about them and no one bothered to speak with them to change that.

Nova glanced at the forest duff beneath her feet, avoiding anything that would rustle or snap under her boots. The planet's light gravity was deceptive and she took no chances. Taking her time, she reached down to check the setting of her gun by touch.

She watched two men and a woman, all of them Human, group nearby to discuss something but could make out no more than a low murmur. A Centauri joined them to show them something on the data unit in his hands and then point at some of the captives. Whatever he had to say didn't seem terribly important and so her eyes shifted to one of the armed men sitting nearby on a supply crate.

It was him. She exhaled slowly to calm the urge to burst from the tangled foliage. His gun leaned on the box beside him and she knew well that his reflexes were honed by years of field experience. He had removed his jacket; she watched him pour water onto a bandanna and lift his thick blue braid to wipe the back of his neck. She wished for some of that; the day was dangerously hot even here in the dense shade. Her tough combat trousers worked against any relief she had found by stripping down to her sleeveless grey undershirt.

The habitable planets of this binary system were either covered in desert or in jungle so densely populated by leeches and reptiles and other things that slithered, bit or sucked blood that most interplanetary visitors declined to settle here. It was precisely the reason it made Phi Six a perfect location for a rebel outpost.

The Delphian picked up his gun and came to his feet, unfolding himself to an impressive height common among the males of his species. She saw his sharp profile when he turned to call something to his compatriots. When he walked to the edge of the clearing she withdrew deeper into the undergrowth to follow him at a safe distance.

He moved slowly, his posture telling her that he, too, was alert to what may lurk in the jungle, whether some native predator or an enemy. Trees were not to be found on this planet but the towering ferns and broadleaf plants closed over their heads much like the forests of Delphi or Feyd or Magra, blocking sunlight and trapping humid air. She kept to the shadows until he reached an abandoned shelter, doorless, its roof sagging and smothered in thick growth. He did a perimeter check and then surveyed the inside of the building.

Nova crept noiselessly to the side of the hovel. She peered around it to see him crouched, examining something on the ground by the door. She grinned and stepped into the open, her gun ready.

At this precise moment the Delphian flung himself up and forward, catching her in midriff to throw both of them across the open space in front of the cottage. The planet's low gravity hurled them a considerable distance before they landed and she grunted when her breath was knocked out of her. A rock or root or something dug painfully into her back. The blue-haired giant quickly straddled her waist and pinned her arms with his knees.

"Today's lesson: Humans think if they can't be seen or heard they're invisible," he said. He yanked the gun from her hand and tossed it aside. The camouflage wrap around her hair had come loose and he pulled it away, spilling the long red strands around her. He twisted it in his hands as if to fashion it into a rope or gag.

She looked up at him, struggling to catch her breath. "Today's second lesson: Delphians expect a clean fight."

He yelped when the ring on her finger made contact with his thigh and a bolt of pain radiated through his body. When he flung himself away from her she followed quickly, soon reversing their position to sit astride him.

Tychon, Air Command Major and commander of Vanguard Seven, was half-laughing and half-groaning as he waited for the pain to subside. "Definitely not fair, Nova!" he protested. "I can't believe you did that."

"Glad I can still surprise you," she said, shaking her hand which had gone numb. The device was imperfect and she had paid the price for using it.

His smile slowly faded. "Come here," he said and tugged on a loose strand of her hair. She leaned down and let him draw her into his arms to kiss her gently. "I've missed you."

She stretched out on his long body. "A few weeks in the field and missed me already?"

He kissed her again, less gently, and rolled her onto her back.

"How about we go in there and I show you how much I missed you, Major," she said with a glance at the dilapidated hovel.

"How about we get back to the others and help process those rebels, Captain. Are you here on your own or did you come with the pickup team?"

"Borrowed a cruiser. Colonel Everett wants us back on Targon on the double, so I volunteered to pick you up. Isn't that sweet of me?"

"Hmm, do we have time to stop on Delphi? I haven't seen Cyann in so long."

"Oh, that's just fine! You don't have ten minutes to fool around, but you can't wait to run home to your daughter."

"Ten minutes!" he said in mock outrage. "I'll show you 'ten minutes' when we get on that ship."

She let her fingers wander to his thigh. "It's a long flight..."

Both of them looked up when someone's feet appeared beside them. Major Bowie Haddad, Commander of Vanguard Two, his fists propped on broad hips, stood looking down at them.

"Captain Whiteside. I was wondering why your cruiser came down without a pilot in sight."

Nova grinned up at him. "Hey, Bowie."

"That's Major to you, Imp." Haddad watched them extricate themselves and come to their feet. He now had to crane his neck to look up at the Delphian. "I have a certain admiration for the way you manage your subordinate officers, Ty."

Tychon pulled a leaf out of Nova's tangled hair. "Not my subordinate right now," he said. "I'm between assignments. I think I'll rest and relax on Delphi for a while. Tracking these rebels has been a chore. You can take them from here."

Haddad nodded. "Casualties?"

"None for us. A couple of Feydans escaped last night, though. They jumped the gate to Pelion before we caught up. Not worth the coolant to follow them out there. We found an interesting communications hub. Want to see it?"

"Please." Haddad turned to Nova. "Help get the detainees out to the pickup point, Whiteside. The shuttles should be there any moment."

She nodded and bent to pick up her gun and did not

resist an urge to throw a salacious glance at Tychon before the men walked away. He pretended not to notice.

* * *

When Nova returned to the clearing where the others waited she found that several more rebels had been rounded up and made to sit on the ground with the others. They huddled uncomfortably, their eyes on the heavy boots of the Union soldiers walking far too close to them. Occasionally, one of the guards prodded a prisoner with his gun.

"Is that necessary?" Nova said to the Lieutenant.

"She called me a Rhuwac's uncle."

Nova did not mention that he was translating the word incorrectly. It probably would not help the rebel if he knew what she had really said. "Leave them be. They have enough problems. Get some water. It's a million degrees here."

He saluted with a striking lack of military crispness and wandered off to follow her order.

Nova looked over the detainees. Centauri, mostly, judging by their glossy black hair and violet eyes. Some Humans among them and three or four of the red-skinned, white-haired Bellacs. A usual assortment captured in raids like these. She walked away to find shade when one of the rebels caught her eye.

"Gods!" she breathed and hurried over to a woman sitting a little apart from the others. Smaller than most Bellac females, she seemed weakened by the weather and whatever rough treatment she had suffered at the hands of the Union's Air Command soldiers. A rash of scratches marked her forehead and cheek and her multiple white braids were a tangled mess. "Medic," Nova called over her shoulder.

"Hello, Nova," the Bellac said with a crooked smile.

Nova looked around and crouched down beside her. "Shh, Acie. Careful."

"Sorry," the woman whispered loudly.

Nova reached up to take a damp cloth and disinfectant from the medic along with a bag of water and waved him away. "I've got this." She considered the other soldiers nearby. Without the two Majors in sight, some of them were bound to take out their boredom on the captives. "Get those people over there down to the shuttle. Yoshida, you will see to it that they'll have not so much as an extra scratch before they get there." She noticed two particularly large Centauri prisoners that looked like they might not be as cowed by Air Command presence here as their compatriots. "Unless they ask for it," she said loud enough for them to hear. "Are we all clear on that, Lieutenant?"

"Yes, Captain."

Nova turned back to the Bellac to dab at the scratches on her skin. "What are you doing out here?" she whispered when the surly captives had been pulled to their feet and moved out of earshot.

Acie took a few deep gulps from the water bag that Nova held to her lips. "Wasn't really my idea. I thought we were going to Feron to pick up some acids. They're always selling us the wrong crap so it's just easier if I can test it there. But we ended up here. And then your boyfriend came down on us. Blew my lab to bits, too. Not that it was much of a lab."

Nova sighed. "Well, that's his job." She smiled and then looked around again to make sure no one had seen. "How did you know he was mine?"

"You two aren't exactly a big secret in my circles." Acie grinned, flashing white teeth contrasting prettily with her deep red skin. "He's a handsome Delphi, I have to say. What shoulders! Those eyes could cut glass. No wonder you fell for him. And you had a baby! How is that even possible! I'm a scientist and as sure as I'm sitting here know that you can't interbreed Humans and Delphians."

"This isn't really the time to discuss biology!" It was not the first time that Nova was stumped by the peculiar wanderings of Acie's otherwise brilliant mind.

"Well, if you'd visit once in a while I wouldn't have to be dying of curiosity, if not of dehydration. We haven't seen you since you were on leave from Ud Mrak. Years ago!"

Nova gestured for her to take another drink. "You know I can't just visit, Acie. Too many eyes on me."

"I guess so. So how did you do it? Were those your gametes?"

"Yeah, she's ours. I... hmm... it's kind of a long story. Some cellular modification that we don't really understand. Between the doctors on Targon and the Shantirs on Delphi, everyone's been shaking their heads for three years over this." She smiled. "Doesn't matter. Cyann is a pretty little thing. You should see her. Blue hair, like Ty, blue blue eyes like all Delphians. And so smart!"

"And so you called her Cyann. That's so cute!"

"Well, for now. Delphians change their names by the week. No doubt her clan will want a proper Delphian name for her at some point. She's growing up so fast."

"And yet you're out here, beating up rebels. How can you stand to be away from her?" Acie looked up at two soldiers walking past them. "Where are they taking us?"

"Zera, for now, and then to Targon," Nova said, naming the Union's primary military base in the Trans-Targon sector.

"Can't you get me out of this?" Acie said. Her expression changed to one of dread as if she only now realized her predicament. "I wasn't even meant to be here."

"You know I can't."

"I'm scared, Nova. I've been arrested before. They're not... pleasant."

"No one will hurt you," Nova said.

"Could you send a message to Vincent? Let him know what happened? He knows how to find Seth."

Nova sat back on her heels when Acie mentioned that name. "Seth..."

"You've not heard from him?"

"Not in years! Saw a report a while ago that tied him to some smuggling thing off Pelion. Do you think he can cut you loose?"

"Don't know. Can you contact Vincent? Please? He's still on Magra. The temple at Naos."

"I know the place. I'll try to send a message. Can you hang in there until then?"

Acie nodded with pinched lips in some attempt to look brave. Nova wished she could hug the tiny woman or offer some assurance that everything would be all right. She could not. Instead, she grasped her arms to pull her to her feet. "Take her," she said and shoved Acie toward one of the female soldiers. "She's not well. Let's not make her worse."

Nova watched as the little Bellac was led away, worried. Quickly, she organized the remainder of the raiding party to gather up equipment and prisoners for the short march to the waiting shuttles. Majors Haddad and Tychon had still not rejoined the group by the time the planes were loaded and ready for takeoff. She cleared the launch, leaving only her own small cruiser and Haddad's Eagle class ship on the ground. She waved to Haddad's two crew members, Vanguard officers like herself, and boarded her plane.

Once inside, she crossed the austere main cabin and dropped into a chair by the communications console adjoining the cramped cockpit. She waited impatiently, keeping her eyes on the external view of the ship, until the relay at a nearby jumpsite was ready to receive her recording. It was audio only. She felt a small stab of anticipation when she thought about the new innovations in the works for these communications. Today, she had to record and encode her message, send it to a relay at the nearest jumpsite where it would be transported through a sub-space breach to arrive at another relay near its final destination. From there, finally, it would be forwarded to Vincent on Magra Torley, never faster than the speed of light. But soon, if things went as planned, new technology would allow for real time two-way connections across vast tracts of their galaxy. It was something to look forward to.

"Hello, Vincent," she recorded. "I don't have much time. Acie has gotten herself into a bit of a tight spot. She's been caught up in a raid on Phi Six and is being transferred to our base on Zera. Don't worry, she's okay for now. Maybe you can call our friend Sethran and see if he can help her. I hope you're doing well, Vincent. Nova out."

Just as Nova entered the destination of her packet to the temple on Magra Torley she heard a tone announcing someone waiting at the ship's main hatch. She sent the message on its way to the relay and hurried to the door to admit Tychon.

He ducked into the small air lock chamber and then followed her into the main cabin. "Thanks for getting the crew off the ground," he said. "Bowie was happy to get out of this heat."

She took his guns and jacket and dropped them to the floor. He had gotten used to her less-than Delphian sense of neatness and said nothing when his utility belt met the same fate.

"So what does Colonel Everett want?" he said.

"Shh," Nova replied. She pushed his shirt off his shoulders and brushed her hands over the smooth expanse of his chest. "I haven't seen you in weeks. Must you talk so much when I'm trying to undress you?"

He hummed with pleasure when her fingers moved through the thin ridge of blue hair growing along his spine to the middle of his back. Even after these years together she was still struck by the warmth of his cold blue eyes when he smiled at her and the heat she felt when his pale lips touched her throat.

His thumb brushed over her cheek and teasingly touched the small metal device embedded at her temple. She, being Human, lacked the Delphian ability to naturally join him in the *khamal*, one of many mental states unique to his people. But they had found the means to connect through the mechanical interface that all pilots used to operate their planes. He only had to touch her neural node to initiate the *khamal shoi*, an ancient way for Delphians, who preferred to outwardly appear reserved and aloof, to share sensations and emotions that made their lovemaking an endlessly astonishing and nearly addictive experience.

She pressed closer to him, ready with a few well-placed touches of her own to break his maddening patience and excite him to begin the mental link she craved.

The perimeter alarm in the cockpit sounded stridently, startling both of them. Nova cursed silently and pulled out of his embrace only after a playful tug on his lower lip with her teeth. He followed her into the cockpit where she dropped into the pilot's bench to activate the screens. "Five bogeys," she said. "Coming from the south."

He sat in the other chair and lowered its crash guard. "Not bogeys. Shrills. Damn, I thought we'd taken them all out. Let's get off the ground."

Nova also secured herself into her bench. She reached for the pilot's headset to connect the neural interface at her temples to the ship's main processors. The control board in front of them lit up to confirm the link to her brain. She ran a rapid systems check and hovered the cruiser off the ground and into the air so that she could engage the shielding. "This is no Eagle," she muttered when she felt a slight delay between her mental commands and the ship's response. "What guns do we have?"

He was busy loading a selection of armament. "Nothing but standard issue." He reached for an interface that also included a visor.

"You want to drive?" she said, knowing that he was the better pilot just as her feel for the outboard arsenal was more refined than his.

"You're not scared of five little Shrills, are you?"

"Hell, no." Nova punched the ship upward, slamming both of them into their pilot couches, and swooped around to head toward the approaching rebel fighter planes. The higher altitude would give them a little more room to maneuver around the more agile Shrills. It would also make it easier for the rebel planes to surround the cruiser.

Tychon wasted no time once the enemy wing came into range. Using the ship's laser weapons, he picked off the fighter in the center. It tumbled wildly and exploded as they passed over it, scattering debris into the cruiser's path. The other fighters broke left and right and screamed past their ship while peppering its shields with solid projectiles. Nova executed an overhead loop to come around again, taking a wide approach to keep the planes to one side. Tychon continued his barrage, rapidly calculating the beams' trajectory with the aid of the ship's processors tapped into his brain. The aim was precise and another Shrill spun out of control toward the ground.

A concentrated volley impacted the cruiser's aft shield. "That one's coming down!" Nova said.

"Keep to port, Whiteside," Tychon said without inflection. By the tone of his calm voice Nova knew that he had dropped into a deeper level of awareness, another khamal, which allowed him to block most external distractions. "Shrill at six."

"I see it," she said, her eyes closed as she focused on the ship's sensors. She executed the defensive maneuver and avoided the enemy's missile lock by a hair. The Eagle class ship that they normally piloted would handle this engagement far more efficiently and it took all of her concentration to succeed. Tychon lobbed a missile at the fighter behind them and destroyed it.

"Beautiful, Captain," he said. "The other two are bugging out."

"Follow?"

"No," he decided. "Let's get out of here. We did not detect that hardware during our last sweep. Perhaps they landed more. I'm not interested in an all-out battle in this tin box with only Vanguard Two still in range."

She nodded and calculated an escape from the planet's atmosphere for the cruiser. "We'll make a dash for the jumpsite to Feyd in case they send anyone after us. It's heavily guarded. We can take the jump to Targon from there."

"Good idea, although I doubt they'll bother. None of the rebels we caught are terribly important. The only useful thing we accomplished here is to take out a really rather sophisticated relay." He paused while directing the ship to request a communication packet for his report to HQ. "You know, if you'd taken the Eagle instead of this boat we could keyhole directly home instead of crawling around in real space to the jumpsite."

She blinked in wide-eyed and entirely counterfeit surprise. "What? You mean this fine ship doesn't have the guts to make it through a keyhole? And that I could have traded a shortcut home for the pleasure of having you exhausted for hours afterward? Dear me! Why didn't I think of that? Now we're stuck with each other for days! What will we do with all that time!"

He laughed. "Set a course for Feyd, then, Captain."

They soon broke away from the planet and headed out into space, toward the jumpsite. Their ship would get them there within a few hours. After the leap through that open site toward the safer parts of Trans-Targon, a leisurely two-day cruise through normal space would see them home. Like Tychon had suggested, using a higher-quality ship like the Eagle would have allowed them to slip through sub-space directly to Delphi air space. But it was expensive and took its toll on the machines as much as the expert navigator required for the maneuver. And so, using an already-expanded, stable and mapped jumpsite like any of the regular commercial flights was still the most economical way to move between sub-sectors.

Nova programmed the auto-pilot while listening to his report, more focused on the gentle tones of his voice than anything he had to say to their Commanding Officer on Targon. Unlike most of his kinsmen, he had spent decades in the military among other species and his words were unaccented.

Still using her interface with the ship's processors, she moved her mental focus to give him a playful, wordless nudge. He responded with a smile but sent no reply. Exchanging words and images telepathically was possible between them but, because she was Human, left him tired and with a headache and so they used it only in times of need.

Humans lacked the Delphians' mild telepathic talents yet, over time, some palpable connection had grown between them that transcended their dependence on mechanical means. It was probably what had allowed him to detect her presence in that jungle even when she was tracking him faultlessly. Nova suspected that the transformation she had undergone three years ago had something to do with that.

She started to ask him about that but then thought better of it. The subject of his son and the events leading up to that terrible day above Shaddallam, while not taboo, often put him into a somber mood from which he was not easily lifted.

And a somber mood was not what she needed from him just then. She waited for him to complete his report and send it on its way. It would arrive at the jumpsite's unmanned relays long before they did. "You'll be on Delphi for a while, then?" she asked. Assured that no one had followed them from the planet, she engaged the auto-pilot and disconnected her interface with the ship. He did the same and lifted his seat restraints.

"Something tells me that Colonel Everett is going to make it a short stay."

"Well," she said slowly. "Yes."

He sat up and put his feet on the floor. "Let's hear it, Whiteside."

She took a deep breath and spoke quickly. "I got approved for the Azon Neural Interface and he wants us both on the test projects before Air Command goes ahead with the contract. Deep space."

As she had feared, the bright blue of his eyes deepened and his brows drew together in disapproval. "I thought you didn't make the cut."

"I didn't. But I'm the only Human with first-hand experience of the Delphian khamal. I guess I'm a sort of baseline. So they want me, after all."

"And you said yes." He lifted a hand to touch the triangular module on his temple. "The ANI is a pretty big leap from this current design. I thought they were going to hold off before field testing it."

"Well, they've tested it as much as they could and now want to test it through sub-space. And I don't want to train with anyone but you."

"I am the only Level Three spanner with that sort of clearance. It's still classified, isn't it?"

She searched his face anxiously, looking for any hint of what he may be thinking. But after his initial reaction he had withdrawn behind that infuriating Delphian veneer of indifference that even she, even now, could not penetrate. "Yes, it's classified," she said. "But even if it wasn't I wouldn't want anyone else."

"Because it's dangerous."

She climbed out of her couch and stood between his knees to wrap her arms around his neck. "No, because we'd be out there for weeks and I'd rather be with you than anyone else they'd come up with."

He looped his arms around her waist. "I know what you're up to, Nova. It's not that easy."

"Yes, it is," she said. He shivered when her lips brushed his ear. "See?"

"What about Cyann? We agreed not to take on that sort of assignment for a while."

Nova pulled back. "We just got attacked by five Shrills! And you're worried about jumping a simple keyhole? She's safe with your clan and with her uncle Anders. You worry too much." She bit her lip. Nagging him about his constant dread that something would harm their daughter was likely not a good strategy at this point. "Besides," she added quickly. "We'll get to take an Eagle. What do you love more than flying that ship?"

"Nova," he sighed deeply. "That's an interesting question, given that my entire field of vision is currently taken up by your very exceptional bosom. I really shouldn't expect a clean fight from you."

"We're not fighting. Are you coming with me or not?"

"When are they doing the implant?"

"Not for a couple of weeks so we can go home for a while. There will be four of us: two Humans, two Centauri. It's not cleared for Delphians yet, on account of your delicate brains." She jumped when he pinched her for that comment. "The lab is out on Dannakor but Air Command is providing security while the project is classified. I guess that means they want to be sure they're the only customer for this thing. After I've got mine we'll leave from Targon for the sub-space tests."

"Where will that be?"

"Don't know. Hopefully somewhere interesting."

He tilted his head toward the lounger in the main cabin. "How about I show you something interesting in the meantime?"

TWO

"I think she's going to look like her mother, don't you?"
Tychon smiled up at the baby balanced on his chest. She
gurgled and drooled and bounced on her diapered bottom
while he held her hands.

"She's but an infant," the K'lar nanny said in very
acceptable Delphi mainvoice. She lounged comfortably in a
chair drawn close to Tychon's hammock, here in a shaded
part of the carefully tended gardens, ready to catch the child
should his indulgence of Cyann's energetic wriggling turn
perilous.

But this was not the first baby he had held and he
managed to keep her both safe and entertained. "She's got
Nova's eyes, in blue," he decided. "And, thankfully, her
nose." He ran two fingers through the fine blue curls drifting
around the child's head. Almost two years old now, already
long-limbed and agile, Cyann was developing at a rate more
common to Humans than his people. Much of her
physiology was Delphian and he hoped that her mental
capacities would develop that way as well. But it was Nova's
face that smiled back at him.

"Nothing wrong with your nose," the woman said. Ever
alert, she turned toward the house when they heard some
voices from there. Although an experienced nursemaid,

preferred by both Nova and Tychon over the often reserved and strict Delphian caregivers, Pryca was, despite her comfortably padded curves, expertly trained in hand-to-hand combat and was a sure shot with several weapons. She was not the only armed guardian installed here, in the sprawling compound on Delphi used by Tychon's clan.

"I prefer Nova's." Tychon turned the child to lie down on his chest where she held a few strands of his hair in one hand and sucked the fingers of the other. "I think she's ready for her nap."

Pryca made to get up. "I'll take her inside, then."

"No, we'll stay out here. Such a beautiful day. Machi has done amazing things with the garden. I wish we could be here more."

"As does your mother, I'm certain," Pryca said with only the faintest hint of reproach. Both knew it was neither the weather nor the garden that kept Tychon out here with his child. She smiled when he kissed the top of the baby's head and closed his eyes. "It was nice to have the both of you here these past few weeks."

"Yes," Tychon said softly as to not wake the child. Nova had undergone her somewhat tedious preliminary physical and psych tests on the Union base located here on Delphi. It had given them plenty of time for their furlough, something they rarely took at the same time, before she departed for Dannakor to receive her new neural implant. "Nova loves it here. But you can't keep her out of a plane for long. She'll be back in a few days and then we're both heading into the outlands for a short mission."

Pryca knew better than to ask about the details of the assignment. "Not a dangerous one, I hope."

"Not especially," Tychon assured her automatically but something about his own words sounded false to him. Was he really sure about that? The privately-developed Azon Neural Interface was not just an upgrade for the neural appliance that he, like any other pilot, carried in his head. Like that one, the ANI allowed them to mentally direct complex machinery but, unlike the previous model, it was also designed for communication. By expanding its access to other areas of the operator's brain, the ANI exchanged brain wave information instantly with another device even through a jumpsite. This would finally make two-way communication possible regardless of distance and render the tedious exchange of relayed packets of information obsolete. Azon Corp, the developer of the new device, was banking on the military contract that was sure to come their way.

The fact that the fundamental concept of the ANI was based on the Delphian khamal used to mentally join individuals did little to convince Tychon that the mother of his child should be experimenting with it.

Two people entered the little grove behind the main house, cutting through the peace of the afternoon with loud, anxious voices. Tychon's hands tightened around Cyann.

"Ty, there's a call from the base," one of the discreetly armed guards called. "They need you there."

Tychon frowned and then realized that he had left his wrist array in the house, likely on purpose to avoid disturbances like this. He sat up and handed the baby to Pryca. "What's happened?"

"It's Anders. He's badly hurt and asking for you."

Tychon leaped from the hammock and rushed to a wall-mounted screen in an open breezeway of the clan home. His bare feet hardly registered the fine gravel of the walkway. A woman in hospital garb awaited him.

"Major Tychon," she said at once. "There has been an... incident. Base command is requesting your presence."

"Is he all right? What happened?"

"It is best if you came here immediately," the medic said with a glance over Tychon's shoulder at Pryca and the guard that had fetched them.

"I'll be there in moments." Tychon hurried into the house to change his clothes without paying much attention to what he pulled on before racing outside again to jump into one of the farm's air cars. It did, indeed, take only moments for him to skim across the open, sundrenched fields of the valley at top speed, startling a few of his neighbors when he cut across their grounds.

Located in the foothills at the opposite side of the valley, UCB Delphi was the only outside installation permitted on this planet and included the only hospital. The local population preferred the effective healing dispensed by the Shantir sect who used the power of their brains to heal injury and illness. But Anders was Human and an officer and so he had been taken to the base clinic.

Tychon barely slowed at the gates to place his hand onto the electronic sentry and had to back up again to give it enough time to scan his eyes before he sped directly to the small hospital wing.

He practically armed the attending staff out of the way when he was shown to the room where his friend waited for him. His steps faltered when he saw armed guards as well as the base commander, Colonel Jervada. "What is going on?" Something in their grim demeanor told him that this was not another accident Anders had managed on his experimental hover sled.

"Major," Jervada held up a hand to prevent Tychon from entering the treatment room. "Captain Devaughn is out of danger, but he is unconscious at the moment. Please step over here."

Frowning, Tychon followed him out of earshot of guards and hospital staff.

"I have dispatched a detail of guards to your family compound. They will be there very soon. We're also setting up a perimeter kit there and requesting clearance of all incoming traffic, whether or not they are landing on this base."

Tychon's face turned so bloodless that the slight blue cast of his skin became clearly visible. But, like all Delphians, he was able to rapidly bring his instinctive reactions under control to deal with this crisis as rationally as possible. "My family?"

"They will be safe, Major." Jervada placed a hand on Tychon's arm as if to restrain him from immediately returning to the valley. He understood that the thought of endangering yet another child in whatever misfortunes the Union's wars had visited upon Delphi was foremost on Tychon's mind even if none of that showed on his face. Few of the long-lived Delphians produced more than one or two children and their families, although small, were of greatest value to the entire population. "We have not been able to get a lot of information from Anders yet. He spoke little when he was brought here. It appears that yesterday some men came to his home and questioned him about you and your family. Since your clan holdings were not breached I'm guessing that he didn't give them your location."

"Or they don't have the means to get past our security." Tychon ran his long hands over his face and considered the possibility that, while he had lounged happily in the garden with his baby, someone may have watched and listened from the nearby hills. It was a chilling thought and he was suddenly glad that he had resisted Nova's teasing and his elders' objections to the guards roaming the compound.

"We will do everything to ensure your clan's safety. I recommend that, for the time being, you move them to the base."

Tychon shook his head. "Thank you, but they won't agree to that. Not this close to the harvest. But I might bring Cyann and her nurse here, if that is acceptable."

"Of course it is. I'll arrange quarters for them."

"How could this have happened?" Tychon said, knowing all too well how easy it would be for someone to land in another part of the planet and make their way to Anders' home undetected. The Union's treaty with Delphi allowed them only to manage traffic destined for the Air Command base. Most visitors, even commercial flights, used the base in deference to Delphi's wishes and to take advantage of an excellent maintenance facility and well-maintained runways. But anyone with a vertical descent plane choosing to land elsewhere was considered a guest on Delphi and not questioned by Air Command. Clearly the day had come, a day everyone had dreaded, when this was no longer possible.

"We are running the logs. Four planes landed off-base over the last eight days, but those thugs could have been here longer. Our agents are investigating. No one has left the planet since yesterday."

"I have to see him."

Jervada nodded. "Maybe you can talk him into coming onto the base as well. I know how much he loves his home but things are changing here."

"I'll try." Tychon went to the door of Anders' room. The two Centauri guards stared a challenge back at him but the Colonel waved them aside. Rarely in uniform, Tychon was not often recognized by off-worlders on this base. As Vanguard members, both he and Nova were stationed on Targon, directly under Colonel Everett's command.

He winced when he saw Anders in the monitoring alcove, parts of his body thickly bandaged, others exposed to devices designed to diagnose or to expedite healing. Both of his eyes were blackened, his lip was cut and a mesh bandage covered most of his short blond hair. One arm, clearly broken, was braced at his side. A medic moved an overhead diagnostic out of the way when Tychon pulled up a chair and sat close to his friend.

Anders, an army brat like Nova, had been born here on Delphi and, except for his education at various academies, had lived here all his life. He had turned into an able ambassador, accomplishing much in reconciling Delphi's traditional sensibilities with the explosive growth of the Commonwealth Union. As a source of water, valuable food products and, most importantly, highly intelligent minds, Delphi represented a priceless ally for the Union despite its isolationist leanings.

Anders' interest in xenobiology had served him well and he looked forward to dedicating more of his time to studying the many races and species that inhabited the Trans-Targon sector. Because of his long history here as well as an appealing personality that even the aloof Delphians found hard to resist, he was one of the few outsiders allowed a private home in the beautiful Chaliss'ya valley.

At age seventy-five if calculated against Human years, Tychon had known Anders for most of Anders' life. He had grown from some small and insignificant creature constantly underfoot into a trusted friend who had changed Tychon's condescending, typically Delphian views of Humans. Because of him, Tychon had learned to appreciate and value Humans for their quirks and follies as well as the emotional depths that guided them with more intuition than intellect. He suspected that Anders had opened the way for Nova in his life and he was deeply grateful.

Tychon smiled when he recalled Anders' first meeting with Nova. She had claimed a place in his heart at first sight and they had been friends ever since that day.

"So you think this is funny?" a rasping voice intruded upon his thoughts. "And why are you holding my hand?"

Tychon blinked, startled. Anders was looking at him through eyes that he was barely able to open, but they were focused and alert. "Gods, Derry," he said, his voice low. "I told you to quit getting into bar brawls."

Anders' lips twitched in a smile. No Delphian polluted their minds with spirits of any kind and a drink was hard to find on this planet. "Stop shouting, Your Blueness. My head's not doing so good right now."

"Talk to me, Brother," Tychon said. "What happened? Who were they?"

"Kinda lacking introductions." Anders rested for a few moments and Tychon waited patiently until he spoke again, his voice slurred by painkillers. "I can hear Phera now. Big Delphi bossman is going to blame us for dragging our rebel problems here. Council's going to shout about getting rid of the base. Again. This'll take weeks to blow over."

"Someone just made you over like a solstice pudding and you worry about work?"

"Well, you know me," Anders tried a grin and nearly succeeded. "Always trying to keep the xenos happy."

"You're the xeno around here, my friend," Tychon said, feeling the old joke stick like equally old bread in his throat. He felt both furious and guilty that his friend had been put in this position. Both he and Nova had enemies by the hundreds and any of them would gladly inflict this sort of damage on them. But how many of them would pursue their friends in this way? "Try to remember. What did they want? Was it a revenge attack? A warning maybe?"

Anders stared at the ceiling for a while. "No, I don't think so." He frowned. "It's a blur. Shouting. And pain."

Tychon turned to the medic hovering by a monitoring station. "Can you unblur him? If it's safe?"

"Being blurred is preferable to being in pain," the medic said, clearly unhappy that his patient was awake at all. "The Captain should be resting."

"Unblur me, nurse!" Anders said. "I need my head on straight right now."

With a look of condemnation for the senior officer in the room, the medic moved to Anders' bedside and adjusted the amount of medication he was receiving. A few minutes passed in silence until Anders winced.

"I see what you mean," he gasped. "Is that what a ruptured spleen feels like?"

"Yes, and if I see your blood pressure go up any further, you're going back under."

Anders rolled his eyes. "See how base personnel talks to me? I get no respect."

"Is anything coming back? What can you remember?" Tychon prodded.

"Three of them. Two Centauri and a really ugly Feydan. Might have been Human. Can't ever tell those apart unless they're naked." Anders swallowed hard and coughed. "Not that I see naked Feydans very often. There was a pretty one at the academy. What was her name?"

"Velara. You moaned after her for weeks after she

dumped you."

"Oh, yeah. Thanks for the reminder."

"Anders..."

"Yes, yes. Give me a moment." His hand gripped Tychon's tightly as he fought the pain and thought back to the previous night. "Kimmie had left and I was getting ready to sleep. I think I went outside to look at the stars for a while. It's so bright here with all those moons that you just don't see them so clearly very often. Such pretty stars..." He frowned. "They came around the back of the house and then we were inside and they started shouting. Pretty sure they were Shri-Lan rebels. Said something about Torley. Don't remember what."

"Shri-Lan," Tychon said thoughtfully. "Could have been to get back at us for the raid on Phi. But this is going to a whole lot of trouble over that. There is no profit in this."

Anders voice was a mere whisper when he continued. "It was about Nova!"

"Nova! What do they want with Nova?"

"I tried to hold out. But things got... fuzzy after a while." Anders grimaced, his brow furrowed as he tried to recall his ordeal. "They are looking for her. Shouting: Where is Whiteside? When did she leave? They knew she was off-planet and that you weren't with her. And they knew that I'd know where she was. Someone's been watching."

Tychon motioned to the medic to leave the room. The man began to object, perhaps ready to recite some hospital policy, but then something in the Delphian's expression seemed to convince him to obey the order.

"The ANI project?" Tychon said once the medic had left. "You think they're after the interface?"

"Yeah, I think so."

"Did you tell them where she is?"

"We'll have to assume that. So much of yesterday is just gone. I guess that's why they came after me instead of you, Delphi. Us Humans haven't figured out how to act stoic when someone beats the snot out of us."

"I'm so sorry, Anders," Tychon said. "What can I—"

Anders gripped his arm with surprising strength. "You have no time to beat yourself up, Ty. I'll shake this off soon enough. But those rebels were after Nova. You have to warn her."

"I'll send her a message and then go to Dannakor myself. As soon as I know Cyann and the others are safe. Jervada offered to keep them here on the base, just in case there is more trouble coming."

"You know as well as I do that no base in this entire Union is safe. Why is there still a guard outside my door? The only safe place on Delphi is the enclave."

Tychon grimaced. "I am not sending my child to the Shantirs. I don't want her mixed up with that lot. Ever." But he knew that Anders was not wrong. The likelihood of rebels or their sympathizers infiltrating any Air Command base was very real, no matter how tight their security processes. Again and again, rebel factions like the Shri-Lan had smuggled their people into a base or simply drew existing personnel to their causes. Even here, even on Delphi, that possibility existed, perhaps more so than in other places.

"You're being obstinate," Anders said. "Cyann will have to study with them sooner or later. You won't deny her that opportunity. They have offered their services and clearly accept her as one of you. Gods, Ty, there are people in every corner of Trans-Targon who'd give up any number of legs and arms if that would get their child a mentorship in the enclave."

"You know how I feel about Shantirs. I'm not asking them for anything."

"Well, get over it, Your Blueness." Anders grinned. He knew his friend well enough to know that he was winning the battle. "I'm going to stay there for a little while, myself. I appreciate the good doctors here but I've grown up with your healers nursing me back to health and it's still the best way to recover. So don't worry so. Her uncle Anders will be there, as will Pryca. We won't let her out of our sight. Look at it as a peace offering. A first step."

"I don't want to make peace."

"Now you're just being stubborn."

Tychon sighed. "Yes, I am. You are meddlesome, as always. And clearly in league with Nova. In this I'm up against both of you."

"Yep. Now let me sleep. We'll be fine in the enclave. You can then chase after Nova without having to worry about the baby. Or me."

Tychon went to the door to beckon to the medic waiting resentfully in the corridor. The man rushed past him to return Anders into a state where his pain was manageable and he began to drowse again.

"Take the *Scout*," Ander said, naming his research team's plane. "We won't need it until the trip to Shaddallam next month."

Tychon hesitated. "Anders..."

"Go! Find Nova. I'll be done here in no time. And I have more pretty nurses than I can grope one-handed in my drug-addled stupor." He shifted his eyes to the medic hovering nearby. "Well, not you. The girl kind, I meant."

THREE

'Interesting' was not the first thing that had come to Nova's mind when she landed on Dannakor, an inhospitable planet in the currently peaceful Mrak sub-sector. Empty of life forms beyond some very hardy lichens and with an atmosphere largely composed of methane and oxygen, the planet offered little appeal to settlers.

But with methane as a power source and gravity suitable for a domed habitat, Azon Corp had staked a claim to the planet's rich resources of rare elements used in the production of laser technology and fine electronics. Dozens of mines dug deep into its crust in search of the premium ore for local use and export.

Less known was the fact that Dannakor's scattered installations also included Azon Corp's main laboratory for research in neural sciences, pharmacology and physics that were often conducted in secret and frequently, as now, under contract by the Union's military.

Most recently, the research facility had added what was probably the shortest jumpsite in space. A nearby keyhole had been carefully mapped to create a stable jumpsite that reached no farther than Dannakor's nearest moon, allowing Azon Corp to lead research into real- and sub-space travel and communication.

Attempts had been made to create a relatively pleasant environment for Azon Corp's workforce here. The domed central hub of the neuroscience clinic allowed the milky daylight to pour over a large recreational area flanked on two sides by banks of airlocks. Secured wings for labs and residential areas reached out from the hub both above and below ground.

"So can I go home now?" Nova said four days after the surgeons had declared the installation of her new implant a success. Threading the microscopic sensors into her brain was no more complicated than implanting any of those carried by thousands of other pilots and machine operators. But this interface did not just link the operator to their machines. The ANI also used communication systems to send brainwave information to a remote recipient's processor. But unlike the tedious one-way packet traffic, the link, once established remained intact to allow for instant exchanges. Approximating the way Delphians used their mental khamal, once the link was established, distance no longer mattered.

What remained to be studied was the possibility that it could also be done via a keyhole, a microscopic, unexplored breach in space which, unlike the gateways they used to travel routinely through sub-space, lacked a stable terminus. Currently, a Level Three spanner was needed to open such a breach and anchor it temporarily to a distant exit into normal space; a talent found mostly among Delphians.

No Delphian had volunteered to risk their highly evolved minds to test the new interface, even though spanning an uncharted keyhole was an exhausting and sometimes even painful process. But their reluctance to join the experiment did not exceed their curiosity or their need to study this new technology. Nova's question was, in part, directed at the blue-haired elder standing silently nearby, observing the last of the tests. Tuain was one of the Shantirs, an ancient enclave of Delphians that served as healers, sages, and spiritual guides for their people. Their mental mastery over certain matter and energy was a source of distrust and even fear among other species and so they usually kept to themselves on Delphi. She had been surprised to see one of them here.

He was not the only observer in the room. Two of Air Command's finest grunts stood by the doors where the only thing that kept them from slouching against the wall in utter boredom was the rank on Nova's insignia. These two had shadowed her since she had received the new implant and her only moments of reprieve came when she attended to personal matters. She had spent a great deal of time in the shower lately.

"No, you can't go home yet," Doctor Unwin replied. "Let's run one more for now."

Nova sighed dramatically and slumped back in her chair. They had been doing the same thing for days. Endlessly. Sent messages to another test subject moving through the short and stable gateway at various speeds and under various conditions. Waited while the experts debated and adjusted and noted and synchronized. Sent more messages. And waited around some more.

"Are you tired? Headache? Dizzy? Anything unusual?"

"Can't you tell? You have enough sensors stuck to me everywhere. They itch." Nova glanced at the silent Shantir. He did not have to shift his blank expression very much to exude his disapproval of the insolent Human. "I'm sorry. Yes, I'm tired. Let's get this done."

Unwin scrutinized her carefully. "You be sure to let me know if anything seems amiss. This isn't like your old unit. It's actually seated in your sphenoid bone to keep the taps in place. We've got those going through natural apertures behind your eyes. It only looks smaller than your old model because more of it is below your skin now. That's a bit more convenient but it can be a drawback."

"How so?"

"It's not designed to break away during an impact like the old one. Once the bone has healed around the anchors, the housing will be part of your skull. The substrate carrying the graphene layer is more securely embedded now. In other words, someone can't just steal it from you without surgery."

"Wonderful," Nova said although she had been briefed on the module's design.

"Captain Luce," Doctor Unwin spoke into his microphone. "Begin, please."

A few moments passed while the Centauri, on a cruiser somewhere beyond the moons, activated his interface. Nova shifted her mental focus to the self-contained processor in front of her. She ran a few exercises as she normally would aboard a plane, checking systems, scanning the simulated vicinity and, just for fun, warmed up a tray for dinner. The doctor ignored the stifled snicker from one of the nearby technicians.

A display screen activated when Nova received a signal from Captain Luce. Or, more precisely, from the processor connected to him that relayed signals from the speech center of his brain. "Incoming," she confirmed.

Nova, she perceived the word in her mind. *Boring out here. Send a dirty joke.* After days of this, his initial awe and excitement over this mechanical telepathy was fading. None of it, of course, was new to Nova who often linked with Tychon without the need for complex processors to translate brain waves.

She smiled and returned a mental image of a mostly naked Rhuwac she had seen in a report somewhere.

Gross, Captain, came the reply. *How about one of you?*
You wish.

"Captain Whiteside?"

Nova opened eyes that she hadn't been aware of closing. "Here."

"We're seeing the same spikes as before. Is the contact solid?"

"Yes, no distortion. He's sending the sample paragraphs. Still has a weird mechanical feel to it. No inflection, really."

He reached up to adjust something on the scanner

suspended over her head. "Remember that you're talking through a processor. The machines, no doubt, have considerable trouble relaying your and Captain Luce's, ah, verbal idiosyncrasies."

Shit.

What?

Nothing. Testing idiosyncrasies.

Stick to the script, Luce.

"Switch languages. Try Centauri," she was instructed.

"We have been, Doctor."

He peered at his screen. "Hmm, pattern is the same. Delphian?"

My Delphian is an embarrassment compared to yours, Luce admitted, using a Feydan dialect. *How's this?*

"He doesn't speak Delphian. Using Feyd."

"Fine." The doctor and his colleagues tinkered with their equipment and conversed quietly as if Nova was no more significant than one of the rodents in their lab.

While Luce continued to talk about nothing, Nova's eyes wandered to the Shantir standing apart from the others. Like his brethren, he wore the traditional blue vest and gathered trousers preferred by the senior members of his sect. His hair was nearly black, hinting at an advanced age that his face did not. The Delphian was observing her without expression and the unblinking gaze from his blue eyes was beginning to unnerve her.

You're not in my head, are you? she tried.

What? Luce returned. *Of course I am.*

Not you. There's a Shantir starting at me. Creepy. I keep thinking he's hearing what we're saying.

Did he touch your interface?

No.

Then don't worry about it. You'd know if he was in your head, wouldn't you?

Yeah. But the Shantirs aren't exactly like your average Delphian.

Well, you'd know better than any of us. Luce sent a mental shrug but also an implied, rather lewd suggestion regarding her contact with the average Delphian.

Watch it, you.

"All right," another technician switched to a different and no less complex-looking apparatus. "One more test beyond surface communication."

"What do you mean?" Nova asked the Caspian that had spoken.

Sao Lok turned his sleek, alien face toward her. His lab coat gaped to reveal a body covered in short, dense hair much like that of the Terran horses bred on Feyd. It was richly patterned in shades ranging from blond to deep brown and so fine and dense on his face that it was barely visible. The intricate markings flanked his long nose and spread out over his forehead and elongated skull. His people disliked to wear clothes at all and did so only when among other species, as here on Dannakor. Lok had chosen a plain kilt for modesty. Nothing covered the outsized three-toed Caspian feet complete with barbaric claws. His hands, in contrast, were small, nimble and endowed with an additional thumb.

He turned off the com link to the distant cruiser so that they could not be overheard. "Try to look past Captain Luce's verbal communication to see if you can pick up anything that he's thinking."

"Isn't that kind of rude?" Nova said. Even her telepathic exchanges with Tychon did not ever exceed the boundaries of what they wished to exchange. Her thoughts were her own and neither of them ever pried beyond 'surface communication'.

"That opinion depends on whose brain you're prying into," he said dryly. "I'm sure Captain Luce doesn't mind sharing his thoughts."

Nova returned his smile. Sao Lok's presence on the project had offered welcome and surprising relief from the tedium here. She had come to know the Caspian over the past few days as their casual chats had turned into long conversations about their vastly different worlds. His wry humor was considerably broader than his colleagues' and she enjoyed the conspiracy that had sprung up between them to eke out a little fun among the tests and experiments. He knew well that she was eager to complete the work here and return home to put the new device into practice.

"But we do want to ensure that you can't do it," he added.

Nova shrugged. "I'll try."

The doctor reactivated the interface.

You there, Luce?

Talking to myself, apparently.

Nova sent a smile. *Keep talking.*

As the Captain launched into a detailed and rather inappropriate story involving his co-pilot, Nova tried to peer beyond what he was saying and into his deeper thoughts. She had to hold back a grin when she wondered what deep thoughts might hover in the back of the young officer's mind.

After a while she shook her head. "Nothing. Just words and some visual cues. Can't get past verbal communication. No abstracts, no emotion, nothing that isn't part of what he's saying and intends to send. And he's not saying anything interesting, believe me."

"Try again," Doctor Unwin said.

She did. Over again. And again. Nothing.

"Enough!" she exclaimed finally. "I'm getting nothing. And you damn well know this isn't new to me. I'm tired. And done with this."

The doctors exchanged glances, clearly offended by their test subject. But Unwin signaled to a technician to remove the sensors attached to Nova's body and to terminate the interface with the processors. Relieved, Nova slid out of her chair and retied her thick ponytail.

"Think you can beat me tonight?" she asked Sao Lok. "You're twenty points behind now."

"Surely you realize I'm letting you win, Captain," he replied without taking his yellow eyes from his displays. "Being crushed by a superior opponent would no doubt affect your performance during these trials." He looked past her to the door. "I believe Shan Tuain wants a word with you. Besides, I am going to be hours yet analyzing Captain Luce's peculiar thought processes."

She turned to see that the Delphian was, indeed, waiting by the door.

"Captain," Tuain finally spoke. "Come with me, please."

She frowned, disinclined to take orders from a civilian and a Shantir in particular but she slipped into her uniform jacket and followed him out of the lab with a quick wave back at Sao Lok. Tuain left the clinic to turn into the hall leading to the recreational area of the complex. She hurried to keep up with his long strides, as did the two guards following them.

He finally slowed when the wall to their left was replaced by a metal railing and they overlooked a pleasant, open area on the ground floor. The designers of the clinic's central hub had created an oasis within the harsh environment outside the dome using greenery and the illusion of natural materials. Real plants and fake nature sounds sought to offer a small reprieve from the metal, stone and plastic found everywhere else here.

The Shantir stopped to look down at a few people relaxing near a fountain. Others were scattered here and there with their work on portable screens.

"Are you comfortable?" Shan Tuain finally said.

"Comfortable?" Nova repeated. "Here?"

"With that device in your head."

"I've had a neural appliance for thirteen years. Of course I'm comfortable with it."

He leaned forward to prop his elbows onto the low railing and gaze down on the little park below. His long, blue-black braid slipped forward and hung over the wall. "It makes you a better pilot," he said. "And now a telepath."

"Not without a whole lot of clunky machinery."

"Unless you're linked to a Delphian."

"Look, if you want to talk about Shan Tychon, this is

probably not the right place or time."

"Shan Tychon left us a long time ago. He's barely had any contact with the Shantir enclave."

Nova turned to wave her guards out of hearing distance. "With good reason. You've caused him a lot of harm."

"So we did. And now his daughter will suffer because of his disdain for us." He continued to show her his profile, as angular and sharp as Tychon's.

Nova frowned. "What do you mean?"

"The child is only half Delphian. She will need us if she is ever going to find what, if any, Delphian mental traits she possesses. He knows this. You know this."

She gazed thoughtfully into the unceasing motion of the fountain below them. "I do. She's just a baby. It will be a long time before we can even consider an interface for her."

"She may not need one, unless she follows your example and becomes a pilot. But unless he allows her access to the enclave we will never know. She will need a mentor."

"Is this what you wanted to talk about? Our child rearing methods?"

A faint smile twitched the corner of his pale lips. "No, forgive the digression. You would be surprised how often she is discussed among us. We are merely curious about the... interbreeding."

"Which you consider an abomination."

This time he actually smiled. "We do not. We are fascinated by it. It's our Clan Council, a circle of elders that would rather not ever have to deal with outsiders, that considers her, and you, an abomination." He paused to regard her for a few moments. "No, the only abomination here is that thing in your brain."

She touched the metal node at her temple. "It bothers you that telepathy is now also possible among our species?"

"We are all the same species, Captain; call it religion if you must. We prefer to point to the science so evident in our DNA." He waved a hand in dismissal of the old argument. "No, we don't care even slightly what you do with your technology as long as it doesn't affect us. Even as you continue to use it to destroy yourselves."

"Shan Tuain, if there is something you are trying to say to me..."

"Tell me, Captain: what else is giving this upgrade such tremendous value?"

She frowned, puzzled. "Well, it will immensely improve our ability to penetrate a keyhole, of course. It's designed to enable us to communicate even through an uncharted breach, if the trials are successful. And if we can communicate for such a distance, it'll also mean that some of us will reach as far as Delphians can to complete the span. And of course once that span is complete, we can jump through it."

"Indeed. It will take you from a simple chartjumper, using other people's maps and calculations, to a fully qualified spanner. No charting required. No following the breadcrumb trails of those who went before. Just open a keyhole and slip through. To just about anywhere."

She smiled. "Yes, I hope so."

"At this time, one in tens of thousands has such ability. And almost all are Delphian. I don't have to tell you that Delphi has a very small population."

"And so...?"

"Since Delphians don't, on principle, deal with rebels, you have a clear advantage in this war. You only need a keyhole to turn an insignificant breach in space into a gateway for your fleet."

"It's what keeps us in power. We cannot continue to rely on Delphi to supply us with spanners. If you, your Clan Council, forbade it, few of your people would disobey. We must find a way of keeping our advantage if that day comes."

"And you propose that creating thousands more spanners, all with the ability to open a jumpsite from any keyhole to anywhere is a good idea? For you and, I will add, your rebel enemy. None of us have the planetary defense systems in place to prevent such unannounced visits. Do you think this technology can be contained? Restricted to a few elite pilots like yourself?"

"Surely this has occurred to the developers."

"Surely they don't care! Their heads are filled with making telepathy possible. They think jumpsites are there to ship ore and tourists from one place to another and that keyholes are of interest only to explorers and scientists. Shan Nova, no one is stopping it! Azon Corp is a private agency standing to gain a great deal of wealth by supplying this device to Air Command."

"We're years away from making this thing available. We've barely started preliminary tests. By the time this is ready for use, we'll have the means to detect breach terminals far more accurately. We will have defenses in place."

"Years? Captain, do you really think you can keep this technology to yourself?"

"Why are you telling me this?"

He turned to look down onto the commons area and toward the air lock entrances to the right. Several cruisers could be seen through the gracefully curving transparency of the dome, one of them the plane returning Captain Luce and his crew. Nova saw him enter the open space but he did not look up to where she stood with the Delphian. More cruisers lined the locks to the left side of the dome. Absently, Nova wondered if some special event had brought so many planes here today.

"Because your government will not listen," Tuain said. "They seek our help and we give it. But they don't heed our warnings. It is true that Delphi cares nothing about what happens to any of you. But a technology like this cannot be contained, no matter how much your Union ambassadors try to assure us. It will escalate your pitiful strife in ways that will no longer leave us unaffected." He thoughtfully fingered his braid before continuing. "Delphi has much to lose if your enemies came to our shores. The only thing worse than your Union with this technology is if your enemies get it first."

"So what do you want me to do?"

"Captain Anders Devaughn, Union ambassador on Delphi, is your friend. He is brother-friend to Tychon. His father is a prominent General. He knows about what's being tested here on Dannakor, does he not?"

Nova nodded. "Of course he does. He got you access to this place."

"Then seek his help in stopping this experiment before it is too late. He has done much to improve the relationship between Delphi and your Union. We trust him. And Clan Council would concede more if that's what it takes to end this madness." He smiled ruefully. "Just don't tell them I said that."

"Don't worry. The Council and I don't have much to chat about."

Tuain straightened up from his casual slouch over the railing and peered into the distance, his head cocked as if listening for something.

"What is it?"

"There is tremendous tension building among those people. I felt it earlier, but it's never easy to taste the mood of a new place. But these people are not at rest."

Nova looked down over the commons. "The uniforms? Or the civilians?"

He pointed a long finger toward the airlocks to the left without taking his hand from the railing. "Those Union soldiers there," he said, "are not Union soldiers."

"What?" She squinted into the direction he had indicated. Three uniformed men and a woman loitered by the locks, still where she had seen them only minutes ago.

"And those." He nodded toward three Centauri by the concourse leading to the base residentials.

"How do you know this?"

"You know so little of the Shantirate, Captain. I can feel them." He lifted a hand toward the people below as if testing the heat of a fire. "Many more in the airlocks right now. I feel their apprehension and their common goal. Their tension and resolve is mounting and I know we are only moments from chaos."

She scrutinized them more closely. He was right. She saw boots that were not standard issue, hands held nervously near gun belts, furtive exchanges of glances. "Rebels!" she gasped, feeling an immediate and powerful surge of adrenaline pump into her system.

"Yes. Ready to infiltrate the clinic and capture your beautiful new technology for themselves. This did not take years, Captain."

"And you said nothing?" Nova looked around for a commanding officer to raise an alarm, too aware that she was not even carrying a gun today. Who else was disguised as Air Command? She beckoned to her guards.

"I knew nothing of it until we came to this spot. But now I'm certain. You are outnumbered."

"Captain?" The two Union soldiers assigned to her had strolled over to where she stood with Tuain.

Nova looked both of them over, trying to find some hint that these two might not be what they appeared to be. "We are under attack," she said. "Raise the alarm immediately. Those planes at the lower locks are carrying rebels."

The two guards exchanged puzzled glances.

"That's an order, soldier," Nova snapped.

One of them, still looking doubtful, activated the communicator on his forearm.

"Give me a gun," she said to the other one.

"Captain, you are not allowed weapons for the duration of the project," she reminded Nova and placed her hand on her holster. "Security protocol states—"

Nova could almost feel Tuain's grim amusement and fought her urge to physically disarm the guard. "Go, inform base command immediately!" She scanned the commons for some sign that anyone else had noticed the imminent raid. Luce was near the fountain, chatting up an attractive junior officer. More uniforms entered from the left bank of locks. In fact, all five gates there were opening to admit more of the disguised rebels. She leaned over the railing. "Luce!"

A furtive movement among the foliage caught her eye and then she saw a small, white-haired woman hurrying through the trees, angling purposefully toward the Captain.

Nova grasped the railing and vaulted it, dropping some distance before landing on a narrow ledge, and from there jumped to the ground. She heard Tuain call to her but she continued to race along a cobbled path among the planters until she caught up with the Bellac.

Acie cried out in surprise when Nova grasped her arm to whip her around. "What the hell are you doing here?" Nova snapped.

"Nova! You have to get out of here! You're in terrible danger!"

"I know that. Are you here with these rebels?" Nova shook the woman, furious over being surprised and unarmed, surrounded and completely without any idea of who was who now. "Spill it!"

"No!" Acie exclaimed. "Gods, no. Well... yes. I wanted to send a message but I couldn't. So I came along to warn you. You have to leave this place! Please!"

Nova threw the little Bellac to the ground when a volley of laser fire sliced through the air over their heads. Shouts and screams reached their ears as utter confusion broke out among the people using the central hub. She dragged Acie behind the corner of a raised planter. "Get on one of those cruisers right now, Acie."

"I'm staying with you."

"No, you're not! Go. Stay low. I don't care what ship you're on, stow away if you have to."

"Nova, I have to tell you—"

"I know, I know. Tuain told me. I'll get out, don't worry. Now go!" She shoved Acie toward the airlocks and then ducked low, toward where she had seen Captain Luce. He had taken cover by one of the exits and tossed a gun to her when she sidled toward him.

"What the fuck is going on, Nova," he hissed. "Those are uniforms!"

"Yeah, let's just assume they're rebels."

"Works for me."

The laser fire abated when the attackers and perhaps the attacked retreated into the tunnels and hallways beyond the commons.

"Grab whoever you can and get into a cruiser," Nova said. "They are after the ANI so we better leave. I have no idea who's on what team so let's not waste time figuring that out." She stepped out of the doorway and waved to a small group of civilian staff huddled nearby. They obeyed, rushing toward them in a panicked scramble. "Into Lock Seven," she called to them. "Now!"

"Where are you going?" Luce said when she turned into the hallway leading under the concourse from which she had jumped.

"Gonna get the devs," she replied and rushed away.

She dodged through the corridor and up a stairway, ducking into doorways when they presented themselves, her senses alert to the uproar taking place all around. Civilians were running every which way and she waved them toward the airlocks when she could, knowing that there were not enough planes to allow them all to escape. Twice she dove for cover when laser fire cut in front of her. When she rounded the corner to the neuro-lab, she was faced with two uniformed Humans. She hesitated, unsure of their affiliation.

That was resolved when one of them fired in her direction. She ducked and returned the volley, cutting him down. The other leaped aside but not in time to avoid her aim. He, too, fell to the floor, gravely injured. Nova continued onward, leaping over the fallen men without another glance at them.

She did stop short when she found another body in the hall. She recognized the blue tunic and pantaloons before she even saw Tuain's face. She cursed and continued onward.

At last, she reached the lab and waved her wrist unit to gain access to the restricted area. "Vanguard," she announced to the empty and silent room. "Anyone here?"

"Yes, don't shoot!"

She saw Doctor Unwin and two of his technicians peer anxiously around a corner. "Get to the south airlocks at once. Avoid everyone you don't recognize. Make that everybody. Don't use the main concourse. Have you seen Lieutenants Betl or Quinn?" she added, naming the other test subjects.

"No, not since the shooting started," the technician said. She was hastily gathering some of their tablets and file boxes, dropping more than she could carry. "Are we not safer staying here?"

Nova went back to the door and peered outside. More shouts and screams in the distance. "You're not safe anywhere. Leave that stuff. Move! Now!" She herded them out of a rear door that she knew led to the service corridors behind the lab.

She turned to look around the now-deserted lab. Their attackers would make their way up to the research level within moments. Is this what they had come for? Rolling her eyes in exasperation over her own indecision, she raised her weapon and blasted the lab equipment, stopping only when it had turned into a smoldering, melting mess.

"What are you doing?" someone exclaimed behind her.

She whirled to see Sao Lok, the Caspian technician, staring in disbelief at the destroyed equipment.

"What do you think? Why are you still up here? Get down to the planes or hide somewhere."

"You can't just... Just look at this!"

"Please, you have to get out of here," she said. "If you people don't have copies of this stored elsewhere you deserve to lose the lot. Now come on, let's go!"

"Who are they?" he stammered. "What... what do they want?"

"Rebels, probably. Please, just come." She grasped his arm, but her tone was gentle. "There are some planes at the locks."

"You won't leave me?"

Despite his eyes of raptor-like intensity, his expression was so woebegone and frightened that she had to fight her impulse to hug him. She put her hand on his shoulder instead, having no idea how Caspians comforted each other. "I promise. We have to get the ANI team away from here. Hurry."

He allowed her to usher him into the service area, through the halls, and down to the airlocks on the lower level. When they reached the bottom of the ramp an explosion seemed to shake the entire dome. Who would be using explosives in an enclosed environment on a planet such as this? What could possibly be at stake here?

Nova had no intention of spending time to find out. She raced to the locks, leaving the rebels to fight the not-rebels and letting any genuine Air Command soldiers figure them out. Her only thought was on escaping with as much of the project team as possible. She reached the locks to find that two of the cruisers had left. Some bodies littered the ground but the battle had clearly shifted to the labs.

"Get into Six," she shouted at a small huddle of survivors. "Go, go, go!"

"Nova! Hold up."

She turned to see Lieutenant Quinn run toward her, dragging her leg. Nova waved anxiously while the woman crossed an open area and cried out in dismay when the deadly beam of an overhead weapon cut through Quinn's chest, pitching the woman forward in mid-stride. Nova flung herself into the cover of a rock sculpture, remembering too late that they were made of synthetics. She ducked, waiting for another shot. None came.

She peered around the sculpture to the causeway above, seeing none of the attackers there now. Quickly, she rolled over to Lieutenant Quinn.

"They took Betl," the woman moaned. She waved a bloodied hand to the locks on the opposite side of the dome. "Dragged him into Gate Two."

Nova grasped her hand. "Can you move? Leesa, can

you..." She ground her teeth audibly when the Lieutenant's body convulsed briefly and then slumped, dead. Another beam passed overhead to scorch one of the planters; someone had spotted her among the greenery. Nova felt for a stylus in one of her pockets and withdrew the small laser tool. Still gritting her teeth, she sliced the skin at the woman's temple, cutting deep. "Graphene layer," she whispered. "What the hell does that look like?" She severed the ANI module close to the bone; the implant was still new and it came away from the anchors fairly easily. She lowered her head for a moment, instructing herself not to throw up. Someone yelled something near the tunnel to the residentials and now the firefight returned to this area. Cursing, Nova turned Quinn's head and used her gun to destroy the other interface before she scrambled to her feet and scuttled into the shelter of the air locks behind her.

Two or three of the civilians were cowering by the gates and Nova hustled them inside, barely waiting for them to clear the airlock before pressurizing. These ships were meant for very small crews and now there were too many people aboard to make any sort of long trip possible. Her only hope was to reach one of the carriers orbiting the planet. "Sit down. On the floor if you have to," she shouted and leaped into the cockpit. "Are there any pilots here?"

She received no answer from any of the stunned escapees staring at her in utter incomprehension of what had happened here.

"Of course not," she muttered and added a few favorite curses. "Sit down I said!" She dropped the pogs that held the ship to the locks and hovered the cruiser away from the dome. Expecting that she would also soon need to engage the ship's guns, she reached for the headset to interface with the processors rather than attempt to fly away from Dannakor manually. Waiting no longer for her passengers to find the floor, she shot away from the installation and into the sky.

She used the ship's sensors to scan the area for other

planes. There were two cruisers nearby, heading into different directions, and two larger ships in orbit. She set a course for the nearest, hoping that some of the others would also make it there. A few frightened screams rose from among the people behind her when she broke through Dannakor's atmosphere. But the ship's gravitational systems did their job and they were not alarmed any more than they already were.

Someone came forward and took the co-pilot's seat next to Nova. She glanced over to see a young Delphian, likely not much older than thirty. His long blue hair hung loose over his shoulders and the clothes he wore were a stylish set of tights and long vest favored on Magra. Although he had attained the long-limbed grace common among Delphian males, it would likely be a few more years before he filled out his lanky frame. He regarded her curiously and in silence.

"Were you with Tuain?" she said to him, her mind on the still-distant carrier.

"He is my mentor," he replied.

"That's not what I asked and you know it, kid."

"That's all I'm saying." He looked over the maze of indicators, screens and control panels that surrounded them, none touched by anything but her mind.

"Don't try my patience. I haven't got much of it left."

"Then Shan Tychon did not train you very well."

She turned to study him. His expression was guarded by his Delphian training as much as his attempt to ignore the blood that stained her hands. "You know who I am?"

He nodded. "My name is Jovan."

"Shantir?"

"Initiate. I have a few years to go."

"Shan Tuain is dead," she said. "I found him near the labs. I'm sorry."

He blanched and she heard a sharp intake of breath before his expression returned to its well-honed indifference. "He knew the risk of coming out here," he said.

"A lot of others are dead, too. He knew something was

about to happen but decided not to warn me. Sometimes your Shantir vows of non-interference are pretty hard to come to grips with."

"Perhaps we can no longer hold on to that." He turned in his seat to observe the frightened people in the rear of the cabin. "Perhaps we need to take sides."

She nodded. He was not the first among Delphi's young people to begin to question the traditional ways of their elders. It was a fairly recent trend greeted with much relief by Union administrators and with dismay by Delphi's Clan Council. "Well, let's hope it's our side." She looked up and shouted over her shoulder. "We are about to lock onto a Union carrier. Expect a little bump." She activated the com after checking the carrier's signal. "*Terius*, come in. Union pilot requesting permission to dock. Priority One." Nova figured that a hold full of people without enough air to go anywhere else constituted a Priority One emergency.

"Been expecting you," came the tense reply. "Lock on Three."

She swung around the freighter to find the unclaimed port. There were bays for five liftplane-sized ships and two had already landed. She nudged the cruiser into its berth and then felt the docking clamps grasp the ship securely.

"We're here," she said when she made her way through the cruiser's cabin, stepping around the people huddled on the floor. She was relieved to see Sao Lok among them. "We hope you enjoyed the flight, please be sure to gather all personal possessions before deplaning."

"This is no time for levity," a Human civilian snapped at her as she passed. "People died here today. You air jockeys might find that commonplace but we do not."

She observed him for a moment, knowing his outrage was well justified. "Are you injured?"

"No."

"Then get up and assist these other people. On the double."

He huffed angrily before turning to help a woman beside

him get to her feet.

"You have a way with civilians," Jovan said sardonically as he passed her in the air lock to help with the door.

They dropped the gate and stepped onto the platform beyond. There were other people there, rushing about, talking excitedly, bleeding quietly, dressed in a variety of uniforms and civilian clothes.

"Captain!"

She turned to see Luce hurry toward her.

"Thank Cazun you made it," the Centauri exclaimed. "What a mess! Who would have expected a rebel attack way out here?"

"Who indeed," she muttered with a glance at Jovan. The Delphian shrugged and wandered away. "Is this all that got away from the clinic?"

"There are more cruisers heading this way but they are not Union flagged. We'll have to assume rebels aboard."

"Are there any officers here?" she asked.

"Looks like you and I are it. I haven't even seen any crew except for some deck hands. Let's get up to the bridge."

She nodded and followed him as he turned into the main corridor leading into the ship's interior. It appeared that the *Terius* was little more than a supply carrier for this outpost. Hopefully, she thought, with enough supplies aboard for them all.

Luce stumbled and nearly fell when the entire ship shuddered under what felt disconcertingly like a missile impact. "Guess now we know who's on those planes," he said when another hit rocked the ship.

They sped up, knowing that, although ships like the *Terius* were heavily shielded to thwart pirates, it would not long stand a continued barrage. Its layout was a universal design for vessels of this class and they soon found the entrance to the bridge. Before Nova was able to request access, the door slid aside.

"Officer on the bridge," someone called.

Nova and Luce looked around, stunned. Only three crew

members were on the bridge, a breach of protocol in a crisis situation.

"Where is the captain?" Nova asked a Centauri woman sitting at the helm.

"Isn't she with you? She went down to the planet early today."

"Damn!" Luce looked over the controls. "Get us out of here. You're not even ready to break orbit. Get busy!"

"I... I tried. I'm a shuttle pilot. I can't even begin to figure this monster out!"

Luce waved her aside and took the helm.

"How about tactical?" Nova looked at the other two. "Does anyone here know how to fire a damn gun?"

"I'm communications," the Human crew member said. He pointed at his colleague. "That's the quartermaster."

Nova stepped up to the tactical station to look over the ship's limited armament. "I see Azon's on a tight budget. There's nothing useful here." She engaged her neural link and saw Luce do the same at the helm. "Give the others a heads up," she said to the com officer.

He leaped to his station and picked up his earpiece. "All decks, prepare for departure." He cringed when something thumped against their hull. "And for impact."

Nova muttered to herself when she scanned the area. Two cruisers were buzzing around them, looking for opportune spots along the *Terius* that might be less heavily shielded. A third, larger ship was arriving at high speed. She took a few shots at the cruisers, having little more firepower than what it took to keep them at a distance.

Luce finally had the ship ready to leave orbit. He punched it up to its top capacity and shot away from the cruisers that immediately set to pursue them. Both Nova and Luce realized that the rebel ships would not be outrun by a cargo vessel never meant for such race.

She turned to the other crew members. "Go down to the docks. See if any of the senior crew is around. First officer, something." She pointed at the com officer while the others hurried from the bridge. "Not you. What's your name?"

"Ryley, Captain."

"Send a distress signal; something tells me you haven't already."

"No, I did! I'll send another. What... what's happened on the planet?" he asked as his hands flew over his controls.

"Damned if I know," she replied. They took another hit.

"Why are they chasing us?" Luce said. "Why would they bother?"

"They're after the interface," she said. "Yours and mine. And the developers, if they're still alive."

"Nova..." Luce said.

"Yes, I know, they're gaining."

"I've detected a keyhole ahead."

"Yeah, so?" She looked up. "Forget it, Luce! You are in no way ready for that! Don't even look at the thing."

"What choice do we have? We're three hours to the jumpsite to Zera. When those cruisers catch up we're all going to be flotsam."

"They don't want us dead."

"They will once they've taken the interfaces. I can do this!"

"Luce, you're a chartjumper. Even if you can crank that keyhole open, you've never worked that sort of calculation before. If it's a long burn we don't even know if this tub has the shields or the processors to make the jump."

"Then you'd better clear the locks and make sure we have full shields around what's left."

She wavered. "Ryley, broadcast an order for any Delphians to come up to the bridge. I know we have at least one."

"There's no time!" Luce said. "Besides, I don't want one of them in my head." He half turned to her. "No offense."

Nova shook her head, aware that they were out of options. She moved to the ship's facilities control and studied the docking ports. The locks were clear and there were no life signs aboard the ships currently attached to the freighter's hull. One by one, she released the pogs and let them drift away from the *Terius*. The enemy ships slowed their pursuit to examine the reasons for casting loose three valuable planes.

"Going negative now, Nova."

"You know what that means, Ryley," she said. He slapped at his controls and the lights dimmed throughout the ship to alert everyone to the imminent leap through sub-space.

She revved the shield generators to maximum when she perceived a change in the keyhole now just ahead of them. It widened as Luce fed it, responding to the ship's energy readily, if not as smoothly as when a trained spanner perform the maneuver. He probed the opening as the ship's processors calculated its depths, looking for its terminus and trying to make the correct choice. "I don't know, Nova..." he said. "I don't see... Oh, there. I think. Be ready to catch us."

"Don't wait for me."

He closed his eyes and the ship shot into the breach barely expanded enough to accommodate its width. Nova dropped onto her heels and squeezed her eyes shut during the breathless, frightening moment when the *Terius* was all that protected them from the unfathomable *nothing* spanning countless light years of space. She saw and heard nothing, felt nothing, until gravity intruded once again and she tumbled forward, across the floor of the bridge.

She rolled, came to her feet and pounced at the helm to slow the ship and arrest its wild tumble through real space. Quickly, she scanned the control boards along the cockpit's perimeter for alarm indicators and saw none. Engaging her interface again, she cast the ship's sensors for some idea of where they had ended up.

"Luce," she grinned. "You did it. I have no idea where we are, but we're in one piece." She turned to him, knowing that a jump like this would have exhausted him beyond measure. He lay with his eyes closed, his body limp. "Come on, you can snooze later. We need to take some inventory here..." She peered at him more closely. "Luce?"

A horrific feeling of dread crept up along her spine when she touched his shoulder to give him a shake. "Luce. Come on, man. Don't do this!" She shook him harder. "Captain! Damn you, don't leave me here!"

Gradually, she had to admit to herself that he had, indeed, left her. Whatever it was that had overloaded his interface had destroyed his brain also. She sank to her knees beside his chair and pulled the ship's neural connector away from her own module. She was alone, possibly the only pilot on a ship full of frightened refugees and she had absolutely no idea where she was or how to get back home.

"Captain," the com officer said nervously.

She turned her head without much enthusiasm. "What?"

"There is another ship. They came through with us before the breach closed again."

"Configuration?"

"Battle cruiser."

Nova came to her feet using the armrest of Luce's chair to heave herself up. "Signal surrender," she said.

FOUR

In the years that Tychon had been a part of the Common-wealth of United Planets, first as an Air Command pilot and then as a Vanguard officer, he had never been made to wait by his superior officers. His exemplary record, mission successes, and skills as pilot and navigator had earned him the respect of even the highest command level. He also suspected that his Delphian heritage and his relationship with Nova Whiteside, a Colonel's daughter, added some of the clout he enjoyed.

Pacing Colonel Everett's antechamber while the brass lolled about on the other side of the closed door was certainly new. Of course, the new commander of the Vanguard division had little interest in befriending his staff, as had Colonel Tal Carras, now retired and living comfortably on one of the moons of Targon.

Tychon pushed up the sleeve of his leather coat to check the data device wrapped around his forearm. Still nothing more from Nova. Why had she not sent a message today? He had dispatched three packets during his trip to Targon and received no reply. The messages had been veiled but by now they had enough language between them to let her know that she was in imminent danger. Also disconcerting was that his inquiry to the Azon administrators on Dannakor had gone unanswered as well.

The last ten hours in-flight from Delphi to their base on Targon had been a torturous exercise to attain and maintain any sort of equanimity and he felt stretched beyond endurance. Her last message to him had been recorded in some lab where she was surrounded by screens and gadgets and covered in patches of tape adhering various sensors. She made one of the technicians demonstrate a scanner that turned her skin entirely transparent, knowing that the sight of that was far more entertaining to her than to him. He smiled at this and let the memory of her antics lull him into the level of khamal he needed.

His recollection was interrupted when the wall at the end of the waiting room gradually turned transparent and he was able to look into the Colonel's workspace. Everett was seated behind his table and not, as it had been Carras' habit, in the comfortable lounging area by the windows. Across from him sat a Major whom Tychon did not recognize and a Centauri woman in civilian clothes. The Colonel raised a hand and gestured for Tychon to enter.

Frowning, Tychon stepped into the room and neglectfully saluted the Colonel. Everett's elbows were propped on the table and his hands were clasped. Tychon noted that his knuckles where white. He glanced at the other two unsmiling people, beginning to worry all over again.

"Please sit, Major," Everett gestured toward an empty chair by his desk and waited until the Delphian had taken him up on his invitation. He made some business of straightening some data tablets in front of him. "These are Majors Cillian and Parsa. Internal investigations."

Tychon raised an eyebrow. His face remained immobile.

"I'm sorry to hear about the attack on Captain Devaughn on Delphi," Everett said. "I understand he is a friend as well as fellow officer."

"He is. Has Captain Whiteside been notified? I have not

been able to reach her at all. Nor her medical team."

"Major Tychon," the Colonel said, clearly not pleased with the task at hand. "I'm afraid we have some bad news."

Tychon inhaled forcefully. The look on the others' faces told him far more than he needed to hear and he was certain there was more to come. "Go on," he said tonelessly.

"Now, we don't have all the details yet. It's a three-day journey to Dannakor from here and our investigators are still in transit. So we can't say for certain exactly what might have—"

"Colonel, please!" Tychon said sharply. He struggled to maintain his composure, using every bit of his lifelong training to subdue his urge to either leap across the desk to shake the information from the Colonel or to run out of the room to avoid it altogether.

"There was an attack. The medical center was taken over by rebels. The facility suffered many casualties but there were survivors."

"And Nova was not among them?"

"We don't believe that she is among the casualties, either," the Colonel said quickly. "But some of the circumstances surrounding the attack are quite extraordinary."

"She is not dead?" Tychon dared to ask.

"We don't believe so. She has disappeared. She escaped on a cruiser but that ship is not on its way back here."

"I appreciate your optimism."

"I will let Major Cillian take things from here," Everett said, gesturing at the plainclothes officer.

She sat up straighter in her chair. Despite her lack of uniform, she looked every bit the officer and not one that took protocol lightly. Tychon felt an instant need for caution when her violet eyes turned to him. He wished that he had worn a uniform. Unarmed, with his long hair hanging loose over his back, wearing scuffed leather jacket and faded trousers, he probably looked like some civilian visitor lost in the administrative levels of the base.

"Major Tychon," she began with a glance at a thin tablet in her hands. "This conversation is being recorded. When was the last time you had contact with Captain Whiteside?"

"Last night, Delphi," he said. "About twenty hours ago, Targon."

She nodded. "What was the nature of your exchange?"

He glanced at Everett. "It was a personal conversation."

She looked at the Major seated beside her as if to silently comment on the difficulty of this subject.

"Major," Colonel Everett said. "I must ask for your complete cooperation."

Tychon frowned. "She is my wife. Three days' travel away. What do you think we were discussing one packet at a time through two far-flung jumpsites? And surely you have access to them, in any case."

Cillian looked at her notes. "You are not actually married according to Delphian customs, Major?"

"No. We are not. That doesn't—"

"Please describe the content of the packets you exchanged with the Captain."

Tychon took a moment to gather himself. "As I recall," he said evenly, "she told me about her accommodations at the facility, that she was bored there but that she had befriended some of the staff, and that she was looking forward to coming home."

"And what did you return?"

"I sent her information about our daughter."

"That would be Cyann?"

"Yes," Tychon said, burying his growing anger behind a mask of indifference.

"And what did Captain Whiteside reply?"

"That she missed us. Then she recorded some words for me to play for Cyann."

"She said nothing more about her activities on Dannakor?"

"No, of course not."

"Are you sure?"

Tychon's lip twitched in a snarl. "My memory is not in any way impaired, Major. The project is classified and Nova would no more record details of it than any of us would."

"No, of course not," she said.

"I really must insist that you fill me in on what happened, Colonel," Tychon said to Everett. "Clearly something terrible has taken place out there."

"Please bear with us, Major," the Centauri investigator said. "When did Captain Whiteside first apply for the new Azon Neural Interface?"

"I'm not sure. Last year, Targon, some time. Almost as soon as we were told about it."

"You were also considered for the implant?"

"Yes. I declined."

"Captain Whiteside did not."

"Evidently."

"What contacts have either of you had with identified rebel factions of late?"

"Major?" Tychon said, startled.

"Just answer the question. Have you had any dealings with rebels outside combat conditions in the past year or so?"

"Of course not."

"Known sympathizers? Informants?"

"None that I'm aware of. We've been on separate assignments for the most part, because of Cyann. When possible we prefer that one of us remains with her."

"So you don't actually know with whom *your wife* corresponds or interacts with?"

"She has no need to explain herself to me," Tychon replied. He decided that he really, truly did not like this woman. "I'm sure she'll let me know if anything interesting happens."

"Are you?"

"What is that supposed to mean?"

She threw another knowing glance at her silent companion. "What follows is classified, Major," she said to

Tychon. She turned to direct a pointer toward a screen on the Colonel's office wall.

A jumble of edited-together imagery moved across the screen. A battle of sorts, people in uniform, in lab suits and in civilian clothes rushing about, shouts, shots and screams. Clearly, a complete mayhem without leadership or discernible outcome.

"We have been able to piece out a few items of interest in all of this, but our technicians are still working on the overall picture," Major Parsa finally spoke.

They watched a segment showing Nova with a white-haired woman in the facility's courtyard amid the confusion of the battle. There was something urgent about their exchange and then they saw her shield the smaller woman from a weapon discharge.

"Do you know that Bellac female?"

"No."

"Her name is Acie Daruen. You arrested her on Phi Six only weeks ago."

"I don't recognize her. There were several Bellac in that group."

"It appears that Captain Whiteside recognizes her quite well."

"Are you faulting Nova for trying to save someone's life, rebel or not?"

"You aren't aware of any relationship between Captain Whiteside and the rebel?"

"No. Why is she on Dannakor if we arrested her?"

"That, indeed, is another mystery for us," Colonel Everett said. "She was released on Zera before her cohort even arrived here on Targon. It isn't clear why or on whose orders."

"We would like you to hear a recording made on Phi Six on the day of her arrest," Cillian said. "This outgoing message was retrieved from the ship Captain Whiteside used."

Tychon listened with growing alarm to the packet Nova

had sent to a man named Vincent, clearly concerned about the Bellac rebel's welfare.

"You can see that this message, along with the fact that Acie Daruen is now at large again, is of the gravest concern to us."

"I can," Tychon said without inflection.

"Continue, Parsa," the Centauri said.

The visual presentation from the clinic on Dannakor played on. Tychon barely bit back a startled exclamation when he saw Nova fire on two men in Air Command uniforms. Then, inexplicably, some video of her destroying lab equipment.

"That is the main data unit for the ANI," Major Parsa said, pausing the recording. "Containing all information about the recent interface tests done on Dannakor. That neural scanner, or what's left of it, was the only one of its kind, build specifically for this project."

Tychon shook his head in disbelief.

"What comes next is simply astonishing." Parsa continued the display. Now Nova was talking to a Caspian standing amid the ruins of the lab equipment. After some exchange, they both left via a rear door.

"Why is there no sound?" Tychon said.

"This is just surveillance video. The project is classified. There are no audio recordings other than those specific to the project. That Caspian is of interest to us."

"Why?"

"Rebel named Sao Lok. We've identified him by his facial markings. Arawaj faction, as far as we know. Expert programmer in just about any Union code ever conceived."

Tychon suppressed a groan. Nova hadn't seemed particularly concerned with the man's presence in the lab. If anything, her hand on his arm had looked really rather friendly.

They tortured him with further footage. This time, it showed Nova bent over a uniformed woman on the ground. The camera was at some distance but they clearly saw her shoot the officer at close range. Then they watched her rush some people into an air lock, two of them in lab suits.

At last, the video stopped. Tychon continued to stare at the blank screen as if he expected something to appear that would explain all of this.

"Among the dead that we know of so far are Shantir Tuain, Doctors Moore and T'lor, and one of the test subjects, a Lieutenant Quinn. Many of the others have not yet been identified. One group of survivors is currently en route to Targon aboard a cargo vessel and two cruisers. Captain Whiteside and the other two test subjects are not aboard."

"Looked to me that she escaped on a cruiser," Tychon said.

"Indeed. According to logs, she and two other planes made it to an orbiting freighter. It subsequently disappeared."

Tychon looked up. "Disappeared how?"

"Keyholed."

"A keyhole? Why would they have a spanner out on Dannakor?"

"We imagine one went out there with the rebels for the purpose of escaping through it. Of course we have no way of knowing where they ended up."

Tychon rose from his chair and paced to the window. He stared out onto Targon's barren landscape, watching a green sunset that looked as morose and tired as he felt.

"Major Tychon," Colonel Everett began. "In light of the evidence—"

Tychon turned abruptly. "Evidence?"

Everett blinked. "Surely, you must agree that what you've seen here is a pretty damning statement concerning Captain Whiteside's recent activities."

When Tychon walked closer to the Colonel's desk the officer actually shrank back, perhaps fearing an imminent assault by the irate Delphian. "You have shown me bits of pieced-together video of what looks to be an extremely disorganized attack by rebels, which is fairly well what all of their raids look like. Perhaps we could spend more on security personnel at these facilities than we do on sub-standard video equipment."

"Major Tychon," the Centauri said. "We understand that you may find it hard to accept—"

He turned his cold blue eyes to the woman. "Captain Whiteside is MIA, Major. That is the only thing I find hard to accept. The rest is utter nonsense. Before you accuse her of whatever you think went on up there, perhaps you need to take a look at her Air Command service. She is an exemplary officer who's more than once put her life on the line for this Commonwealth."

"Sit down, Major," Everett said. "Please."

Tychon shook his head in frustration but dropped back into his chair. "Of what, exactly, are you accusing her?"

"It appears that her aim was to provide the rebel enemy with information pertaining to, if not an actual working model of, the Azon Neural Interface. She is currently at large with some of the developers, her own device as well as the one she pried from the other test subject, and possibly with a copy of the design files of the project."

Tychon tipped his head back and closed his eyes. "This is getting more ridiculous by the moment. I know she wanted the interface so that she could make Level Three spanner. She didn't say so but I know. It's been on her mind for years but she doesn't have the aptitude for it. Few of your people do. And now that goal is finally reached you accuse her of treason? Of being a damn rebel?"

"You have to admit that what we've seen here has put her into a very bad light."

"What about the attack on Captain Devaughn on Delphi? Clearly, they were looking for Nova. Why would they, if she was in league with them?"

"I think you are grasping at straws, Major," Cillian said. "New rebel factions spring up as fast as we can take them out. Few of them even know what the others are doing. It's not unlikely that more than one of their groups is trying to get the ANI design before we can put it in place. They fight each other as much as they rebel against the Union."

Major Parsa leaned forward to put his notes on the Colonel's desk and then sat back to fold his hands over his knee. "Major Tychon, are you aware of matters contained in Captain Whiteside's restricted files?"

Tychon frowned. Now what? "I know there are two classified cases that don't also include me. I don't know what they were about."

"She never discussed them with you?"

"No."

"You never asked?"

"I did. Once. There are some small scars her arm. When I asked her about them she said it was classified. I thought she was joking. But she insisted."

"Well, at least that is commendable."

"I really don't like your use of the phrase 'at least', Major. Captain Whiteside is not the sort to turn military secrets into pillow talk."

"We also cannot discuss these cases with you," Cillian said, ignoring his objection. "But we can tell you that this is not the first time she's been involved in rebel activities. If you are wondering why we are skeptical about her motives for being on Dannakor, this is why."

"That is absurd!" Tychon snapped.

For the first time during this interview, the Centauri Major's expression softened. She regarded Tychon with puzzlement and a hint of sympathy. "I believe we are done here for now. Major, I understand that you are very much attached to your... to Captain Whiteside. But given everything we have shown here today, can you truly say that she is blameless?"

Tychon came to his feet. "Yes, I can." he said. He turned to Colonel Everett. "Colonel, if you have nothing further, I would like to leave Targon now."

Everett stood up. "I'm afraid we have more bad news,

Major. During the current investigation and due to your close relationship with Captain Whiteside, I am forced to temporarily remove you from active duty. You can move freely but I have rescinded your access to Air Command facilities and security clearance."

"You are accusing me of collaborating with rebels?" Tychon said, incredulous.

"I am following protocol. Of course, we will continue to extend our protective measures to your family."

"Who is doing the investigation? Are they aware that the Arawaj faction operates mainly out of Pelion's moons, not Caspia? Vanguard Three was out there not too long ago and probably know who's doing the thinking for them these days. Is the facility on Dannakor closed off? You'll want to get that keyhole charted to see where they may have gone."

"Major," Everett said with an air of a man at the end of his patience. Tychon thought that slugging him might have some therapeutic value for both of them, but as always restrained himself from acting on impulse. "Air Command will investigate thoroughly, I assure you. Leave this to us now."

* * *

Once outside the Colonel's offices, Tychon muttered string of expletives all the way to the elevators. He had learned from Nova long ago that an outburst of temper could at times offer just as much relief as escaping into the soothing meditations of the khamal. And so he cursed.

He hurried through the halls with long strides, his mind on Nova. What could she have gotten herself into? Where was she now? The possibility that she might be injured or worse tried to get his attention but he pushed the thought aside before it could distract him any further.

When he reached the flight decks and Anders' ship, he wasted no time in requesting liftoff clearance, doing so by simply waving at the controller behind his glass wall at the end of the parking hall. He had no intention of filing a flight plan nor did he need one – at least not until the flight crew was told about the loss of his Vanguard privileges. Once aboard, he reached up to tie his hair into a braid and vaulted into the pilot seat where he settled a headset over his interface nodes.

"Ready to go here, Flight," he said.

"Cleared, Major Tychon. Have a pleasant day."

Normally, this would have made him smile but today he simply raised a thumb at the camera above him before shutting it down. He hovered the ship into the chute leading to the exit in the cliff that formed the edge of the base. Once clear, he calculated a course directly for Odar, one of Targon's several habitable moons.

He did not announce his arrival until he was ready to land on the small, shared apron outside a sprawling residential complex. Odar's thin atmosphere lacked the rich oxygen mix required by most of their species but its gravity and easy access to Targon's resources made it habitable. Residents lived under vast, flat domes or simply used portable oxygen when wandering outside them. The almost fantastic biology of purple, yellow, orange and blue plants and rich sources of water made it a whimsical and desirable place to live.

Today Tychon had little appreciation for Odar's eccentric flora. He snapped up an oxygen tank and left the ship to hurry to a row of waiting skimmers just inside the dome. From there it was only a few minutes before he set the air car down in front of a pleasant, single-storied building tucked cozily into a riot of orange and red foliage. The door opened before he had even found a bell.

"Tychon!" he was greeted by a stout elder of Centauri origin. The man was clearly unprepared for a visit by the Delphian with so very little notice. He wore a comfortable lounging suit and his black hair was disheveled as if Tychon had disturbed a nap. "Come inside, come inside."

"I'm sorry to come down so unexpected," Tychon said as he followed his former commanding officer through the small home and into an outdoor area. Here, too, plants grew in abundance, many of them in calmer shades of blue and green. "It is urgent that I speak with you."

Carras gestured to one of several comfortable chairs before calling back into the home. "Theresa, would you bring some of that wonderful *arooja* juice for our guest, please?"

Tychon raised an eyebrow. "Theresa? Wasn't that the name of your aide on Targon?"

Carras settled into his chair with a bland smile. "She decided to retire as well," he said, the sparkle in his violet eyes revealing more than his words. "Where is our lovely Nova? I have not seen either of you in months. When was the last time? Solstice on Delphi, I think. How is little Cyann?" He paused and leaned closer to Tychon to read the Delphian's expression. "What's happened, son?"

Tychon who, in years at least, was older than the Centauri in front of him, hesitated. "I need to speak to you in absolute confidence," he said and, with a glance at the house, added, "and privacy."

"You have it, Ty. What's on your mind?"

"Nova's in trouble. Terrible trouble."

Carras' first impulse was to chuckle at that. "Not an unusual condition for either of you," he said but then his expression sobered. "You would not be here with such short notice if you did not need my help this time."

"I need classified information."

The Colonel sat back in his chair and gazed over his small garden. "Well, now..." he said. "Surely you can't mean that. I may be retired but I am still bound to my oaths."

Tychon nodded. "I will tell you what happened. As much as I can, anyway. And you choose how much you wish to tell me."

"Seems fair."

Carefully, Tychon began by telling Carras about the attack on Anders and then went on to the raid at the Dannakor base. He described what he had seen of Nova there without mentioning the location or the specifics of the project itself.

He included the puzzling message she had sent from Phi Six to the man on Magra and ended with his own banishment from active duty.

Tal Carras said nothing for a long while after Tychon finished. The woman who brought a tray did not join them when he glanced up at her and some silent signal passed between them. He poured the tart, warm juice but neither he nor Tychon picked up their cup.

"This does sound like a whole lot of trouble," he said finally.

"Do you know this Bellac woman? Acie?"

"No."

Tychon unfolded his long legs to stand up, feeling restless and caged; an unusual sensation for him. "Look, Nova is impulsive and temperamental and sometimes she pushes the rule book a little past the literal meaning, but she is no traitor! She is a soldier and she takes that very seriously. You know this!"

"Apparently Colonel Everett does not."

"Fine time for you to retire, Tal," Tychon said, looking past the thin shield of the settlement's dome to the hills beyond.

"I'm not sure if protocol would have allowed me to do anything differently," Carras said. "He's new to the job. You Vanguard are not like the other wings and he'll come to realize that, I hope. But he'll have gotten top-level directives on the matter if it involved a classified project. So what can he do but try to contain the damage? Frankly, he could confine you if his doubts were greater."

Tychon nodded and sighed. "Yes, I suppose you're right."

"I'm sure further investigation will show the truth, whatever that may be. Once the witnesses are interviewed they will know more."

Tychon turned back to him. "And meanwhile Nova is missing in action. And no one seems to care! She could be in rebel hands for all I know. Or injured. I can't wait around to see what their team might or might not find out when they get there! That could be days yet."

Carras pursed his lips, pondering. "From what I'm hearing you say, these weren't just pirates looking for loot. The only force with the resources to successfully take down an Azon installation are the Shri-Lan. She could be dead by now."

"No," Tychon said at once. He tapped his forehead. "I'd know that, Tal. If she were gone, I'd be missing something. She's still in there. She's still with me. I know this."

Carras regarded the Delphian silently, realizing that no off-worlder would ever truly understand his people. Perhaps Nova did. But Nova was as tightlipped about Delphian secrets as she was with military matters.

"She's not without wit and resources, Ty."

"I know that. Can you at least tell me what has Everett so convinced that she's a collaborator?"

"No, I can't. But he is not wrong. There is enough in those files to cloud his opinion of her."

Tychon froze. "What are you saying?"

"I'm saying that I can't say anything. But I know she's an excellent officer and I do not want to believe that she'd give classified information to rebels."

"You sound doubtful."

Carras inspected his folded hands, choosing his words carefully. "I've seen a lot in my years, Ty. It has given me doubts about many things. I have no certainty about anything and I've learned to live with that."

"We've fought the rebels for years. One faction is worse than the next. Nova has every reason to loathe them, besides an actual professional duty. Nothing would ever convince either of us to further their cause." Tychon touched the sickle-shaped scar under his eye, a gift from a rebel leader, and then ran a fingernail over the edge of his interface. "I've been inside her head. There is no treachery there. I *know* this."

Carras smiled sadly. "There is much power in the love of

a man fighting for his family," he quoted. "So also true for Delphians, I see."

Tychon shrugged. "You won't find a Delphian admitting to that, old man, so don't start with me."

The Centauri chuckled. "Too late for that, young man." He turned serious. "But don't let it blind you, either. You are wired to trust analytical investigation and empirical evidence. Don't lose sight of that."

"She is the mother of my child. You know what that means to us. And I've learned the value of trusting my guts, too."

"From her, no doubt!" Carras said. "If you asked me what my guts were telling me, I would say that you are correct. Her loyalties are with the Union. And with you."

"Is there nothing you can tell me?"

"I will do more than tell. I will give you this Sethran that she mentioned in her message to Magra. He may know how to find the Bellac woman, if she escaped the attack. Or he may know why she was there, or how she knows Nova. Any of that may help."

Tychon returned to his seat. "Who is he?"

"Sethran Kada." Carras hesitated. "He is a bit of an enigma. Centauri. Pilot. Probably as good an ethnologist as Anders, mostly because he moves around so much. Probably speaks more languages that you do."

"But he's not one of ours?"

"Hard to say. Technically not any more. He has done work for us. Mostly black ops, I'm afraid. Maybe some for the rebel. Generally for himself, I think."

"Sounds like a fine specimen. How does Nova know someone like that?"

"Yes, well." Carras leaned forward to pick up his drink. "I'm not too sure. However, I think I know how to find him. I will send a message today to ask him to contact you. I'm also going to see if they'll let me take an interest in this matter. Perhaps I can get clearance to get at some of the information you need. Considering my experience with

Nova, they may well allow this. It's the best I can do." He observed the Delphian's troubled face for a moment. "Now, since you're here, stay for a meal and tell me how the planets are turning out there! Did they get to an agreement with Feyd over the extra property? Did your Council figure out the rights to the North Slope? And how is that pretty little daughter of yours?"

FIVE

Darkness. Cold. A metal floor beneath her and the unpleasant sounds of the ship's mechanical workings too close to ignore. Nova sat up and scrubbed her face with both hands before making yet another futile attempt at escaping the bonds that tied her wrists together. Had she fallen asleep? Passed out after yet another kick to her midriff from that miserable Centauri? The whole thing seemed a little blurry.

She groped around the dark, moving slowly to avoid another bruised hip. When the two grunts had first tossed her into this box she had stumbled around and finally decided on the floor after colliding with a number of metal edges. This room was little more than an umbilical space between the freighter itself and its cargo modules.

Nova slumped in a corner, listening to the rhythms of the machines that drove the life support and gravity systems. None of them sounded particularly well-maintained and she wondered if anyone on the bridge was monitoring them.

She closed her eyes and tipped her head back against the metal bulkhead and wondered what had gone so terribly wrong yesterday.

Ryley, the com officer, had stuttered their surrender out

to the rebel ship and then more or less collapsed beside his console, awaiting his fate.

"Get up," she had told him when she came to look at his displays. "Haven't you had instructions about pirates or hostile boardings?"

"These aren't pirates!" he whimpered. "These are rebels. Killers, anarchists, rapists. They'll murder us all."

"Some pirates are worse than rebels, believe me," she said, her eyes on the ship's sensors. There were thirty people on the freighter, still near the locks. The enemy ship appeared to have about seventy life forms. And heavy armament. "You're going to have to pull your pants up now, Ryley. Let's join up with the others."

He shook his head.

"Fine. Stay down, don't annoy them, do what they tell you. Clear?"

He nodded.

Nova left the bridge and hurried back along the main corridor of the supply ship to where most of the others had gathered. Along the way she shrugged out of her flight jacket and threw it into one of the cabins along the hallway. Belatedly, she remembered the interface module she had taken from Lieutenant Quinn and retrieved it. It was small enough in the secret fold of a pocket flap on her fatigues to escape whatever search she could expect at the hands of the rebels.

She arrived near the locks to find a mix of civilians and uniforms, either speaking excitedly or huddled as frightened and shocked as the com officer on the bridge. A quick look around the crowd assured her that Acie was not among them.

"People," she raised her hands to catch their attention. "Listen, everyone!"

Gradually, the excited babble ceased and their faces turned toward her. A few more civilians arrived from a side chamber.

"I need you to stay calm now," she said, looking from

one confused and anxious face to the next. She was unaccustomed to dealing with civilians and suddenly felt utterly unqualified to manage a survival situation that was sure to turn hysterical at any moment. She took a deep breath. "We escaped through an uncharted keyhole. At this point we don't know exactly where we are." She raised her hands again to calm the panicked voices that rose from the small crowd. "But the breach is stable and we haven't lost contact with it."

"So can you jump us back, then?" a Centauri woman close to Nova said.

"Not right now. You're about to feel a collision against the hull of the ship. That is a cruiser locking on to us. It also came through the breach with us." She paused for a moment before delivering the rest of the news. "It's a rebel ship. They followed us from Dannakor."

Nova took a moment to look around the group, ignoring the terrified wails and questions hurled at her. She noted some lab coats, some of whom she recognized, several civilians and a number of uniforms. Near the back, Jovan, the young Delphian, leaned against a bulkhead, arms crossed as he surveyed the situation. His expression gave nothing away but Nova was sure that she saw amusement in his eyes. She gestured to the soldiers to join her. Most of the others fell silent when she addressed them.

"I am Captain Nova Whiteside, Vanguard Seven, stationed on Targon under the command of Colonel Dom Everett. We're outnumbered, so don't be playing the hero. Look after the civilians as best as you can. Keep only your long guns for them to take and hide your side arms somewhere. See if you can find any other weapons aboard. That does not mean I want you attacking anyone, clear?"

"Yes, Captain." Two of the soldiers collected their guns.

She looked to the others. "Any crew members here?" A few of them raised their hands. "You, go with the Lieutenant and cache the weapons."

"Aren't they going to take us to their ship?" someone

wanted to know.

"I don't think so. They won't have room or air for that."

"They'll just kill us all," the Centauri woman exclaimed. Her violet eyes flickered like a faulty light bulb as she blinked nervously. "If they're lost, too, they'll just kill us and take our air!"

Nova frowned, mainly because the woman was likely correct. Unless the rebel ship, for some inconceivable reason, had a Level Three spanner aboard, they were as lost as everyone else here. How long they would last on the available air, food and water would all come down to everyone's interest-level in keeping each other alive.

"The important thing is to keep calm," she said, all too aware that nothing they did now would make any difference to the rebels about to board the freighter. Her only hope was that the they had pursued them because of the value of the ANI project team aboard. Whether for ransom or for the interface technology, it would give them another chance for survival. They soon felt the thump of a large ship locking onto one of the bays, momentarily jarring the gravity depth of their ship.

"They have to come through that lock," a Lieutenant standing beside Nova said. "We can pick them off one by one."

She turned to him. "You will follow my orders, soldier. You can take out a handful and then what? They'll disengage the cruiser and blast us out of the sky just for spite. Your priority is the civilians."

He seemed unconvinced but decided to stand down.

"Do nothing," she addressed the others. "Do not incite them and maybe we can get out of this. Please just stay calm."

They all stared anxiously at the air lock gate when it finally opened to admit the boarding party. The civilians crowded back against the bay walls when they saw four Centauri and two Humans, likely chosen for their size and menace, step through the door. They were heavily armed, weapons ready. All were dressed in a mix of body armor, combat uniforms and civilian clothes, as patched and scuffed as their scarred faces and arms.

Nova winced when one of the Union soldiers took a step toward them.

"Drop that gun, boy," a Centauri rebel barked. The Human beside him was not so accommodating. He raised his gun and shot the Lieutenant. The soldier was thrown back into the huddle of civilians cowering behind him. The Centauri scowled at the Human before speaking again. "The rest of you, hand over your weapons."

Nova and the remaining soldiers complied. Another rebel quickly collected their guns and returned to the air lock. Moments later a different Centauri emerged from there, accompanied by an elaborately tattooed Feydan woman. He still wore the Air Command uniform that had disguised him on Dannakor, proclaiming himself as Major. It was one normally issued to Human soldiers but the short sleeves and trouser legs didn't seem to strike him as awkward. His violet eyes moved slowly from one of the escapees to the next as if taking measure of each of them.

"Who is the captain here," he said finally.

After a silence one of the crew members spoke up. "She was on Dannakor. I think the com officer is still on board somewhere. Other than that it's just regular crew here."

The Centauri nodded. "Didn't expect an admiral on a cargo plane. Who is your spanner?"

There was some uneasy shuffling of feet and a few stolen glances in Nova's direction.

"He's dead," she said quickly. "Still at the helm. Didn't survive the jump."

The Centauri turned his glowing eyes to Nova and stepped closer to her. He reached out and pinched her face in his hand to turn her head, bringing her neural interface in view. "You're a pilot."

"I am," she said and pulled out of his grasp.

"Let me save you some time." They turned when Sao Lok

stepped forward. Two of the rebels turned their guns on him but he waved his hand to shoo them aside. "That pilot is an Air Command officer. The interface you see there is the new ANI model. I am Sao Lok, of the Arawaj, and was on Dannakor to obtain a copy of the interface and the files for our leader, Pe Khoja."

Nova rounded on him. "What?" She reeled with the information the Caspian had so casually tossed into the room. Not only was her new acquaintance a member of a rebel faction, but what was that about Pe Khoja? "Pe Khoja is dead," she said. "I was there."

"Thank you for confirming that, Captain," Sao Lok said. "And in time you'll pay for your part in that. His mission, and that of the Arawaj, is not dead."

"Shut up," the Centauri leader snapped. "Both of you." He glared at the Caspian. "I don't give a damn about your leader. Right now we're just looking to get back to Trans-Targon." He turned back to Nova. "And you will get us there."

"I can't," she said. "I don't know how. I'm a Level One chartjumper. If I tried this we could end up in an even worse place. I have no idea how to get us back to Trans-Targon."

The rebel leader raised his hand and struck her across the face. She stumbled backwards and resisted an urge to retaliate. The guns pointed at her helped to fight the impulse.

"Stop that at once," Sao Lok said. "That implant is new. You'll only damage it by hitting her."

The Centauri leader looked over the semi-circle of people. "How many more on board?" he asked.

"Someone on the bridge, three down that hall. Couple in one of the cabins," a rebel with a scanner told him.

"Which of you were working on the ANI project?" the leader demanded and saw a few hesitantly raised hands. He gestured for them to move toward the corridor. "Medics?" A few more joined them. He scrutinized the remainder, civilians and four Union soldiers, before gesturing to Jovan to step aside, as well. Delphian hostages were easily sold back to their families at very worthwhile rates. He pulled a few more people from the group and Nova realized that all four of them were attractive women.

"Look," she said. "We have other options. There may be habitable planets around here. Or we can try to send a message back to Trans-Targon. That's what the interface is designed for, after all. Just ask Lok. Leave these people alone."

The Centauri grasped Nova's arm and shoved her toward one of his men. "I told you to shut up. I don't intend to risk my neck on an unexplored planet or let you send a message to Air Command." He gestured for his men to herd the selected group away, toward the cargo areas, before speaking to the brutish Centauri holding Nova in a painful grip. "Lock her up somewhere. Maybe give her something to think about." He started to walk back into the umbilical to his own ship. "Get the others to quit breathing my air."

And so she found herself, hours later, cuffed and alone in the dark. And dreading the return of the Centauri who had thrown her in here.

He had struck her but had pulled his punches to avoid serious damage to the one person that might see all of them home again. Her wrists were tightly bound with an elastic strap that immediately cut into her skin. Finally, he had searched her for weapons and took away the laser tool, a knife and her communication array.

She cursed when he moved on from checking pockets to exploring her curves. When he thrust a rough hand between her thighs she twisted away and tried to reach his gun. In answer he whipped her around and shoved her against the wall. He outweighed her by half again and she felt his large body press against her back and his hot breath on the nape of her neck. Centauri liked to use their teeth when aroused but there was nothing playful about the bite that now sunk into her neck.

When she felt his hand fumble with the fastener of her trousers her fury overtook her training. To hell with passive resistance, never mind that an all-out fight would only bring more rebels into the assault. This was personal. She struggled to maneuver her bound hands to activate the little ring she still wore on her thumb. Twisting as far as she could, she pressed her hand to his face.

A surprised shriek broke from the rebel's throat as he recoiled, clutching his face. Nova leaped aside and barely avoided the full force of his fist as he swung blindly in her direction. She ducked low and swept his legs out from under him, lurching out of the way when his hefty body crashed to the ground. His head slammed into the wall where he had pinned her and she saw with some satisfaction a splatter of blood left behind.

The door to the hall opened. "What the hell are you doing to her?" a Human rebel exclaimed. He grabbed Nova's collar and shoved her back when he saw her haul back to kick the prone Centauri. He laughed harshly when he understood the situation. "That was you screaming like a little girl, Lef?"

Nova jerked out of the Human's grasp and retreated, clenching and unclenching her numbed fingers.

"Bitch!" the Centauri swore, still holding the side of his head. "She stung me with something in her hand. Get it off her."

She did not struggle when the rebel twisted her hand to remove the ring. A broken finger was not something she wanted to add to her problems right now.

"Making you work for it, is she?" he said. "Looks like you're done with her for now. Rakh wants us to get the others rounded up."

The door shut behind them, leaving Nova in perfect darkness and aware that only luck had saved her this time. She crumpled to the ground, gasping, trying to fight back the memory of a less fortunate incident so long ago on Bellac Tau. Long ago, dealt with, gotten over, she told herself. The doctors had said so.

According to Air Command manuals there were worse

fates to suffer at the hands of an enemy. All female Union soldiers received training in how to deal with the physical and mental impact of violations such as this until it was reduced to little more than an unpleasant occupational hazard. Nova understood all too well the need for desensitizing and of the tedious post-mission psych evaluations that all of them underwent. But preparing for this and living through it were not even in the same sphere of reality.

All that had been hours ago. No one had come back since. She had stayed in a corner of the room, curled on the metal floor and had sought escape from her pain in sleep, grateful for the Delphian training Tychon had passed along to make that possible.

Nova sat up, wiped her face on her arm and tried to assess the damage to her body. She ached everywhere but it felt mainly like bruises. Her shoulder had been scratched by something sharp along one of the walls or perhaps on the floor and she suspected that she was bleeding from the Centauri's bite. But everything seemed to work when she moved.

Tychon had been foremost on her mind when she had felt the rebel's rough hands on her body. His intervention had saved her from one of the barely-sentient Rhuwacs a few years ago; something that still haunted him more than her and it had take a while before she had told him about Bellac Tau. His first wife had died horribly in rebel hands and it would surely kill him to lose her, too. He would never know how close she'd come this time, she promised herself, knowing quite well that the threat wasn't over.

The thought of Tychon, always seeming so rational, so calm, even when upset or angry, helped her organize her thoughts. He would assess the circumstances, ignore the pain in his body, and look for opportunities to resolve the situation. Of course, all of these things seemed to come easily to Delphians, who simply dropped into another level of consciousness when the current one wasn't up to the task.

But what would he do, floating around in the middle of nothing with a pack of Shri-Lan rebels and a bunch of frightened, abused civilians? She bit her lip hard enough to hurt. He would not give up, that was certain.

She had no allies here and by now the rebels would have eliminated the handful of poorly-disciplined soldiers that had escaped the facility. Her options were non-existent. The only thing, she realized, that would help any of them was to try to make the jump back to Trans-Targon. Perhaps she would be luckier than Luce if she took her time and relied on her experience with more complex ships than he would have piloted.

She squinted when a sharp slice of light cut into the darkness. The door to the corridor opened and then someone used the control in the hall to turn on the overhead lamps. She blinked and raised her bound arms over her head to shield her eyes before realizing that she now appeared to be cowering in fear. She dropped her arms again and looked up at the Centauri.

She gasped in surprise when he pushed the Delphian youth she had met earlier into the room. Jovan stumbled over her legs and nearly fell.

"Get her fixed up, Delphi," the Centauri barked. "Rakh wants to talk to her."

Jovan crouched beside Nova. "What, by the Gods, did you do to her?" he exclaimed, like the Centauri using the common trade language of the Trans-Targon sector.

Nova bared her teeth, about to snap something caustic at the rebel when Jovan passed his finger over his lips. She remained quiet.

"Teaching the Human some manners. Get on with it."

"She is practically catatonic! How can you possibly expect her to jump any site, not to mention an uncharted one, if she in such a state? Just look at her!"

Nova kept her eyes directed at nothing and mumbled something unintelligible.

"I barely touched her," the rebel said without conviction.

"Go immediately and fetch some clean bandages and disinfectant," Jovan said sharply, with all the arrogance of a Delphian among lesser creatures. "I'll see what I can do to make her coherent before your master sees what you've done to her. I suggest that you keep your hands off this woman if you expect to find your way home again."

Incredibly, the Centauri withdrew and slammed the door behind him.

Nova looked up at Jovan. "Nice work!" she said, speaking Delphian. "Have you actually ever talked to a rebel before?"

He collapsed to sit on the floor beside her. "I've not ever been so frightened!" He laughed nervously. "And I've never been away from Delphi before, since you seem to be alluding to my lack of experience."

"You did that well, Jovie. How did you get in here?"

"It's Jovan," he pointed out. "I told them I was a Shantir. Most of them seem to think that means healer. I figured they'd get rough with you." He had spotted the smear of blood on the wall. "Are you all right?"

"Yes, all's well. That's not mine. Thanks for worrying about me." She held up her wrists and winced when he tugged on her bonds to untie them.

He shrugged. "You're Tychon's mate. I don't want to see you harmed."

She came to her feet. "Thanks, kid. Not wild about Humans, either, are you?"

"They're all right," he said with an air of someone who has met hundreds of them. "He must have good reason to have taken up with you."

"How do you know him?"

"I don't," he admitted. "I've seen him once or twice. He came by the enclave when Lord Phera stayed with us a while. Some of us waited around to get a look but we didn't speak with him. He sort of nodded when he went by. Sami was going to say something to him but then she changed her mind. I think he frightened her."

Nova smiled. Air Command actively, if discreetly,

recruited Delphians for their unfailing ability in combat and vast capacity for mathematics and engineering. Those who joined the military tended to work in more crucial parts of the Trans-Targon sector and rarely returned to Delphi except to meet familial obligations. Tychon, like other Delphian officers, had taken on heroic proportions among their younger kinsmen. It irritated him as much as it amused Nova.

"There is always much talk about him in the enclave. He has seen so much, done so much. And he takes a Human woman and cares not one bit what the Council thinks of it! A Human soldier, at that!" He contemplated for a moment. "Is it true you used a lava flow to save an entire city?"

"It was a smallish city."

"I've wondered what it's like being off-world, fighting rebels, seeing new places. It sounds so fantastic."

"Well," Nova said, testing the air lock on the other side of the small chamber. The key plate beeped encouragingly but kept its secret as to what was behind the door. "You get beat up a lot, I can tell you." The display near the lock told her that the cargo pod behind it was depressurized. "And shot at. A lot." She looked around the small room, seeing nothing but bare metal and sealed doors. She slapped her hand onto the one leading to the hall. "And locked up when what you really want is a toilet!"

He gasped. She suspected that interacting with Humans had not been on the Shantirs' daily lesson plan for him, after all. Off-worlders tended to overestimate the younger Delphians whose intellect and education easily surpassed those of most other races. She reminded herself that they aged emotionally and physically at a much slower rate and this boy, in particular, had likely not experienced much outside the confines of the enclave.

She half-turned away from him and pushed her hair out of the way. "How does that look back there?"

He peered at her neck. "Bad bruise. That rebel did that? Are all Centauri such monsters?"

"Most of them aren't a bad lot." Her shirt had adhered to the blood on her shoulder and she hissed when he tugged it away.

"That one could use some tape," he said. "Your face is bruised around the eye. Are you hurt anywhere else?"

She shook her head. "How many rebels are on board the freighter?"

"Just a few on the bridge. Most of them left to go back to the battle cruiser. We can move around the cargo bays. They found the guns and they took all the food." He stared at nothing for a moment and took a few slow breaths. "They... they killed the soldiers and some civilians. It... it was..."

Nova watched the troubled look on his face dissolve into a distant expression formed by both his training and his adolescent need to appear unaffected. She knew better than to try to comfort him.

"How many are left? Of our people?"

"I'm not sure. No more than a dozen."

"I'm going to have to jump us," she said. "Back to Trans-Targon."

He wrinkled his brow, puzzled by something. "This is all very new to me. How much harder is it to go through a keyhole than through a regular jumpsite?"

"A lot. All jumpsites used to be keyholes, of sorts." Nova looked around. "That door there is like a jumpsite. Someone made that door; you can go through it. It's not that hard and most pilots can do it. Your ship does most of the work. But going through a *keyhole* is like finding your way through the molecules of that wall and then making a hole big enough to hop through."

"And that's difficult."

"Very. The non-Delphians that can do it would probably fit in this room, in case you need confirmation that your brain is special. But even for you it takes a lot of energy and concentration to do this. And it's expensive because of the coolant we use to keep the ship's processors running. Those help with the math and of course we need the ships to shield us during the trip. Not all ships are equipped for this sort of travel."

"And so those ships use the regular jumpsites."

"Yes. Like the one you came through to get to Dannakor. When we find a keyhole in a useful place, we chart its exits and turn it into a jumpsite by recording and sharing the information needed to get through it. It becomes a door. It's actually more like a funnel. Entrance on the narrow end and a whole bunch of exits on the wide end."

"So there is a keyhole outside this ship and nobody knows how to get back in it?"

"We can go into it. But I have no idea where to leave it again because no one's mapped the exits yet. I don't have the ability to find the right one. We were hoping this new interface will let us do it."

"But the interface does not work?"

"I don't know. I don't think so. A miscalculation would have torn the ship apart, or left us in the breach, not kill the navigator. There are safeguards for that. The ANI is designed for communication. Everything else is speculation. Likely, they weren't even ready yet to test it for any jump, never mind one like this into an uncharted site."

"Then it seems a dangerous thing for you to try."

"Yes," said. "It is. But there is no other way."

"You don't think we'll be found? Won't someone come after us from the other side?"

"They'll try. But jumping through sub-space leaves no trail to follow. They won't know where we came out."

Just then the door opened and the Centauri returned. He threw a box of medical supplies and a few food packets at Jovan and then stood by the door, his back turned to them.

"Listen," Jovan said to him, again using the supercilious tone that had worked on this rebel before. "This woman needs to clean up properly. There is a decon chamber just over there."

The Centauri turned briefly and grunted his assent. "Don't be babbling in that Delphian. Talk so I can understand you."

Jovan moved between Nova and the rebel and looked meaningfully at her neural interface. Guessing his intent, Nova nodded. He hesitated before lifting his hands to place his blue-nailed fingers onto the nodes. He closed his eyes until he had created his link to her.

How did you know this would work? she asked when she felt his tentative touch in her head.

More rumors in the enclave. That you can share the khamal because of the interface. About Shan Tychon teaching you things. Maybe things he shouldn't.

He's been respectful, if you're worried about that, she replied. *And he's not a Shantir. This will give you a big headache, by the way.*

I'm already there.

They sidled past the Centauri's gun and across the corridor where Jovan waited outside the little chamber while she cleaned up.

"This is crude," she commented through the door.

"I noticed," he replied. "There isn't even a hygiene program for Delphians. I had to use the one for you people. I itch."

"That one works perfectly fine," she assured him. "Although when there isn't an option, Tychon likes the Centauri decon. He says it works better for your hair."

"I really don't need to know about Shan Tychon's bathing habits."

"Hey, it's educational. You want to keep your tail trail nice and soft for the ladies," she added mischievously, using Delphian slang for the narrow line of hair growing down his spine. It was a most sensitive part on any Delphian's otherwise hairless body.

"You are outrageous!" he exclaimed.

I need you to do something, Nova projected.

Oh? came the cautious reply.

Do you know what they did with the other pilot, the one that died on the bridge?

Yes, they took all the bodies into one of the cargo pods. To freeze them.

Nova opened the door to the room. "Need you to come in here and fix my shoulder, Jovan," she said loud enough for the Centauri to hear. "It's bleeding again."

Jovan stepped inside, looking nervous when she pushed her shirt from her shoulder. She turned her back to him and he carefully placed a clear patch of tape over her injury. "I don't think I've ever seen a Delphian blush," she smiled. "Does this bother you?"

"Of course not," he said, forcing a careless tone. "I have touched a woman before, you know."

"I'm sure you have," she grinned. Delphian society was sexually permissive and all youths received instruction by more experienced mentors before choosing their lifemates. It was another part of Delphi's culture that few outsiders were aware of. She pulled her shirt back up. "But not a Human one."

"Certainly not!" he said quickly. "I'm sorry. I sound... I know how I sound. I meant no offense." He cocked his head when some revelation seemed to strike him. "I know what you're doing. You think I'm traumatized and your teasing will distract me like some child lost in the woods."

"Is it working?"

"Actually, yes. Although your brand of humor is a strange thing, Human." He backed out of the coffin-size room. *What do you want me to do?*

Huh? Oh. Right. I need you to find Captain Luce's body and retrieve his neural implants.

His eyes widened. *You can't mean that!*

Yes, I do. See if you can find that cargo pod. Just make sure the temperature in there hasn't bled out too much. If you can get in there, break the external parts off his head. They will come away from the taps fairly easily, especially if he's cold.

That is sickening!

Nova looked into his horrified face and berated herself for her callousness. This was no soldier. This was a Shantir to whom corpses were still sacred vessels. *Can you do this?*

He pressed his lips together until they formed a thin white line. *I'll try.*

The Centauri in the corridor looked Nova up and down when they returned to her makeshift cell. She crossed her arms when his eyes lingered too long on her body as he perhaps considered last night's unfinished assault. His violet eyes gleamed in the fleshy folds of his scarred face but when he saw her glaring at him he addressed Jovan as though she wasn't there. "Don't go back in there. She's going to see Rakh on the other ship."

"She is not well," Jovan reminded him. "She is weak and badly disturbed by your behavior. I suggest you let her eat something." He retrieved some of the emergency food packets the rebel had tossed at him earlier and handed them to Nova. She did not have to pretend to be famished and broke into the packaged and tasteless rations with more enthusiasm than she thought possible.

I need to break this khamal. Jovan grimaced. *My head is going to explode.*

Try to get some sleep. It'll help. Then make sure to find the nodes, she reminded him. *Destroy them when you do. Just hit them with something hard. Should be enough to damage the contacts.*

He sent his reluctant agreement and quickly touched the side of her head to release her from his mental link.

"Come on, come on." The Centauri grabbed Jovan's shoulder and shoved him aside. "That way, Human."

Nova was pushed and prodded along the central corridor of the cargo ship to the docks. They stepped through the umbilical and boarded the rebel vessel which didn't look in much better shape that the *Terius*. It, too, had seen too many battles, too many badly-navigated jumpsites and too many crew members who cared nothing about denting and defacing the interior. The gravity here was something to get used to and the air quality spoke of extreme conservation.

She stumbled when her guard grabbed her arm to stop her from walking past a door. "In there. And watch your mouth around Rakh. He's not in a mood to piss around with

Union scum."

"Maybe I'll tell him you broke my interface. See if that improves his mood."

He raised his fist as if to backhand the insolent Human but then seemed to think better of what consequences that may have. He punched the door's entry panel instead. It slid aside to reveal the battle cruiser's bridge.

Nova stepped ahead of the guard into the dim space. Her eyes adjusted to reveal Rakh, the Centauri rebel leader, and a few others seated around the bridge. Surprisingly, Sao Lok, the Azon technician who had claimed to be an Arawaj rebel, was among them. To her left, against the wall, knelt three of the civilians from Dannakor, their heads down and their hands tied.

Rakh swiveled in his bowl-shaped chair when the light from the hall momentarily brightened the space. He sprawled lazily, apparently not concerned about further damage done to the scuffed captain's chair by the boot he had drawn up on the seat. He studied her for a moment. "Looks like you haven't been having any fun." He grinned at her guard and waved him out of the room.

She scowled at him. "Are you Arawaj, too?"

"Watch your mouth. This is a Shri-Lan ship." He glanced at Sao Lok and then equally sternly at the other rebels here. "And I'm the commander and can choose who I want to work with."

He turned his chair and his back to her. The others were not so incautious and he probably knew it. Several guns were pointed her way. "We've been having a look around," he said. "We're precisely nowhere. There isn't even a planet around that we'd reach in a lifetime. Unless you like swimming in melted iron. The only way back is through that breach."

"I'm just a chartjumper," she said, as if talking to someone with limited comprehension. "That keyhole is uncharted. I can't get us back to Trans-Targon any more than your own navigators can. I'm sure you've been trying for hours. It could kill me if I used the ANI for this."

"I'm not concerned about your health," he replied. He turned around again to hand her a data tablet.

She studied the display. The keyhole was definitely stable, which offered some hope. She would be able to open it and hold it for the ship's passage. But then what? She linked her interface to the computer to test the processor. It was considerably more powerful than the one aboard the *Terius*, but it was still just a processor, no more able to discern one exit from another without the guidance of a conscious mind.

"I'm sure you're plenty concerned about your own hide," she said and handed the unit back to Rakh after breaking her link with it. She glanced at Sao Lok. "This is suicide."

"Just yours," Lok said. "If you do it wrong. But you have more brains than your recently deceased colleague. And more experience. Don't forget that I am quite familiar with the workings of the ANI." He directed a friendly smile at the three civilians huddled near the wall. "As are some of these individuals who have graciously supplied us with information."

Nova glared at the Caspian. "Even if I live through that I am not likely to drop us anywhere near where we want to be. I just don't see how."

"I will tell you how," Rakh said. He raised his hand and she saw a gun, now pointed at the civilians.

"Stop!" she snapped. "Don't do this!"

"Too late," he said. "A lesson must be taught." He smiled as if driven by some perversity when he trigged the weapon and shot one of the men precisely between the eyes. The other two screamed in terror and cowered back against the bulkhead. Rakh swiveled back to her. "Did you understand the lesson?" When she did not immediately reply he aimed his gun again.

"Yes!" she said. "I understand."

"That does make me happy," he said. "I think we're going to need some of our hostages for later. Would be a shame if you wasted them all." He came to his feet and gestured at the helm. "Take us home, Captain."

"What? Now? I can't! I need to study this thing."

Rakh glanced at Sao Lok who nodded. His almost congenial expression shifted into anger territory. "How much time will that take?"

She shrugged. "Days, probably. Depends on your sensor range."

Rakh turned to a Centauri manning a console near the front of the bridge. "How much time do we have?"

There were some calculations, some thought, some discussion with a Human sitting next to the rebel. "If we cut the freighter loose, got rid of a few more breathers, maybe three days. We have air for more, but if she's going to ramp up the processors we'll have little power left for basic life support. Might have to give up gravity."

The rebel leader nodded. "You heard him, Human. You've got two days and then we jump."

Nova's mind churned with rapid calculations. Assuming that Rakh was using standard time, two days will have given Air Command time to figure out what had become of them. Surely there were survivors, video records, even. Tychon would have been notified and would be mobilizing the entire Vanguard to turn the keyhole inside out. Would they reach them in time? "I'm going to need the Delphian," she said.

"Who? What for?"

"He's a whelp," Sao Lok said. "What do you need him for?"

"He's a Shantir and you know it," she said. "He can make all the difference in finding our way through this."

"Fine. Whatever. Find the Delphian. Lock them up until they get their heads together." Rakh loomed dangerously over Nova who refused to back away. He had to step around her to reach the door to the corridor. "I want you back here and mapping day and night or you'll have more blood on your hands."

"I will try. That's all I can promise. Just keep your rapist goons away from me. I can't concentrate if I have to worry about getting beaten up at every turn."

His hand shot out and clamped around her neck. "You are not in a position to make demands."

"She's got a point," Sao Lok interjected. "Let's see what they can come up with. There's nothing to be gained by harming the girl."

Rakh snarled. "Get her out of my sight."

Nova left the bridge, aware that Sao Lok followed her and the guard that soon pushed her into a narrow cabin on the lower deck. They passed a number of rebels, both male and female, of Centauri, Feydan and Human origin. Few of them were Caspian. Sao Lok stepped into her new prison and closed the door behind him.

She looked around the room, seeing nothing but a set of bunks and a metal storage bin here. At some point someone had scribbled something on the wall and someone else had tried to erase it. She stared at the incomprehensible words, fuming silently. At last she turned to face him. He had discarded his lab coat and now wore only a loose pair of breeches to fully display the swirling patterns on his gleaming hide. "Whatever you want, Lok, I'm not in the mood to discuss."

"I can understand that you're angry."

"Angry?" she said. "You played me! What was the point of that? Do you always get friendly with your targets before you carry out your mission? A few games of Points to pass the time? Trade baby pictures before you stab them in the back?"

"Captain, I assure you that I enjoyed our time together on Dannakor. I had not expected you to be quite so interesting. Please, I want you to believe me."

"I don't give a damn what you want. You gave me up to that Centauri bastard without a second thought."

"My *only* thought was of you! He's killed all of your Air Command colleagues. You'd be dead now if Rakh hadn't immediately grasped your value to all of us."

She frowned. He was probably right. "And what you said

is true? You're Arawaj? A rebel?"

"That is what you call us."

"What's your interest here? You had no idea the Shri-Lan were coming to raid the station, did you?"

"No, I did not. I was there to, ah, invite you to visit with us a while and to obtain the schematics. Unfortunately, you blasted the lot before I had a chance."

"Pity."

"But I still have you. That's a whole lot better. You will be of great service to the Arawaj. Once we find our way home, that is."

"Arawaj!" she scoffed. "Your group is a pitiful faction of dissidents hiding in holes on Caspia. You don't have one tenth of the Shri-Lan's fire power."

"That is not going to matter much longer. The Shri-Lan are surviving only by making use of whatever hardware remnants were left in the wake of Tharron's passing. Once his group crumbled there was no one left to keep the ledgers balanced."

"You're talking about Pe Khoja. The only one of Tharron's people with any sort of vision. Even in a demented rebel sort of way."

"There is no need to resort to name calling," he said primly. "But, yes, when we lost Pe Khoja we lost much of what gave any sort of cohesion to our battle against your Union, our oppressors. We splintered, and now we fight among ourselves instead of rising up against your control of our worlds. That must stop."

Nova shook her head and sat on one of the narrow cots in the cabin. "Caspia is allied. We don't even have a base there. No one wants to control your planet. And the Shri-Lan have as many Humans and Centauri as they do indigenous members. They don't want freedom. They have no ideals. They want to take over everything that the Union has built in Trans-Targon."

"What the Centauri have built. Foreigners whose home planet is so far away that most of them have never even been there. Who flattered and bribed those who actually belong here into joining their empire. Followed by the murder of those who refuse. It's not a Union. It's exploitation."

She threw her hands up, a tired gesture. She was well aware of the Union's shortcomings and their reliance on Air Command to keep enemies at bay. But it was still largely a trade organization and most worlds prospered by their membership in the Commonwealth. And the pirates, thieves and rebels who helped themselves prospered, too. "I've heard all this before. You even sound like Pe Khoja. Did he leave notes?"

"It's sad to see you reduced to mockery, Captain. It's beneath you. You have far greater purpose and potential."

"What are you up to, Lok?" she said, not expecting an answer. She was surprised when he actually seemed to consider her question. He looked at the door as if preparing to leave the room, and then back at her. A few silent moments ticked by before he stepped around the other cot and sat down.

He leaned forward. "You can make a difference in all this, if you wish, Captain," he said slowly, as if choosing his words with care. "You know the Centauri don't belong here. And neither do you. But more importantly, you don't belong in power here. Your Union has the guns and the wealth to make it so, but that doesn't make it right."

She shrugged, having had to listen to rebel lectures before this day. But his didn't sound like the usual disjointed harangue she had heard before. There was a quiet tone of reason in his voice that intrigued her.

"That slice of graphene in your head can change everything," he said.

Nova blinked. "What?"

"Do I have your attention? The ANI will shorten the distance between us all even more than the stable gates already have. Some day it may even reach to Centauri in a single jump instead of two years. Is that what we want? Can you imagine the horrific escalation of our wars? Do you think the Shri-Lan are going to sit idly by while you overrun more of our worlds?"

Nova felt a little transfixed by the large yellow eyes that were focused upon her with fierce intensity. She had heard this not so many hours ago when Tuain had said much the same on Dannakor. And now Sao Lok, a rebel, also seemed desperately afraid of what the new interface would mean to all of them.

"What do you want from me?" she asked, as she had asked Tuain.

Sao Lok drew back and his eyes shifted away from her face. "There are ways to stop all of this. You can help us stop it."

"Me?"

"Yes. You do not have to spend your life in mindless service to your Union. To Air Command. There are other paths you can take."

She raised both eyebrows, nearly amused by his suggestion. "You are asking me to defect?"

"It may be a good choice for you." He looked down at his hands and thoughtfully twisted one of several rings on his thumbs. "When my kinsmen heard that you were going to be part of the ANI project, I was directed to, ultimately, hand you over to them. To Pe Khoja's clan. Their need for justice requires it." His eyes returned to hers. "Eventually they will find you. And Major Tychon. But I want to convince them that you hold far greater value! You are an immense source of information. You have access to places we cannot go. You have skills that we need. But there is more. I've read about you. Heard about you. You are resourceful and you have proven that you are more than just a soldier. You can have great influence and power among my people."

"You've studied me?"

"Yes, of course," he said, apparently not aware of her discomfort at that revelation.

"Then you should know that power doesn't interest me. Wealth doesn't, either."

"I do know that. What matters to you is the stability of Trans-Targon. But I don't think I'm wrong to believe that it wouldn't matter to you *how* this will be accomplished."

"It cannot be accomplished your way! You're as destructive as the Shri-Lan, except that you don't have the means to be really good at it. You are as murderous as they are."

"And you? Are you not? If you had a gun you would shoot me and everyone else here without a second thought. Maybe killing rebels is so easy for you that it does not even require a first thought! How many have you killed? Can you even still count them all?" He paused briefly as if waiting for an answer. "You don't even consider or understand the difference between Shri-Lan and Arawaj. We don't seek wealth like common pirates. We just want the Union gone. We want this sector to return to the peace we knew before you showed us how to pollute other worlds with our presence."

"You really believe that is possible?" she asked, more curious than derisive.

"I do," he said. She gasped when he actually took her hands in his and squeezed them for emphasis. "I really do! Tell me, Captain, if it were possible, would you not give up your life to end these wars? To bring peace into this sector?"

She tilted her head. "Yes," she said. "I would. And many of us do. Every day."

He nodded. "So is it then such a big leap for you to change the way you view us? And the way you view your own people? With people like you on our side we can start over. The right way."

She pulled her hands out of his grasp. "Your way! Arawaj ways."

"The Arawaj is only the part of Caspia that is desperate for a solution. Our homeworld is peaceful. We want it to remain that way."

"Now you sound like the old Delphians. Except they just ignore what they don't like. You want to destroy it."

"Before it destroys us. As it will destroy Delphi. The interface you carry is the next step in that process. What if I told you that you can help us bring peace to this entire sector? End these wars. Start all over again. Peacefully."

"How?"

He stood up. "I will not tell you that now. I want you to think about what I said. You know I'm right. We, the Arawaj, are not your enemy. Not like the Shri-Lan who are so busy collecting war trophies that they have forgotten what they are rebelling against."

"I am not a traitor."

"I don't care what you call yourself, Captain. I am offering a way that you can actually make a difference in this world you've created." He opened the door to the hall. "Think about it. Then let me know when you're ready get over your single-minded loyalties and listen to reason."

"I'll be sure to do that," she said, aiming for sarcasm but missing the mark.

He smiled thinly. "Believe me when I say that I hope to make you see us for what we really are. I hope, if I may be so presumptuous, to be your friend. I like you, to be blunt. But I will not underestimate you. Do not try to cross Rakh. Remember that I know how the ANI works. You won't have access to communications."

"You would rather die out here than risk capture by Air Command?"

"Yes. Stop trying to make your people out to be any more noble than those contemptible Shri-Lan. If you manage to send a message through that keyhole and if that leads Air Command here, we will be captured. Rakh will probably murder every one of your people before giving up. And then your commanders will simply blow this ship to pieces. The Union has no interest in filling its prisons with rebel foot soldiers and you know it."

Nova said nothing. He was right. Rakh's rabble was worthless to Air Command. And Azon Corp had a staff of thousands. Every last civilian on board was replaceable.

"I will make sure that you remain unharmed. You and the young Delphian in any case. I am not concerned about the others. It's up to you to keep them alive a little longer by cooperating."

She held up her hand. "No. Not with threats, Lok. If you are so much better than the rest of us, show me. Promise me that no one else will get hurt while I consider what you've said."

He tilted his head. "Bargaining, Captain?"

"Yes. They are civilians. They did not ask for this."

"I will try. But this is a Shri-Lan ship. Their fate is in Rakh's hands."

"I am pretty sure that you have his ear by now. You are persuasive."

He smiled. That smile was every bit as friendly and attractive as it had been on Dannakor when they had shared a leisurely breakfast what now seemed ages ago. When she had liked him for his knowledge and wit and the certainty that he belonged on her team. "You are the only one I'm hoping to persuade," he said. "But I will try to manage that Centauri's baser instincts. If you do your part and get us home."

Nova kicked the bunk on which he had sat as soon as the Caspian had left the cabin. "Bloody hell, bloody rebels, bloody stupid Luce!" She drew her knees up and wrapped her arms around them. She was to blame for this, too, she knew. She should have tried harder to stop Luce from making the jump. Would the rebels have destroyed the freighter? Or would they now be hostages also, but at least in a safer part of the galaxy?

And what was Sao Lok planning? Was he really hoping to recruit her to his cause? He seemed so very convinced that he had some critical answer to all of their troubles. Was it possible? Clearly, the man's intelligence and cunning had gotten him past Azon Corp's security processes to get him a position on Dannakor's ANI team. Of what else was he capable?

She sat, brooding and planning, for what seemed like hours, until the door opened and Jovan stepped into the cabin. He looked around the cramped space and did not flinch when the door behind him slid shut with more force than necessary. He leaned against it and regarded her for a while. "At least on the other ship I wasn't locked up," he said finally.

"They're going to cut the *Terius* loose," she replied. "It's taking up too many resources."

"I assumed that."

"Did you get a chance to find the other interface?" she whispered.

He shook his head. "I made it into that... room. They had them stacked up like they don't care. Just piled up! It was so cold in there. I could barely breathe. I found your Captain Luce. There were only holes in the sides of his head. But very precisely cut. Someone knew what they were doing."

She grimaced. "I'm sorry, Jovan. That must have been awful."

"Yes," he allowed. "It was." He sat on the other bunk and folded his hands between his knees as he leaned forward in a posture eerily similar to Sao Lok's. "What's your plan?"

"My plan?"

"You didn't have me locked up in here with you just because you miss Delphian company. And from what I know about you and Shan Tychon, you're not the sort to take orders from rebels. So you must have a plan."

"We don't really have any options. We're going to have to jump us back home." Nova nodded toward the door and then surreptitiously pointed at her interface by scratching the side of her face.

He winced. Another khamal with the Human so soon after the last one was surely going to hurt. Reluctantly, he reached out as if he, in his capacity as Shantir, was examining her bruised cheek. His fingers touched her interface and she soon felt his presence inside her head.

How are you holding up? This is all so alien to you.

He sent a mental shrug and again she was reminded of Human teenage attitudes. She hid her smile along with her worry for him.

I don't think the interface can make the long spans possible, she relayed. *It'll likely kill me as it killed Captain Luce and then it may not bring us any closer to home, anyway. But I am being forced to try or they will kill the others. Those that are left.*

You want me to help you with the jump?

No. I won't ask that of you. It's too dangerous. We're going to try to reach Shan Tychon.

He blinked. *How?*

I think I can do it. If you help me.

That is not possible! You cannot begin a khamal without a physical connection. It just cannot be done. And at such a distance!

Distance is nothing, she sent. *You should know this by now. Even your sect's own teachings are clear on that.*

But how will you touch him?

I don't think I need to. There is some connection between Tychon and me that we haven't really explored. But it's there. I think it's because of what happened back before Cyann was born.

There are rumors about that in the enclave. That it changed you. Physically. That you're a transgenic mod. That you're not really Human any more.

I've heard that, too. Don't mind the rumors. I'm all Human and proud of it.

You don't seem convinced.

Can we talk about my plan, please?

If you wish.

I think together we can reach Ty. If we can get his attention he will join us and then there will be three of us working together. Right now no one even knows where we are, or if we're alive. If we can connect with Trans-Targon they will come for us. We just have to stall for time. We'll pretend to work on the jump.

He seemed skeptical. It was clear by his narrowed eyes and tight-lipped expression that the pain in his head had already reached an uncomfortable level. *It's going to hurt. Will it damage me?*

It doesn't seem to harm Tychon. We will be in a deeper khamal most of the time. I just need you to help me stay focused. And some of the time we can just pretend to be working together. We just need more time!

Very well, then.

Nova glanced around the room. Would they have video surveillance in here? She pretended to scratch another itch while hooking her fingers into a pocket.

I have a copy of the interface. Maybe it's best if you kept it safe. They're not likely to search you. If they do, try to destroy it.

He smiled tiredly. *Swallow it, perhaps. Like a proper spy would?*

Nova remembered cutting the device from Quinn's head and bit back a comment. Perhaps some of her Vanguard squad mates would see the ghoulish humor in that; Jovan would not. *Well, let's hope you don't need to.*

She put her hand on his knee and he patted it comfortingly until she pulled it away, leaving the small metal device behind.

"You know," he said after breaking their mental link. "Sometimes I've wondered about maybe joining Air Command. I can see the base from my balcony in the enclave on Delphi. All those planes taking off to places I might never see. What you do sounds so incredibly exciting. Hearing about Shan Tychon and some of the other Delphians who've become pilots and engineers and explorers makes me wish I was doing those things, too."

"Why don't you?" she said. "If your head is good enough for the Shantirs, it's more than good enough to be a top level spanner. You could take a ship anywhere. At your age Tychon had dreams of exploring, of deep space, too. Things worked out differently for him, but I know he still sometimes thinks about it. He could help you with this. We both could."

She shrugged. "Shan Tychon's contempt for the Shantirate is well known. He'd want nothing to do with me."

"You don't have to be a Shantir," she said carefully.

"I have a duty. I was never meant to be anything but a

Shantir. You know there is no higher station among us. It's a privilege I can't discard lightly."

"But is it what you want?"

He was silent for so long that she thought he might not answer at all. "It's what I love. But I have only my dreams to compare it to."

"You would not be the first Shantir to leave Delphi."

"Leave Delphi?" He shook his head at that notion. "It's a dream, nothing more."

"Just for a while. To explore and to learn. We need people like you off-world. Ambassadors, scientists. Your abilities are needed elsewhere as much as in the enclave."

"Recruiting, are you?"

"Yeah. They'll not run out of Shantir initiates so quickly on Delphi. But imagine the sort of Shantir you can be if you spent some years exploring other places. You would be worth so much more to your sect. They will not stop you."

"The Council might." He stared into the distance somewhere a few light years beyond her left shoulder. "I've dreamed of flying. Piloting I mean. Like you... like Shan Tychon." He gave her a shy smile. "Seeing you in that cockpit, trying to save everybody, knowing that we were being chased. It... it was so unimaginable. So frightening. And yet the thought of taking a ship to some faraway place is more wonderful than anything I can think of."

"Then do it!" She looked around their dreary cabin. "You don't have to join Air Command if these accommodations aren't up to your tastes."

He surprised her by laughing at that. "You have a way about you, Human. I can see why Shan Tychon chose you."

She smiled back at him. Once relaxed and less intent on disguising the distress he must surely be feeling aboard this rebel ship, his handsome face lit up with warmth and kindness. "Well, think about it. I can help you find a place to start your studies."

His smile faded. His vague gesture encompassed their surroundings. "If..."

SIX

Walking here, along the high fence that cordoned off the Air Command base allocation from the rest of Delphi, where fences were used only to control livestock, had always given Tychon a feeling of being in two worlds at once.

He looked to his left, across the flat, deserted expanse of the airfield where a few military and civilian planes parked cozily side by side. Not far was the base itself, also well-maintained because Delphians wouldn't have it any other way even if few of them ever set a foot inside. And then he looked to the right, through the fence and over the shallow bowl of the Chalyss'ya valley, flanked on two sides by soaring, snow-capped mountain ranges. A single city nestled at the opposite end of the valley, close enough to feel the protection and convenience of the Union base, yet far enough away to make a point.

He threaded his fingers through the links of the fence and breathed deeply of the cool, moist air rising from the valley. Several of Delphi's moons illuminated the farms and fields below him but the silvery light did not seem to dispel the dark up here.

"Did you want me to notice you or are you really so

inept?" he asked the shadows.

"Was waiting for visiting hours to be over," came the reply, spoken with a lazy drawl. The man who had silently followed Tychons since he left the base hospital came into the light of the moons. As smooth-featured and black-haired as all Centauri, he moved with feline grace made all the more catlike for the eyes that seemed to reflect the moonlight. A scar marred his forehead above the right eye.

"Sethran Kada, I'm guessing." Tychon said.

"That's me, Cap'n," the Centauri replied.

"Major."

"Right."

"How did you get onto the base?"

"I asked nicely. Carras seems to feel that you need to see me in a bad way."

Tychon shrugged. "Not you. I'm looking for a friend of yours. A Bellac woman. Didn't he tell you that?"

"He did. In a way that was missing a lot of details. Let's go to my place." Seth tipped his head toward the far side of the airfield. The men walked silently, uncomfortably, until they had reached the Centauri's cruiser.

Tychon's practiced eye moved along its contours, easily making out its armaments and modifications. "Nice," he said, recognizing capabilities likely rivaling those of an Eagle. He ducked into the small cargo hold that also served as air lock and followed Seth into the main cabin. That was less nice, featuring well-worn, bare essentials and the careless clutter of someone not terribly concerned with housekeeping.

Seth perched on a stool by the small galley near the cockpit and gestured toward a low, comfortable chair. Tychon picked up a jacket and tossed it onto a lounger before seating himself.

"Now we're all cozy," Seth said. "Carras told me your lady is missing in action and that somehow Acie has something to do with it. Let's have it, Major."

Tychon continued his appraisal of the pilot, making a

mental note to find out who had cleared the man for landing on UCB Delphi and then allowed him to walk about the base unaccompanied and fully armed. The nondescript black shirt and well-worn combat pants gave no hint about where he might have been recently although a wide bracelet on his wrist looked like it was made on Bellac. "Carras mentioned that you had some dealings with Captain Whiteside in the past," he said.

Seth nodded.

"What sort of dealings?"

"Went to school together."

Tychon sighed, already tired of the rogue's impertinence. "Surely more than that?"

Seth grinned. "Like what?"

"You had some contact with rebels. Like that Bellac woman. Acie Daruen. Nova knows her and Carras told me that you do, too."

"I do."

"I need to speak with her."

"Why?"

"That isn't really your concern."

"Acie is my friend. I'm not too clear on what *your* concern is."

Tychon ran his hands through his hair, wondering how much to tell this man. Anything at all? Everything? Did it even matter? Every moment that passed was another moment that Nova was in danger. "How does your friend know Nova?"

Seth leaned back and propped his elbow on the galley counter. "Why don't you start by telling me what happened? In case you're wondering, I am not a rebel, in the way you label these things. I was Prime Staff, working for Factor Baroch before he dropped dead. On your watch."

"That incident is classified."

"Apparently."

Tychon considered. To be Prime Staff meant working exclusively, and outside military authority, for the Ten

Elected Factors, the highest level of government that ruled Trans-Targon and the Terra-Centauri systems. Those agents lived in anonymity and with complete immunity as the Factors' proxies. Spies and assassins, in other words. How would Nova have been mixed up with this group?

He stood up and paced across the small space, stopping to look down into the cockpit. It completely invalidated the casual messiness of the living area with a spotless array of features that would put most battle cruisers to shame. Clearly, the Centauri was either very adept at collecting some very high-quality gear or he had easy access to government-issued technologies. "Feeder interface," he murmured. "Foursquare crossdrives. Shields to handle that, I'm guessing."

"Aye. I call her the *Dutchman*, although there might be a gender problem with that."

Tychon leaned against the bulkhead beside the cockpit entrance. "All right, Kada. This is what I can tell you. Nova was testing some classified equipment. There was some sort of attack. It's not clear what happened but the recordings that went out with the distress signals showed her shooting Union officers, destroying equipment and talking to rebels, including your friend Acie Daruen."

Seth's eyebrows had slowly risen toward his shaggy hairline as Tychon recited Nova's deeds. He stared speechlessly at the Delphian when he had finished but managed a whistle.

Tychon raised his hands, waiting for a reply.

"Are we talking about the same Nova?" Seth said finally. "Whiteside? Redhead? Vanguard pilot? Expert marksman, career soldier and really bad cook?"

Tychon nodded, almost amused. "That one."

"And you believe any of that?" Seth asked, incredulous.

"Command does. She's wanted and I'm off duty because of all that."

"And Acie was there?"

"Not just there, but a few weeks ago Nova was caught

sending a message about Acie to someone named Vincent on Magra. The Torley side of Magra. That's when your name came up. And then Acie was accidentally misplaced on Zera. Strange coincidence, don't you think?"

"Yeah," Seth grinned. "Funny how these things happen, isn't it."

"Not really funny."

"You Delphians have no sense of humor."

Tychon crossed his arms and slouched comfortably against the wall, prepared to bide his time until the Centauri was ready to deal.

Seth said nothing for a while and drummed his fingers against the counter, a little unnerved by Tychon's unwavering gaze. His patience broke long before the Delphian's, which didn't surprise either of them. "Acie is just a dissident," he said finally. "Not really a rebel."

"That's not much of a distinction."

"It is when you consider that people like her and Vincent are no more enamored by your Union than they are with the Shri-Lan and their kind. They do what they feel they must. Peacefully, if possible. She's been living among the rebels, mostly on Magra Torley, for years. Sometimes she acts as an informer. For your side. As far as the Shri-Lan are concerned, she doesn't get involved in anything heavy. Mixing explosives, analyzing whatever bio materials they can steal from Union labs, doctoring, breeding a better Rhuwac. Who knows. When she can she engages in a little sabotage. Sabotaging rebel initiatives, I mean. Faulty ammo, drugs that don't work, stuff like that." He thoughtfully chewed on his lip. "Not sure how much longer she's going to get away with that. She's running on pure luck by now."

"Your side," Tychon said.

"Eh?"

"You said 'your side'. Not 'our side'."

"Did I?" Seth shrugged. "Interesting. I guess I haven't really thought of myself as being on anyone's side since I left Prime Staff."

"How about now?"

Seth contemplated the question for a moment. "I'm on Nova's side."

Tychon nodded. "That's good enough for me. Who is that Vincent that Nova mentioned?"

Seth smiled. "Acie's nanny. Acie may be brilliant but I doubt she knows friend from foe half the time. He makes sure the doors get locked at night. I'm surprised she was even out there. She doesn't go on raids. She's a big brain in a tiny body. You don't jeopardize that in a firefight."

"I'm hoping she'll tell me more about what happened. What factions were involved. Where they came from. Any of that might help me find Nova."

"I received a message from Vincent yesterday. Acie's ship is on the way back. From Dannakor, your classified place."

Tychon's upper lip twitched in what was neither a snarl nor a smile. "Where can I find her?"

Seth shook his head. "Round about Aikhor. But if you want to see Acie, it'll be on my terms. We can get there in about twenty hours if we jump past Magra."

"I wasn't planning to arrest her."

The Centauri shrugged.

Tychon sighed and came to his feet. "How are you set up for coolant?"

"Processors are fine although I won't feel imposed upon if you can cadge another tube or two from the ground crew. Why?"

Tychon tapped the data array embedded in the thin sleeve on his forearm. "Because I know of a keyhole in this system that'll get us to Aikhor in nine hours. Long burn though."

Seth grinned. "Damn, I love having a spanner on board!"

"I won't be long," Tychon went back into the ship's air lock. "Get us cleared for takeoff."

* * *

Tychon's estimate had been accurate; after making the jump through the promised keyhole, they approached the waterlogged planet in just under nine hours. He had opened the breach with enviable efficiency, using the *Dutchman*'s generators without waste. Seth had covertly watched the Delphian's calm face as he lay in the pilot's couch, his mind tethered to the ship via his interface to probe deeply into the unknown void to find a suitable exit. He had felt his way carefully, guiding the ship's calculations as one possibility after another was suggested and then discarded. It was some time before he perceived and understood the location he meant to find and punched the ship into the breach.

Seth had taken over to slow the *Dutchman* when it emerged into real space, knowing that the tremendous strain of the jump would nearly incapacitate the Delphian for a while. He steadied the ship to find that their coordinates were true and they had come through the vast distance as unscathed as if they had never left Delphi. Tychon had risen from the pilot bench and moved to the cabin lounger like a man twice his age. He had dropped into a silent, motionless khamal, as close as Delphians came to sleeping, and had not opened his eyes again until Seth put the *Dutchman* into a high orbit over Aikhor.

"New again?" Seth asked when Tychon rejoined him in the cockpit.

Tychon had changed into a loose Feydan pullover and a worn cloth jacket over combat pants that were not out of place on civilians on Aikhor. He tucked a gun into a pocket on his thigh and reached up to braid his hair. "Fairly."

"I don't understand why you people volunteer for this job. I once saw a guy get a nosebleed from trying to make a jump. Torture."

"Beats hanging around in normal space for days on end," Tychon replied. He looked up at the display screens. A considerable amount of traffic buzzed the area, coming from and going to this neutral planet that welcomed rebels and renegades more often than Union members. "Where are we landing?"

"Ath Kier. She's holed up at a temple on the north end of

the island. Oh, look! It's raining."

"Those people wouldn't know what to do on a day that it doesn't rain."

Seth stood up and went back into the main cabin. "I think I need to dress up a little," he said. "Might be folks there that don't need to see me." He opened a bin near the cargo area and sorted through it. "You inspire me, Delphian. Let's be kinsmen."

Tychon watched him pull a few items from the bin and then reach up and carefully retrieve a long blue wig from an overhead compartment. "You're joking." He stood up and came into the cabin to perch on one of the galley stools.

"Nope," Seth said. "Physically, Delphians are the closest to us. Well, I suppose Humans are, too, but they're short and this is much more fun." He held the blue head of hair toward Tychon. "Braid that for me? You guys have the knack for that."

Tychon grimaced. "I think not! That's someone's hair. You're not going to tell me that someone actually gave that up? Voluntarily?"

"I didn't ask. Maybe not all Delphians are as fussy about their hair as you are." He put the wig aside and pulled a small case from the bin. Tychon watched in fascination while Seth fished through the case and retrieved a set of lenses that he fixed carefully over his eyes. He blinked a few times and when he looked at Tychon his eyes were of a deep blue.

"Still glowing, though," Tychon said.

"Hmm, yeah. Let's hope I don't have to hang out in any dark places. Usually this works fine."

"You do this often?"

Seth shrugged and lifted the wig over his head, carefully tucking the glossy black waves of his own hair beneath it.

"Don't cover your ears," Tychon could not help but comment when Seth tried to gather up the long strands. "Pull it back over the top of your head or you'll look like my grandsire." He stood up and, with a dramatic sigh, took over from Seth to tie the hair into a loose braid. "This is without doubt the strangest thing I've done in a long while. Let's hope you don't have to fool a real Delphian with this getup. You're not pale enough, either."

"Do you really think the average Aikhor rebel is going to notice that?" Seth took a paint stick from the bin. "If they had more brains they wouldn't be hanging around that dump." Carefully, he added a shade of blue to the corners of his lips and then slipped on a pair of gloves to hide his fingernails. "There. Am I pretty?"

Tychon returned to the cockpit. "Let's get on with this. Please."

They brought the *Dutchman* down on a crowded airfield located precariously close to the edge of a deep fissure running nearly all the way across Ath Kier Island. Tychon had looked into it as they approached, seeing no bottom except for a thick layer of yellow mist below them. The walls of the fissure were made of some dark stone that glistened in the constant drizzle. The planet's low gravity assaulted them as soon as the ship came to rest north of Kiertown, a city as dense and grey as the rest of the island. An inhospitable, greenish sky loomed low over their heads when they walked to a boxy pre-fab building at the edge of the airfield. There they paid for the use of a domed skimmer that took them down a winding path away from the city and into canyons of jagged cliffs running along the island's chasm.

They found a scattering of cone-shaped buildings housing whatever supports were required by a massive structure perched on the edge of the trench. The temple was so roughly-hewn that it appeared to be part of the cliff face, its sharp angles and panes simply an extension of these walls. Some of the yellowish fog emitting from whatever vented in the depths of the gorge added a pungent smell to the misery here. It was only partially held back by a protective stone wall separating the temple grounds from the canyon.

"Pleasant," Tychon said when they climbed out of their air car. He observed some of the natives moving on all four of their gangly limbs among the round buildings. None of them even looked their way, apparently not startled by the sight of blue-haired bipeds. Or perhaps they just didn't care. "This is a church?"

"Of sorts," Seth said, his voice low. "A retreat. Belongs to the Shri-Lan. Didn't I mention that?"

Tychon frowned. "No, you did not. Can you be a little more forthcoming? You just dumped a Vanguard officer in the middle of a very nasty rebel faction."

"Would that have stopped you?"

Tychon turned to cross the cobbled courtyard in front of the temple. "A little notice would be polite."

"It's not much of a rebel hangout, anyway." Seth hurried after him. "This is mainly just a religious enclave, like yours on Delphi. Except this has more gods and less neuroscience."

"You know a little too much about Delphi," Tychon muttered. He walked up the broad ramp leading to massive doors, his eyes on the sharp peaks above them. The panel he tried rolled on small wheels as it moved aside.

It was cold inside and he hadn't expected it to be different. A vast hall appeared to make up most of the building's interior. There were no prayer benches for the faithful making the journey to this place but the floor was a magnificently tiled masterpiece of intricate patterns. He suspected that people were invited to sit or kneel to receive whatever instruction was dispensed from the stage at the far end of the hall. The ceiling disappeared into vague shadows into which the light of the hall's few lamps did not reach.

Seth pulled a torch from his pocket and lit it. It was common knowledge that Delphians did not see well in the dark and the extra light hid the telltale glow of his Centauri eyes. They walked cautiously across the patterned floor toward some doors to the right of the stage.

A figure wearing a long kilt emerged from there and moved toward them. The shambling, splayed gait told them that this was a Caspian, as did the click of his nails on the tiles, before they saw his face. He did not extend welcoming arms but held a short walking staff defensively across his chest. Seth and Tychon halted at a respectful distance, their hands not far from the guns at their sides.

"We not often see Delphians among us," they were greeted in the language of the Caspians. The man displayed narrowed yellow eyes and bared teeth, making it clear that the greeting was not meant to be welcoming. The dense hair on his chest and shoulders was patterned in light patches found among the people of equatorial Caspia.

"Indeed not," Tychon said, using a trade language. "We are here to find someone."

"You come well armed."

"It seems prudent. Is there a Bellac woman here? Name of Acie Daruen?"

"Yes, she has taken refuge with us."

"Refuge from what?" Seth said, sharpening his Centauri drawl as he spoke.

"From the dangers of these worlds, pilgrim. From herself, perhaps."

Tychon scanned the dim recesses of the temple and wished, not for the first time, for the keener night vision that blessed other races. "What do you mean?"

"I fear she's been... compromised by the evil influence of the Commonwealth Union, your overlords. Be gone, Delphi. There is nothing here for you."

"We have come for Acie," Tychon said firmly. "What has happened with her?"

"The woman has been seduced by your masters' promises and their lies. There are those among us who wish her harm, to punish her for the secrets she has whispered into the enemy's ears. And others seek to extract what information she holds by means that will surely destroy her frail body and spirit. She is a traitor and she will not live much longer unless she comes to see the way of the Truth."

"Where is she? What have you done with her?" Seth said.

Tychon grasped Seth's arm. "Is she safe here with you?" he asked the priest.

"She is hidden. Her safety is a question of circumstance. Even here not all are in agreement over her fate. She has value but she is no longer trusted. For now she is under my protection."

"Can we see her? Please."

"What can you possibly want with one such as she? Your people's understanding of the sciences is far greater than hers. We need her more than you do."

"She is a friend," Tychon said "We are concerned. We want to help."

The Caspian hesitated. He wrung his hands around his staff as he seemed to consider Tychon's request. But then something behind the two visitors caught his attention and his eyes widened in surprise. Both Tychon and Seth turned to see what approached.

"Crap," Seth said under his breath.

A dozen or more people, male and female and mostly Centauri, had loosened themselves from the dank shadows of the sanctuary and were approaching from all sides, silently and heavily armed. Walking toward them from the entrance was a woman carrying a compact data unit in her hands. Her short black hair was streaked with purple and silver dyes. "Tychon," she said, sounding amused. "Major Tychon, Vanguard Officer under Colonel Dom Everett, UCB Targon." She smiled at Tychon. "Have I got that right?"

He snarled and said nothing.

"Just because we are isolated here on Ath Kier does not mean that our surveillance systems are merely decorative. Or did you fail to notice them? Is it too dark in here, perhaps?" She turned to Seth. "You, however, were not recognized, whatever you are." She grasped his long braid and snatched the wig from his head. The Caspian priest gasped audibly when Seth's black strands fell over his forehead. "But unless you're ill with something, Centauri, your core temperature is a little hot for a Delphian."

He smiled and shrugged as if caught stealing a pastry from the dinner tray. They were searched and their guns and communicators were taken.

"Let's drop them off the cliff and be done with this," one of the rebels said. "Them and the Bellac traitor. The vent eels will love the treat."

"The Bellac has sought sanctuary with my sect," the priest said to the woman. "Do what you want with these spies. Outside. This temple is for those who come to find peace."

"Sadly, your comrades don't agree, Rebel," Tychon said angrily.

"Rebel to you, perhaps, but we here work to bring peace to our people, just as your own clergy does, Delphi. All wars are evil, no matter whose beliefs you hold."

The rebel leader regarded the priest with cold eyes. "We shall let Ros Talac decide the Bellac's fate when he arrives." She turned to Tychon. "We have a long list of grievances against you, Major. You've been hounding us for years. The Shri-Lan will celebrate when you've been purged from existence. You don't mind if we invite the others to watch you die, do you?"

"By all means," he hissed.

Tychon's eyes were on the walls and deep-set windows of the stone temple as they were led along a damp corridor and down into the lower levels. Aikhor's murky daylight faded entirely and now only a few and widely-spaced lamps helped them forward. He felt the air move in the direction they were going, indicating open windows, if not doors, to the temple. He shook his head in a minute gesture when he saw Seth studying the distance between himself and the nearest of their guards. There were too many of them, and too heavily armed.

They were marched into a small room near the end of a corridor, apparently some sort of storage. He made out barrels and boxes stacked along the walls but most of it was lost in the gloom to him. He was relieved when one of the rebels lobbed Seth's torch at him.

"Here," she said. "Let it not be said that we're without compassion. This might keep the pets from chewing your feet." She slammed the door and they were left alone.

Tychon looked around the room before facing Seth, wondering about the measure of the man. Surely, as a former Prime Staff member, he was well-trained and experienced and not likely to crumble in this situation. Physically, he seemed as fit as any Union agent. But he had a quick tongue and a belligerent nature that may well prove dangerous to both of them.

Seth raised his hands. "Yes, don't say it. I should have known better than to take a Vanguard officer in here. Not my fault you're so damn recognizable, though."

Tychon walked to a small window, little more than an air shaft, set into the deep wall. "Covert operations are generally not our mission." He tried the door into the corridor. "A percussion charge would work nicely on this. But the one I had seems to be missing all of a sudden."

Seth hitched a hip onto one of the crates. He peered at the stone floor. "What do you think she meant with 'pets'?"

"Will they be able to find your plane?"

"Doubt it. At least not quickly. That airfield is busy. I didn't bring the remote com with me, so they won't know which one is mine."

Tychon nodded. "Then we'd better get back there fast."

Seth pointed at the locked door. "After you, Major."

"They have to come back sooner or later. Look around for something useful. I can't see a damn thing down here."

Seth smirked and hopped off his crate. "Probably a good thing. That bug in the corner looks hungry."

Tychon turned to make out a creature scuttling along the stone wall. It seemed to be an insect, carrying a ridged black and green carapace, but it was likely the largest beetle he had ever seen. Indeed, he had known people who kept smaller pets than this. He saw two long mandibles on one end and what might be a stinger on the other. "Let's not assume that thing is non-poisonous," he said.

"Sounds sensible." Seth began to peer into boxes and along some of the shelving. "Mostly food stuffs. None of it terribly appetizing. Maybe to our friend there." He jumped back with a curse when another one scurried from behind some jars.

"Let's see if we can take that shelf apart. Those metal uprights look fairly sharp." Tychon grasped the corner of the shelf to give it an experimental tug. He halted when something caught his attention. "Did you hear that?"

"No. What?"

Tychon frowned. A headache had begun with a jab and now radiated from his temple around the side of his head. He closed his eyes for a moment and then it had passed. "Nothing," he said. "Imagining things."

They worked without speaking for a while and managed to pry some of the supports from one of the shelves lining the walls. Tychon continued to feel some odd presence intruding upon his thoughts. It was faint, no more than a feeling that there was something to be remembered or some task left undone.

Seth hefted the metal bar in his hand and feinted about the room. "En garde!" he exclaimed. "Now if everyone's guns quit working we'd be almost dangerous." He whirled and stabbed the bar to the floor, impaling one of the pets. It made an unpleasant hissing sound as it died.

Tychon sat on a crate and lowered his head into his hands.

"What's the matter with you?"

"Head hurts," Tychon said. "Gravity getting to me, too. Don't shout."

Both of them looked up when they heard a sound by the door. It first seemed like the scrabbling of another insect but then the bolt was pulled back and the door opened. They raised their makeshift weapons to greet whatever was coming at them.

"Acie!" Seth exclaimed when the small Bellac slipped into the room and closed the door behind her. She wore a stained pair of coveralls but otherwise did not look very much imprisoned. "This is a little unexpected."

She ran across the room and flung her arms around his waist. "You're here! You made it!"

He took her head into his hands and kissed her forehead. "Well, for what it's worth. Not sure how we'll leave again, though."

"Nar Tosh told me that the others had taken you down here. He left my door unlocked. I'm thinking he wants me to leave." She giggled and then squinted at Seth. "What happened to your eyes?"

"So cold down here that I'm turning blue," he grinned. "Speaking of which, meet Tychon. We forgot to disguise him, too. He'd make a fine Rhuwac."

She peered at Tychon from the safety of Seth's arms. "Air Command guy," she said. "That's Nova's boyfriend, isn't it? What's he doing here? His people broke my spectrometer on Phi. No way can I afford another. Did Nova make it back from Dannakor?"

Tychon rubbed his hand over his face. "Look, can we get out of here now? Obviously, the Bellac knows her way around this little chapel. Maybe we can chat about your beakers later?"

Seth looked at Acie and soundlessly mouthed "Delphian", as if that explained Tychon's curt request.

Acie nodded. "Yes, we don't have much time. They've sent for their boss. He's somewhere in Kiertown so it won't be long before he gets here. He's a mean one." She went to the door and along the way nudged one of the insects out of her way with her foot. "Shoo, beastie! We'll go down the hall this way. There is a passage down into the ravine from there. Leads to the outside of the wall. Take that torch with you. We'll get Vincent on the way."

"Ravine? You mean that bottomless pit of putrid fog that runs through this valley? And why is Vincent here?"

"He came to get me out of that pinch I was in with the Shri-Lan. That didn't work out so well. I'm not leaving without him. And it's not bottomless. It's just smelly. Sulfur pits down there. And dead things. And things that eat them.

Bring your sticks."

Tychon sighed. What was wrong with these people? His head throbbed and what they said seemed to make little sense.

Seth explained. "They don't have graveyards here. Too much stone. So they chuck the corpses over the edge. And us, if we don't get moving."

Acie inspected the hallway outside and then gestured for them to follow. She sped ahead of them, white braids bouncing with every step. The floor under their feet was slippery and the men moved more cautiously until she stopped by another door. "He's in here. But this door needs a key. Vincent!" she added in a loud whisper.

They heard someone move on the other side. "Acie?"

"I'm here. Seth is, too."

Tychon examined the lock on the wooden door and then wedged his metal bar under the crude latch. Seth also leaned on the lever until the entire faceplate of the lock came away from the door with a dull clank. They froze and listened for anyone that might have heard.

Acie pulled the door open and they quickly stepped into the monk's cell beyond. They found a Human elder whose broad smile rearranged the deep furrows in his face when he embraced the Bellac woman. "Acie! Child, I was so worried! And hello, Sethran! It's been a few years."

Tychon rolled his eyes at Seth. This old man was Acie's guardian? And why did these people constantly have to hug each other? Did no one here understand their peril?

"He's wickedly efficient with a gun," Seth assured him. "And more protective of her than a grush cat is of her babies."

"We have to keep moving," Tychon replied. "Someone is bound to come looking for us soon."

The Human squinted at Tychon while he stepped into a pair of worn boots. Acie handed him a long, rough-spun vest. "Who do we have here? A Delphian! And by his bearing a warrior. A rare combination among those folks.

That would make you a Union agent, seeing how none of you will have dealings with the likes of us."

"You have a good eye, Elder Brother," Tychon said and turned to open the door by a fraction to peer into the hallway.

"This is none other than Nova's mate," Acie said to Vincent. "The famed and feared Tychon of Delphi. His squad totally ruined Phi for us. But now it seems that he's finally fallen into rebel hands." She giggled. "Isn't it just utterly twisted to have two of Nova's lovers here together like this?"

Tychon's back stiffened and he turned very slowly to glower at Seth. After a long, breathless moment during which Acie's smile faded to nothing he said, "You didn't find it necessary to share that bit of news?"

Seth reached over and yanked one of Acie's tangled braids. "You know, sometimes you are a little loose in the general lip-area."

"Uh," she grimaced. "Oops. Why didn't you tell him?"

Seth shrugged. "It doesn't matter now, does it?" His question was for Tychon. "Was a long time ago."

Tychon regarded the Centauri wordlessly. He found it hard to imagine that Nova would take up with this rogue. There were some physical similarities between the two men; their height and long-limbed build had made it easy for Seth to pass as a Delphian. Their genetic link, although unexplained, was undeniable. But, he thought, that's where the comparison ended. What did Nova see in this man? Once again, he felt confounded by the complexities of Human emotion, reminded again that, as well as he thought he knew Nova, there was much more to learn.

He winced when he reminded himself that standing around here and speculating about her past relationships was probably not the way to get out of this place and on his way to finding her. There were four of them now here behind enemy lines. The woman little more than a civilian and the old rebel not looking any less frail. And not a single gun between them. He hefted the metal bar in his hand, feeling exceptionally underequipped for escaping a rebel hold.

"Yes! Five years, I think," Acie said quickly. She looked nervously from Seth to the makeshift weapon in Tychon's hands. "That's a long time, isn't it?"

Tychon turned back to the door. "Let's get out of this place now," he said. "Acie, lead the way. Quickly." He herded them into the hall, alert to sounds in the distance.

The Bellac woman darted past him, followed by Vincent who, despite his apparent age, moved with agility and speed. Seth fell into step beside him as they hurried along the dimly-lit stone passage.

"In here." Acie had stopped beside a low arch from which a narrow tunnel led somewhat downhill. "Goes to the outside. They dump garbage down this way. Don't worry about the jazzies. They don't bite unless they're hungry."

"Jazzies?" Seth said, ducking into the tunnel. Both he and Tychon had to stoop to fit into the small space. Something crunched under his boot and hissed. "Never mind."

They moved quickly downhill, mindful of the slimy ground and whatever it was that dripped from the ceiling. Soon a gust of air moved over their heads, bringing with it a smell of sulfur and offal that became stronger until it blasted their faces as they stepped outside. The opening of the tunnel was swathed in yellowish fog. Above them hung a heavy, hinged grate held to the ceiling with a lever.

Tychon grasped Acie's arm to stop her from moving forward. "Stop," he said. "Wait."

They paused and watched the dense clouds move past them until a strengthening breeze pushed them aside.

Seth whistled. "Good call, Major."

Only a few steps in front of them lay the massive ravine that dissected the island, sloping downward at a dangerous angle into dense fog. The decline was strewn with jagged boulders and a scattering of what looked disconcertingly like bones.

Seth looked upward for something recognizable above

them. The temple behind the massive wall reached high into the cloudy sky and he could make out a row of dimly lit windows. "I think the front of the sanctuary is that way. It faces toward the town."

"Wait," Acie said, her hand over her nose to ward off the smell. "Let's close this exit up."

Seth looked up at the grate. "Yeah, that'll slow them down by about a minute."

She shook her head as if amazed by his simple-mindedness. "The gate opens outward. Get your rod behind that rock over there and see if you can pry it free. Then just drop the gate and wedge the rock between it and that boulder."

"I vote we put Acie in charge," Seth said. Vincent and Tychon lowered the gate while he put the rock in place.

"All right, let's move." Tychon nodded toward the ledge snaking between the ancient wall and the side of the chasm. He pulled his sleeve over his hand to cover his mouth and nose. "What a stench!"

"I'm going to throw up," Acie moaned.

Vincent removed his vest and tore his shirt into strips which he handed around to the others. Once they had fastened the cloth around their faces it was a little easier to breathe and Acie's impulse to give up her breakfast seemed less urgent.

Tychon walked at the rear of their small column, keeping his eyes on his feet, but his mind was elsewhere. Something kept nagging at him. Had he forgotten something? He used his rod to push one of those nasty beetles out of his way and over the drop-off. "What?"

Seth, just ahead of him, turned. "What what?"

"Did you call me?"

"Why would I?"

Tychon frowned. "Someone called me."

"No one's said anything. Makes it easier not to taste the crap in the air." He coughed into his sleeve to muffle the sound.

Tychon looked back over his shoulder. "Let's try to move faster. I want to get off this planet. Something isn't right. Doesn't feel right."

Seth raised an eyebrow. "A lot of things aren't right. But since when do Delphians go by feelings?" He turned when they heard shouts behind them and above. A bright light shone overhead, stabbing into the fog. "I think someone noticed we left the premises," he said. "Hurry, Acie. Pick it up."

"Keep to the wall," Tychon said. "They won't take hovers down here. Too risky with all these rocks. Move faster."

They clung to the cliff wall, alternately looking down at the uneven ground and out into the fog where the beams of the searchlights continued to probe. Aikhor's heavy gravity hindered their progress as much as did their desire not to have to gulp the foul air.

"They'll be waiting for us up ahead at the end of the wall," Seth said.

Tychon nodded. "Yes, we're not so important that they'd bother coming down this way. Into this mess."

"You don't know Ros Talac, then. He's the worst of a bad lot."

"We've had to deal with his group a few times. He's a—" Tychon clutched his head and stumbled forward when a deep, stabbing pain drilled into his brain. He groaned loudly and slumped against the stone wall.

"Tychon?" he heard someone say. It might have been Vincent. "What's wrong with him?"

"My head," Tychon said. His vision began to fade but there was something oddly familiar about this pain and its location in his head. It had never been this bad before.

"Maybe there's something here that Delphians can't tolerate," Acie said. "Shouldn't be the sulfur, though. Wish I had my kit with me. Who knows what else is in the air."

Tychon sat heavily on the rocky ground and lowered his head into his hands. "Nova," he gasped.

"What about her?" Seth asked. He looked up when

another beam of light strafed over their heads.

"She... she's here. So far away... How?" Tychon closed his eyes and concentrated on the distant signal that felt so very familiar. "Is that you, Nova?"

"What is he talking about?" Acie said.

"That's a khamal," Seth said. "But how? Don't Delphians have to start one of those mind links up by touching?"

"This is not a good time for this!" Vincent said.

Tychon no longer paid any attention to them. He felt Nova in his mind as clearly as if he had touched her just moments ago. He smiled despite the pain when she tried to send her words.

Ty? I found you!

He groaned. *Easy. I hear you. It hurts a whole lot.* His lips moved silently as he formed the words in his mind to give them substance. *What happened? Are you well? How did you reach me?*

I don't even know! I opened the keyhole. We've been trying for a long time now. There is a Delphian here with me. Can you feel him?

Yes. Tychon paused a moment to focus on the youth. *That's a Shantir.*

Well, yes. A novice, though. He's helping me reach you. He's in a lot of pain, I think. This can't last.

Are you all right?

We're on a rebel ship. Shri-Lan, mostly. We don't know where we are, any of us. We went through a keyhole near Dannakor and I don't know where we came out. I don't think the new interface works. It killed the spanner who got us here. Now they want me to jump us back. I don't know if I can, Ty!

Don't do it. Please, Nova. Just don't.

I have no choice. The ANI team is here, too. They've killed everybody else. They said they'll kill more if I don't get us back. This isn't about hostages.

Tychon swore silently.

And they have a copy of the interface.

Forget the damn interface, Nova! We have to get you back!

No, listen. I mean that the Shri-Lan that attacked Dannakor, the ones that are still in Trans-Targon, have a copy of the interface. They took Lieutenant Betl, one of the other test subjects. They will force him to use the ANI to jump. They could have a fleet appearing anywhere.

But if it doesn't work...

Betl is Level Two. And he won't be as panicked as we were.

Understood. We will warn Air Command.

I have to go. Jovan is going to pass out or something.

Yes, I can feel that. You didn't answer me. Are you all right?

I... I'm fine now. They won't hurt me while they think I can get us back.

Tychon ground his teeth, knowing that she was hiding something. He cursed himself for not having insisted on also joining the project, choosing instead to laze around on Delphi. He could have taken the time to at least accompany her to Dannakor. His position within Air Command would have allowed him that privilege as an observer. But he had to make a point of his disdain for the entire project. *I'm so sorry—*

Don't do that, she sent. *I can feel that. If you had been here you'd be dead by now. I'll be all right. Jovan has convinced them that I'm very delicate and that they have to be nice to me.*

I will come for you, he promised. *Please don't try that jump. Wait till I get to Dannakor. We'll find a way to get you back. Please! You have to hold them off.*

I'll try. He felt their mental communication fade. *Kiss Cyann for me. I miss you so!*

Tychon hesitated only a moment before leading her into a deeper khamal, one they shared far more often than the one used to exchange words. He felt the pain in his head recede as both of them sunk into a blissful mental state that few people outside Delphi were aware of. With a silent apology to the Shantir linked to her, he sent a gentle touch from his mind to hers that grew in intensity as if they were not separated by a vast piece of galaxy. For an instant he felt every cell in her body and it seemed as if they were a single entity occupying the same space. She responded with a touch of her own that forced a groan of pleasure from his lips.

I'm going to need you to do that when you're back here, he managed when his body felt like his own again.

I wish I was there with you now.

Tychon had doubts about that. *I will find you. Don't do anything foolish, Greenie.*

She sent a smile. *It's been a while since you called me that, Major.*

He felt her fade away until nothing remained but the pain in his head. He opened his eyes to see three puzzled faces loom over him.

"What was that about?" Acie asked.

"Shri-Lan's got her," Tychon said. "They jumped to nowhere."

"Cazun," Seth whispered. A pilot like Tychon and Nova, he was able to grasp the implication of having left sub-space without a mapped target. Even the most highly skilled spanner flying the best of the fleet never lost sight of the terrible possibility of emerging at some point of no return. Or not emerging at all.

Tychon accepted Seth's arm to pull himself up. He looked uphill and then bent to pick up his metal rod again. "Time to get the hell out of this cesspit," he said. He gestured to Acie and Vincent. "You two stay down here. Follow us only if you hear anyone coming from behind. How many rebels are at the temple?"

"Not sure," Acie said. "If more of them haven't arrived from Kiertown I'd say maybe a dozen."

"Does that include the priests?"

"No, they're not fighters. Pacifists, in a rebel sort of way. They won't care if we're caught or not. They just want us gone." She grasped Seth's sleeve. "You're not gonna go up against them all, are you?"

Tychon nodded for both of them. "I'm tired of slinking through this sewage. Someone's ass is going to get kicked."

Vincent chuckled. "Now I know you've been talking to Nova." He put his arm around Acie's thin shoulders. "Let's get behind these rocks."

Tychon and Seth moved quickly along the path, following the crumbling wall that encircled the temple proper. The fog allowed only a short distance's visibility and they kept their pace within that, alert to the rebels that were surely waiting where the path joined the plateau.

Tychon raised his arm to stop Seth when they reached a sharp outcropping that nearly blocked their passage along the ledge. "We must be almost there. They'll have the advantage in the open." He kicked a few rocks over the edge. They tumbled noisily before the sound was swallowed by the mist. "You two try to keep up," he said in a louder voice as if calling to Acie and Vincent.

Seth looked up and stepped behind the outcropping when, only moments later, a Caspian rebel dropped from the top of the wall. Another followed and then they saw the shapes of two Centauri rush along the path toward of them. He wasted no time in grabbing the Caspian before he had even found his feet to toss him into the gorge. "Thanks for stopping by."

Tychon used his metal bar across the other rebel's throat to pin her against the wall while Seth took her gun. He flung her into the ravine and then stepped aside while Seth shot the two approaching rebels.

Stopping only to pick up the fallen men's weapons, they moved onward but now the rebels, more cautious after their compatriots had not returned, fired blindly into the fog without showing themselves.

"Back," Tychon led the way back to the outcropping they had just passed and motioned to Seth to boost him up. He found a ledge just over his head and heaved himself up against the planet's high gravity and then turned to pull Seth up as well. Within moments they had reached the top of the wall and peered cautiously over it.

Below them four rebels huddled behind a tomb of some sort, all of them Caspians. Near the end of the wall that separated the courtyard from the ravine, three Centauri, fleeter of foot than the Caspians, waited expectantly for the escapees to round the corner. Tychon nodded to Seth and they edged over the top of the wall to drop noiselessly onto the stone tomb. From there it was only a short jump onto the rebels.

What the Caspians lacked in surefootedness they made up with strength and both Tychon and Seth were bruised and bleeding by the time they had subdued the rebels. Gasping for air, they paused a moment, hidden behind the crypt.

Seth dabbed at his bleeding nose. "You're fierce for a Delphian."

Tychon turned when the unconscious rebel behind him groaned and started to move. He used his gun to silence him. "Someone put his hands on my wife," he growled. "That is making me just a little bit irate."

Seth winced. "Umm, like I said, that was a long time ago..."

Tychon scowled at him but then, reluctantly, his angry expression softened into a grin. He shook his head. "You're in a class of your own, aren't you?"

"Yeah. Look, they won't hurt her if she's a hostage. She wouldn't be alive if they didn't need her for something."

Tychon edged to the corner of the tomb and looked across the square. "I saw... hmm, I saw a Centauri when she talked about them. He was like a monster in her mind. She was afraid."

"There are some nasty-looking bastards among us," Seth allowed.

Tychon shook his head. "It was more than that. That one scared her. She doesn't scare so easily. She doesn't fear getting into a fight."

"Nope, not our Nova," Seth agreed.

Tychon turned and held a forefinger close to Seth's nose to get his attention. "Don't push your luck, Kada," he said before grabbing Seth's collar to pull him to the side. "Get down!" He shot over Seth at a rebel that had come up behind them. The beam of his weapon lit the mist like a beacon in the perpetual twilight. Seth rolled out of the way and leaped for the edge of the tomb to fire at the rebels racing across the yard.

"Shit!" Seth jerked back when a projectile whined off the stone by his face. "Sons of Rhuwacs! More by the stairs."

Tychon took out the approaching Centauri so that they were able to take shelter on the other side of the tomb. "How many is this now?"

"Nine or ten."

Tychon sprinted along the wall while Seth fired rapidly at the rebels hiding behind the open temple door. One fell to his aim and tumbled down the ramp to the cobbled yard. Tychon drew some fire before he dove around the corner of the building, giving Seth another clear shot at the rebel who stepped out too far in his eagerness to target the Delphian.

Both Tychon and Seth waited cautiously after the continuous firing of both laser and projectile weapons had stopped. The silence of the courtyard was broken only by the sound of the wind soughing through the peaks above the temple. One of the priests risked much by stepping outside to glare at them angrily. It was Nar Tosh, still gripping his staff. He said nothing but the contempt for them and all that their Union Commonwealth represented was clear on his streamlined face.

Seth jogged to the end of the compound wall to retrieve Vincent and Acie while Tychon returned to their skimmer. It was not long before they sped silently away from the dreary enclave and back to the airfield of Kiertown. No one met them along the winding road but they soon saw several planes glide overhead, toward the temple, surely carrying more of the rebels.

They did not bother to clear their takeoff with anyone at the airfield and were soon aboard the cluttered, tight confines of Seth's ship and heading toward the nearest jumpsite.

Tychon, in the cockpit with Seth, waited until they had left Aikhor's atmosphere before he went into the main cabin. Acie and Vincent had settled in a sleeper set like a padded shelf into the wall. He took a seat in a low-slung chair facing them. "Talk to me, Bellac," he said.

She sat upright and then glanced uncertainly over his shoulder at Seth who had also left the cockpit.

"He looks meaner than he is," Seth said. "We need to know what happened on Dannakor. Why were you there?"

"Well, I'm sure he's not mean. Nova wouldn't put up with that."

"Nova is in a lot of trouble, in part because of you," Tychon said. "So help me help her."

"I went up there to warn her," Acie said. "With the Shri-Lan. But it's the Arawaj that are after Nova."

"Can you back that up a little for us, Acie," Seth said.

"Sure," she said brightly. "Couple of days ago some Shri-Lan came by the..." she glanced at Tychon. "By the Place to talk with Perris. They were going to steal something and wanted someone to come along to make sure they were stealing the right thing. So Perris said I could go. So I went."

"Without letting me know. I was worried for days!" Vincent said. "Especially after what happened on Phi!"

"You would have just fussed and fretted endlessly," she said. "Besides, there wasn't time. They said they beat up someone on Delphi for the info and they had to go right now." She halted briefly when Tychon made an unclear sound deep in his throat and then hurriedly continued. "The Shri-Lan don't care so much about that new com system. They want the new interface because it'll let them open any old keyhole instead of having to use the charted sites. Obviously they don't have a lot of Delphians on their side to span for them."

"None, I would hope," Tychon said.

"Well, they want to level that playing field by getting a hold of the ANI before anyone else does. Perris went, too, and on the way to Dannakor he told me that the Arawaj were already there. He's easy to get information from when he's drunk."

"The Arawaj and the Shri-Lan don't work together," Seth

said. "Those two factions have been at each other's throats since Tharron disappeared."

"Exactly," Acie said. "The Shri-Lan had no idea that there were other rebels on Dannakor already. Except that the Arawaj weren't attacking. They planned to kidnap Nova quietly."

"Why would the Arawaj want Nova?" Tychon wondered. "There were four test subjects. All officers, all pilots. Are you sure they singled her out?"

"Yes, they wanted just Nova."

"Maybe they, the Arawaj, aren't after the interface," Vincent said. "They could want her for any number of reasons. Information. Revenge. Just ransom, even. She's a prominent officer."

"They wouldn't wait until she's at a secure location," Tychon said. "Under guard. Monitored. She wasn't even supposed to be there."

"What do you mean?"

"Nova wasn't on the short list. But they picked her, anyway." Tychon stared up at the ceiling and then closed his eyes. "Gods! Somebody on the ANI team is a rebel! Or working for them. Someone with access to the list of approved pilots."

"That's what Perris said. They got one of their own people in there, working as a technician or something. Anyway, when we got to Dannakor I went down to the surface to warn her."

"You are not trained for ground combat," Vincent said. "That could have been very dangerous."

"Well, it was. Lots of people died in the attack. It was terrible! Nova told me to get back on my ship. She didn't listen and there was no time to explain before she ran off again. I lost her in all that but I managed to get back aboard. Some of the Shri-Lan heard me talking to her and figured me for a spy. I spent the trip back in a box."

"Perris contacted me and we got her to the temple before they decided to lynch her," Vincent said.

"This Perris is also a spy?" Tychon said.

Acie looked up at Seth. "How much do I have to tell this man?"

"You're doing fine, Acie," Seth said.

"Well, not so fine. I guess my job is done. I can't go back to Magra. They'll shoot me, after all this."

"Then maybe it's time to get out, dear," Vincent said. He placed his hand over Acie's. "You've dodged around the edges of this thing for long enough. You've been lucky, but luck runs out." He smiled ruefully. "And I have to admit that I'm getting tired. It's not been easy keeping you out of trouble these past years."

"You've got plenty left, Vincent," Acie exclaimed and hugged him quickly. "Don't talk like that!"

"I'm just not as spry as I used to be." He looked up at Seth. "Can you land on the Union base on Magra Alaric? It's the closest to here."

"Sure. No one's been looking to arrest me lately," Seth replied.

Vincent turned to Tychon. "Can you get us amnesty, Major? If we can stay out of sight on a base somewhere I'm sure she'll be soon enough forgotten."

"She could also tell them about what happened on Dannakor," Seth said.

Tychon shook his head. "Tell them what? They're not going to take the word of this Bellac, a rebel of questionable loyalties, that Nova hasn't absconded with the interface voluntarily. We don't know where she is, or with whom. Or where the rest of the ANI team is. We know nothing at all." He gestured at the cockpit. "I imagine you have ways of getting a message to Colonel Carras on a tight band?"

Seth reached over Acie's head to fetch a thin tablet from a shelf there. He handed it to Tychon before moving to the cockpit and its com panel. "I'll get a packet ready."

Tychon thought a moment and then began his message. Acie watched curiously as his long fingers flew over the input screen, entering words, moving symbols, combining ciphers that normally weren't part of the display. "What code is that?" she inquired.

"Known only to Vanguard," he answered and corrected the placement of one of his symbols. "Asking Carras if there is news about Nova. For all we know they've found out for themselves what went on there. And to let him know to expect our Shri-Lan friends to pop out of any one of a thousand uncharted keyholes at any moment. He'll like that part."

She poked a finger at the screen. "Shouldn't that be a repeat of that one?"

Tychon paused and exhaled sharply.

Vincent chuckled. "She's a sharp one, the little minx."

"Well, he didn't say not to read it," she said to him.

"You can read that?" Tychon asked. "After just looking at it now?"

"No, but I see the pattern. I could probably figure it out."

He regarded her thoughtfully, taking in the dirty coveralls, the deeply red skin smudged with grime and the mess of white braids springing up from her head. "You're that smart?"

"She can handle any physical science and mathematics you can throw at her," Vincent attested, as proudly as if she were his daughter. "I've always said she was wasted on Magra, patching up wounded rebels and repairing lasers. Don't be fooled by this slip of a girl. Brightest mind this side of Targon, if easily distracted."

"A GenMod?"

"Natural!" she exclaimed. "My people don't hold with that. GenMods are loopy."

Tychon had to smile. "You're wasted on a military base. I can get you some work on Delphi if you're serious about giving up the rebel business. Xenobiology. There's an expedition leaving for Shaddallam soon. They can always use more experts. And you'd be out of sight for a while."

"I've not been to that place yet," she said, considering. "Xenos, eh? Sounds interesting." She looked up at Vincent, a question on her face.

He shrugged. "Where you go, so shall I, child."

Tychon finished his message. "Let it fly, Kada."

Seth transmitted Tychon's coded message at light speed to a relay station near a charted jumpsite not far ahead of them now where it was forwarded through sub-space to Targon. There another relay would send it along to Colonel Carras on Odar.

"This will be so very much easier once we get those new interfaces in use," Seth said. "Now let's hope the Colonel is home." He tapped another screen for information. "Kinda late there now."

They did not have to wait long. An incoming message announced itself before Seth had fished handing around strong cups of tea. Acie had cleaned up a little and was returning from the ship's tiny comfort station when the missive from Odar appeared on Tychon's screen.

He read it silently and his brow grew increasingly furrowed with every block of code deciphered. The others exchanged worried glances when he muttered a colorful oath.

"What's he saying?" Acie tried to peer over his shoulder.

"He knows nothing more about Nova or what went on at the Dannakor labs. It's actually worse now. The ship she took away from Dannakor was traced to a rebel hangout on Magra Torley before they stripped it. So now they think she's there, on Magra."

"Surely the Colonel will report that she's keyholed God knows to where with the others!" Vincent said.

"Yes. But when he tells them *how* he knows that they won't believe she was able to reach me here. He'd have to find a Shantir to declare that it might be possible but I don't know if any of them would consider it. *I* don't even know how she did it!"

"They wouldn't accuse *you* of lying. Of covering for her."

"Carras wouldn't. Everett would. He barely knows us and he's bent on protocol."

"Vanguard doesn't exactly operate within protocol."

"He'd prefer if we did." Tychon's attention returned to the display in his hands. "More survivors have returned from Dannakor but no one knows what went on there. Sounds like sheer mayhem. There is a team there now, investigating. They assume that rebels were disguised as Air Command personnel but they didn't leave any bodies. At least not rebel bodies."

"Well, that's something," Vincent said. He sipped his tea and lifted his eyebrows in appreciation of it. "Makes her appear less guilty of shooting officers, at least."

"Perhaps, but they aren't spending energy looking for the missing. Seems that Nova's right about them having gotten their hands on the new interface. There has been a lot of chatter about an impending attack and they've recalled all the spanners. Something massive is brewing."

"Where?" Seth asked.

"No clear target. Just a lot of very recent noise about rebel mobilization and plans to attack. Until they figure this out the entire Air Command fleet is on alert. Including the Vanguard wing. Every last one of them is being called in."

"What about you?"

"Still not wanted on the payroll."

"Well, that's good, then," Seth said.

Tychon frowned. "I was hoping to get my Eagle back. And a few of the Vanguard teams to back me up, at least."

"Yes, but if they give you back your plane then you'll also be put on standby. How are you going to find Nova if you're babysitting UCB Targon?" Seth grinned and tipped his head toward the cockpit. "I say we go to Dannakor. We'll take the brain with us."

Acie threw him a playful punch. "Be respectful, Kada!"

He hooked his elbow around her neck and kissed her face wherever his lips happened to land. "I have every respect for your brain."

Tychon looked from one to the other. How had he ended up here, on this pirate's ship, with a Human elder, a flighty

Bellac, all of them with rebel leanings, and only a very distant, retired Colonel to back him up? It seemed that, once again, Nova's ventures had catapulted him out of the ordered, disciplined military routines he valued so much. A slow smile appeared on his face. If nothing else, these people were more committed to her than Air Command would ever be.

"Let's jump," he said.

SEVEN

Nova jolted out of some endless, tedious, unpleasant dream that seemed to have little purpose but to make her glad that she was no longer asleep. She stared up at the metal ceiling, aware of a dull headache and a gnawing emptiness in her stomach. There had been little water and even less food allocated to the captives and the only reason that they were not also freezing was that the cargo ship had now been cast adrift and everyone, rebel and hostage alike, were crammed aboard the Shri-Lan's battle cruiser.

She turned to look over at Jovan lying on the other bunk. He seemed to be still deep in whatever khamal allowed him to escape the pain in his head and the horror of their situation. He was too young, she thought, too sheltered by his well-padded life among the Shantirs of Delphi, to be dealing with any of this. At least they had been given this tiny cabin apart from the others, where they were allowed to rest between their attempts to penetrate the keyhole and find a way back to Trans-Targon.

She sat up and leaned over to him to touch his forehead. His skin was cool and he breathed evenly. "Are you awake?"

"Don't want to be."

"How's the head?"

"Attached."

She scrubbed her face with both hands and sat in silence for a while. Tychon would come, she knew. He would mobilize the entire Air Command fleet and every Level Three spanner. By now he'd have half the Vanguard fleet on its way to that keyhole outside Dannakor. They would be found.

Jovan sat up. His eyes were a very pale blue now, something she knew to mean that he was either ill or still terribly exhausted. Mechanically, slowly, he untied his braid and then retied it neatly, perhaps not even aware of the fussiness of his task. "I've never done that before," he said after a while.

"Done what?"

"Touched someone like that. The way Shan Tychon touched you."

She smiled. "You got some of that, did you?"

He nodded. "I've joined with many people before. My people, anyway. But not like that. It was so... I mean, I should not have been..."

"Yeah, I love it when he does that."

"You don't understand. This is Shan Tychon! To feel him touch you like that was like... like..." He looked at his hands. "I should not have been part of that."

"Was nice though, wasn't it?" she teased.

"Captain!"

"He knew you were there! If it didn't matter to him, why should it matter to you?"

He rose from his bunk and went to the door. "If I were the gossiping sort it would be quite the tale for my fellow novices." He knocked loudly on the door to the corridor. "Is there any food on this ship?" he shouted. "How are we supposed to concentrate if I am lacking the basic sugars required by my undeniably superior brain, you Centauri degenerates."

"Easy!" Nova said. "Are you all right?"

"No, I'm not. I have never been locked up in my life. This is intolerable. My head pain is intolerable."

She reached across the small space and took his hand. "I need you to hold it together, Jovie. He'll come. I know he will. Now they know we're alive and they will send help. They won't leave us out here like this."

He pulled his hand away. "And your very Human and excessive optimism is also intolerable." He returned to his cot and closed his eyes. "Don't wake me until they drag us back to the bridge."

The door opened. "Why the noise?"

Nova looked up at the Centauri and wondered why it was the thuggish-looking ones that were either drawn to or recruited by the Shri-Lan. This one kept his hair shaved, exposing a large burn scar covering most of the side of his head. His nose had been smashed long ago and never repaired. "We need food. I can't think when I'm hungry. And we need to think. Your boss wants us to think."

"Stop your babbling, Human."

"I wouldn't babble if my brain was working right."

He grimaced. "There is food where the others are. This way. No, leave him here. Just you," he added when she turned to Jovan to rouse him.

Nova followed the rebel a short distance to another locked room where he fumbled for a moment with the key plate. The door finally opened onto a cabin crowded with the escapees from Dannakor, most of them trying to be as comfortable as they could on the bare floor. There were only a few cots and some chairs here, all of them occupied. The air had been breathed too many times and Nova felt an urge to escape back into the hall. An armed rebel seemed a less daunting opponent than the accusation and mistrust she saw in these people's faces. "Good luck getting them to give up their grub," the Centauri laughed and shut the door behind Nova.

There was a brief silence before one of the women at the rear of the room spoke up. "You're the officer that got us into this," she said.

Some of the others looked uncertainly from the Centauri that had spoken to Nova.

"Well, technically, no," Nova said and looked around for any of the ANI team she might recognize. "But if you need to blame someone, that's fine." She moved to one of the cots where a young woman lay curled up in the comforting lap of an older Feydan female. She made no response when Nova gently moved her hair to look at the bruises on her face. "Just this girl?" Nova said.

"One other taken by a Centauri," the Feydan said. "She's been gone hours now. I see they've not been kind to you, either."

"None of them are. Don't try to fight them. We're only alive because of the ANI. Pretend you know more than you do, that you have value. Is this all that's left? Are there any other hostages?"

"No. They've killed everybody else," someone nearby said. Nova did not recognize him. "You're not in charge here. So don't start giving orders."

"Fine," Nova replied. She spotted Leon Rhys, one of the tech team, sharing another cot with a colleague. She smiled encouragingly at the Feydan woman and then stepped around the others to reach Rhys. He looked up at her with far less hostility and moved to let her sit with them. The other technician even offered her an almost full foil wrap containing a gritty nutrient paste that was probably designed to be eaten hot. She ate silently, waiting for the rest of the group to return to their desultory conversation.

When the noise level had risen sufficiently, she leaned closer to Rhys. "I've been able to make contact with Trans-Targon," she murmured and raised her hands when he started to reply. "Say nothing. Let's not get anyone excited. I'm hoping to stall a while until they've figured out a way to track us down."

Rhys nodded. "Like you said just now, they'll keep us alive for a while, anyway. They want us to duplicate the interface hardware once we get back to Trans-Targon."

"What about the program that goes with it? Don't they need that?"

"Not really. It's not much different from what we have now. It's just designed to access communications systems as well as navigation."

"They have Captain Luce's interface," Nova said. "But I don't know if it's the Shri-Lan or the Arawaj that have it."

"Won't be enough. They'll need the schematics of where the taps go in your brain. That alone took years to figure out. Without contact with a brain the device itself can't be activated. They'll want to scan your head for that. Luce's will be too deteriorated by now, even if they didn't dislodge the nanowires during the removal. These are prototypes. We haven't even started to modify them for the sort of field conditions you pilots encounter."

"Do they know that?"

He grinned. "Not likely. At least not Rakh and his band of rats. Sao Lok is another matter. He sounds like he knows what he's talking about."

"He obviously knows enough to fool the neuro team and get himself a job on Dannakor! Who knows how long he's been there." She folded the remainder of her small ration and tucked it into her thigh pocket for Jovan. "I don't know what he's up to but the Shri-Lan probably want the ANI to give them access to keyholes."

"Our biggest tactical advantage over them."

"Yeah. I think the Shri-Lan were able to grab Lieutenant Betl on Dannakor. To use as navigator. Right now they only have a few spanners and those can't visit grandma without us knowing about it. Having a working ANI could change all that."

He shook his head. "You saw what happened to Luce. Turning a chartjumper into a Level Three is just fanciful thinking right now. We thought there might be a chance but the latest tests just came up empty. You still need a certain brain to handle all that and the sad fact is that most of us don't have one of those."

"Really? This is never going to work?"

"I won't say never, but we'll have to find a whole new way to work with the capacities we have among non-Delphians. I don't see that happening any time soon. So let's not piss off any Delphians in the foreseeable future."

She scowled. "That's disappointing. Really really disappointing!"

"Yeah, but you still get to be a telepath. With the right equipment."

Nova nodded. "So what did happen to Luce, exactly?"

"He was being an idiot, exactly," the engineer said. "Should never have done that. Azon Corp will have to create a failsafe to prevent hotshot navigators from going into places they shouldn't. We've got our bets on a total neuron overload. Would have happened even if he had found the right exit. Heed my words, Captain. Do not attempt to jump us back. And let's hope that Betl, wherever he is, won't try it, either."

"So if they're planning an attack somewhere, using the ANI to jump there isn't going to work for them?"

"Oh, it will. But just once."

"They probably envision jumping Betl through one keyhole after another to open the way to multiple attack sites. Without the sort of toll that usually takes on a spanner."

"Not going to happen. Still, even a single jump will land them without warning some place where they can do a whole lot of damage before any sort of defense can be launched. They could pick Targon, even."

"They'll be on alert there. Listen, don't tell Rakh about the ANI not working. Just say that Luce didn't have enough training, which is true enough. I've convinced them that I need the Delphian to help me with it. We're just trying to buy time."

"You got it." Rhys pulled apart the edges of his remaining rations bag and carefully licked what little was left in it. "You think you can get out of this, Captain?"

"Vanguard, remember?" she said with confidence that sounded almost convincing to herself. "I'm not trained to give up. Just make sure these people here hold together. Is anyone hurt badly?"

"We've got some medics here," he said, but his eyes were on the devastated woman on the other bunk.

"They'll find us, Leon," Nova said. "You've got to hang on to that thought."

Both of them, along with a number of the other hostages, turned when the door opened again. Nova rose, assuming this to be her guard, here to return her to her cabin. But it was another and not one she had seen before. He looked around the room and then carelessly gestured at a few of the civilians. "You, come with me. And you two over there. Going to put you to work while you're enjoying the fine free room and board here."

Nova grinned and winked at Leon when she sidled her way into the group of hostages now slowly and uncertainly coming to their feet. They shuffled ahead of the rebel who periodically jabbed one of them with his gun. Nova kept her head down and tried to look as tired and dejected as the other five in her group.

They arrived at a narrowed junction of the rebel ship. A corridor to the left was lined with doors that appeared to be crew cabins. An airlock portal opened to their right to allow them to enter a cargo pod. "We're going to cut this one loose," the rebel said. "You people are going to clear out those bins there. Take the stuff across the hallway."

The others looked vacantly about themselves before approaching the bins. The weakly pulsating light from above revealed the ship's supply of food containers and a number of unmarked packages.

Nova fell into step with the others and made a few trips carrying the heavy boxes from the pod to a nearby cabin until the chore had become monotonous, more so for their guard than the prisoners. He barely watched them and only cursed now and again when one of them complained or slowed down. She dropped out of the line and waited in the new storage area to see if he'd notice that she had not returned. One of the Azon Corp technicians frowned at her quizzically but didn't care enough to question her.

She looked around, finding nothing useful in this cabin until a panel beside the door caught her eye. She flipped it open to see if anything interesting might be found in there. Something sharp, perhaps, that she could smuggle back into her prison.

"You Shri-Lan have a firm grip on sheer laziness," someone said outside in the hall.

Nova picked up one of the bundles, prepared to look busy, and stood by the door. The slightly rasping voice belonged to a Caspian and she was certain it was Sao Lok. He sounded amused.

"I just like watching a bunch of brain surgeons get their delicate hands dirty," their Centauri guard replied. "Still think we should break some fingers. Teach 'em a lesson."

"A lesson in what?" Sao Lok inquired.

Apparently, the Centauri had no answer to that and after a moment's silence said, "What are you doing down this way, anyway, Arawaj? Your cabin's by the crew dorm."

"I'm looking for Rakh. I'm told his room is here somewhere."

"Yah, that way, go left at the end there. Third door. Probably with his woman, though. You don't want to be bothering him, believe me."

Nova ducked aside when Lok's voice sounded closer. "Let me worry about that," he said as he passed her.

She peered into the hall once the sound of his talons scraping the floor had faded. It was empty in the direction Lok had gone and to her other side she saw only her fellow captives milling about in disorganized fashion. When a few of them had blocked the sight line between her and where their guard might appear at any moment, she hurried away from the junction and then around the corner.

This area was slightly cleaner and in better repair than what she had seen here so far. She sidled along the wall to the third door and soon made out voices behind it. Male voices, but also a woman who sounded Human. Her voice was strident; clearly she was displeased with something.

Nova noticed a narrow metal door beside this cabin. Something hummed to itself behind there but no sound of movement indicated that someone was breathing on the other side. She touched the key plate and winced when the door moved aside with a tired wheeze. It did not quite open all the way. She peered inside and smiled when she saw a utility room that gave access to some of the ship's maintenance sub stations.

Just as she slipped into the room, Rakh's cabin door opened and Nova now heard the woman very clearly. "I must have been crazy to even agree to leave Pelion at all. Just get us the hell home!" She continued to complain to herself as her voice faded away and down the corridor.

Nova moved to the end of the utility room and pressed her ear against the wall, expecting them to be fairly thin between these crew cabins. She was not disappointed.

"I suppose now I'm sleeping alone tonight," she heard Rakh grumble. His voice was slurred by whatever he had been drinking since the day before. "You better have something interesting for me, Lok."

"I've come to strike a deal with you."

"What sort of Arawaj deal would interest me? You have nothing to bargain with."

"I want the girl once we're back in Trans-Targon."

"What girl? You mean the officer? The jumper?"

"Yes."

"Out of the question. We've come a long way to get that interface. With or without a Human attached to it."

"You said yourself that your people were able to grab the other pilot on Dannakor. So you have a copy of the ANI already. Let us have her."

"I have no intentions of letting the Arawaj have this

thing. What good is it to you, anyway? You have no fleet to speak of. I doubt you even have more than a handful of ships capable of spanning without charts."

"That is true, but we still want the girl. Look, I'm willing to trade you this."

There was a pause and Nova wished for even a few bits of the surveillance equipment tucked away aboard their Eagle uncounted light years away from here. Cameras disguised as insects, wires of nearly invisible gauge capable of conveying sound, sensors that could penetrate just about any material or distance. And here she was with her ear to the wall!

"Where did you get that?" Rakh said, sounding very alert now.

"From the navigator that got us into this mess to begin with. The one that didn't make the jump. He didn't object to giving it up."

"Is it broken?"

"No, just missing the taps. I am very familiar with this unit, don't forget. It is intact. You only need to scan the other pilot already in your possession to duplicate the implant."

"Why do you want the girl so badly, anyway?" Rakh said after another pause. He seemed to be considering the prospect.

"She and her people killed one of our own. Revenge. Nothing more."

Nova frowned. Was this Lok's way of ensuring that she would not be harmed by the Shri-Lan once her purpose had been fulfilled? Was he really so naive as to trust Rakh?

She ducked down beside the door when she heard heavy footsteps in the hall. Someone cursed at full volume as he stomped past her hiding place. Perhaps it was wise to return to her chain gang. She waited a few moments before she hurried back to the storage cabin where her fellow hostages were still at their slave labor. There was not much time to spare before the rebel assigned to her burst into the room.

"What are you doing down here!" he thundered.

She put her heavy package down and pushed back a few wayward strands of hair with the back of her hand. "Being a good prisoner," she said.

He grabbed her arm and yanked her into the hall. "You were to get some food, not go for a walk," he growled and strode down the hall so fast that she had to practically jog to keep up with him.

"I just do what I'm told. It says so in the hostage survival manual."

He stopped in front of her cabin. "That would have been my head rolling if Rakh had found out you were out of your room, you stupid bitch." Nova cried out when he punched her arm hard enough to numb it. "Get your Delphian and then go to the bridge. Now!"

* * *

Sao Lok had barely looked up when the rebel in the corridor had interrupted them with his crude expletives. Things had settled down out there and no immediate emergency seemed to be brewing. He held the small interface module between his thumbs. "What do you say, Rakh?"

"I say you have something else going on in that pointy skull of yours," Rakh said but his eyes remained on the ANI even as he reclined in his chair and casually propped his feet onto the edge of the cabin's unmade bed. "If revenge was all you wanted you'd have had your chance on Dannakor days ago."

The Caspian sighed, tired of this game. "You're right. Let's get on with this." He flipped the unit into the air and at the surprised Shri-Lan who barely managed to catch it in time. "You're planning an attack on Union domain, correct?"

Rakh looked up from the interface in his hand, clearly amazed that it had come to him so easily. "What of it?"

"I'm going to guess that you Shri-Lan planned to grab an ANI for the single purpose of jumping to Sidara Ber for a little surprise visit to four of our esteemed Factors currently meeting there."

Rakh's eyes narrowed. "How'd you know that? Took hours to beat that location out of the envoy on Delphi."

"Our methods might be a little more subtle than yours, but no less effective. Of course you must realize that by now the meeting will have been called off, considering that three of the ANI test subjects and their valuable little plugs are missing. Losing four of the top Commonwealth governors isn't a risk they'd take."

The Centauri shrugged. "Not if our people moved fast enough. For all we know, Sidara is a pile of dust by now."

Lok perched on the edge of a garishly-colored storage unit, wanting to sit down. Like those of many Caspians of his age, his callused feet ached by the end of the day. But he realized the value of having the rebel continue to look up at him. "I don't believe that. And I'm going to propose something far more devastating to our Union. You can launch an attack the entire sector has never seen before."

"Is that so? Air Command outnumbers us twenty to one."

"And I say that we can wipe out most of their fleet with one single stroke."

Rakh's broad lips twitched in a derisive smile. "How will you manage a feat like that, Arawaj?"

"The girl is the key. Her interface is able to communicate with anyone that is currently listening. Meaning anyone whose interface is also linked to a transmitter, be that on a ship or a station."

"Yes, that *is* the point of the ANI," Rakh said. "So far I'm not excited by your news."

"Captain Whiteside is a Vanguard officer. Her ANI will have clearance to open a link to anyone operating a Union ship. It's hard-coded into her neural appliance so all she needs is a processor that can relay her signal."

"And...?"

"We have developed a new program. The moment Whiteside links her ANI to our processor, a fatal signal is transmitted from there, using her access code, to anyone receptive to that code. Meaning any Union pilot or operator of any interface model."

Rakh was momentarily speechless. "Any model," he said finally. "That also means anyone operating a Union relay, communication array, scope or any other equipment with a neural interface."

"Correct," Sao Lok said, beaming. "Anyone that would give clearance to a Vanguard officer. This is why she was chosen for the project. Or, rather, that is why we made sure that she was chosen."

"And your program works only with this thing?" Rakh gestured with the module in his hand.

"Indeed. There is a reason why these things aren't wireless. They're designed precisely to prevent outside tampering. That works fine if you're using it to point a plane or a gun at something. It's a whole other matter if you're leaving a closed system. The ANI just forwards information to a transmitter. You can do that much with the one on your arm. So that is the point where my new code enters the loop. She sends a signal, our program takes over and multiplies the new signal to all receivers it can reach, cranks the amplitude to the point where it'll blow out the receiver's brains much in the way that other test subject experienced. To his detriment."

The Centauri rebel frowned. "That is a beautiful plan, Lok, but you forget that she's going to have to get us home, first. The odds are good that she's not going to live through that. None of us might."

Sao Lok waved that aside. "That was an accident. She's got more ability than he had. And she has the Delphian. She'll hold it together. And, frankly, if she doesn't, none of this will matter to any of us."

Rakh thought about this for a while. "So how do you plan to use her, should we get back to Trans-Targon?"

Lok strolled to a small window set deep into the ship's exterior wall. He looked out into nothing but the pinpricks of distant stars. "I went to Dannakor to steal one of the units for ourselves. But then it was decided to remove her from Dannakor and take her to Gramor on an ore transport. All she has to do there is initiate a contact with Air Command using our processor and transmitter and her job is done." He waved a hand in the air, indicating this ship. "Your unexpected visit changed some of my plans, but perhaps for the better."

"How so?"

Lok turned his back to the window. "Once Air Command realizes what we have they will simply change Whiteside's access codes. So this was never meant to be more than a single strike, perhaps two, where we'd cause as much damage as possible. Eventually, they'll install more fail safes and that'll be the end of this."

Rakh nodded. "Still, a good way to take out a number of pilots, perhaps capture their ships. A very expensive strike."

"Yes, but if we do this together we can do much, much more."

"I'm listening."

"Shri-Lan is already planning an attack. Air Command will be on alert. If your people do, indeed, have the other test subject, no one will know where that's coming from or where you're going to hit. They'll be spread thin and they'll be out in force."

Rakh grinned. "Damn right. They'll have every pilot in the air. And plugged into their machines!"

"Exactly. And that's when we'll make sure that Captain Whiteside finds herself unguarded and within reach of a transmitter. Her first thought will be to alert Air Command. If we make sure that no relays are available to send a message packet, she'll have no option but to use the ANI. She won't even think twice about that."

Rakh threw his head back and laughed. "And that'll launch your clever little program and she'll end up killing every Union pilot and operator that's also linked to their processors."

"That's the plan. So the more hysterical you Shri-Lan can

get Air Command, the more planes will be in the air. Appear to send ships to every keyhole reaching to likely targets and make sure they know it. They'll expect strikes on Feyd, Bellac Tau, Magra Alaric, Zera, Delphi, Aram and maybe Mrak Four, with no idea of where you'll be coming from. We could wipe out most of the fleet with one single transmission."

"Oh, you can be sure that we'll add more noise to the intel the minute we get back." The Centauri's eyes returned to the interface module in his hand. He played with it for a moment. "So what's in this for you? She kills the pilots, Shri-Lan can move in and capture the planes without a single shot being fired to damage them. Even if your plan doesn't work we stand to bag at least one valuable target. What do the Arawaj want?"

Lok shrugged. "We want the Commonwealth out of this sector. That has always been our goal. We're not fighting their tyranny out of greed like… like some of the other factions."

"Like the Shri-Lan, you meant to say?"

"Take it to mean what you wish. Do we have a deal? You have the girl jump us to Gramor Bejo, leave her with me and start rattling sabers."

Sao Lok watched Rakh's expression, knowing that he had convinced the Shri-Lan rebel to hand the woman over to the Arawaj. The captain's face, for the first time since they had been dumped into this situation, had lost its constant scowl and exhibited something akin to hope. And greed, of course. The idea of capturing so much of their enemy's fleet at no cost to their own lives and equipment was almost too phenomenal to imagine. No doubt he would be handsomely rewarded for this coup as well as for the additional ANI unit held tightly in his fist.

How easy it was to move people, Lok thought. One only needed a key, some sort of inkling of an opponent's desires to set things in motion. Challenges may appear, conditions may change, events can turn. But, ultimately, things moved in one direction and a few nudges often pushed pieces into place.

He'd have the girl, the girl would help him pull the teeth out of Air Command's bite and then soon the Union would crumble, much weakened and even defenseless in some sub-sectors.

What Rakh didn't know was that most of what Lok had told him about Nova's communications access was nonsense. The truth was that Nova, as a Hunter Class pilot and Vanguard officer, was cleared to operate just about any ship ever built by the Union, including every last fighter plane and every last immigrant tub plying the gates between Centauri and Trans-Targon. Few ships were off limits to her and she had navigational access to some of the mighty battle ships, even if she could not pilot them by herself.

He gave Rakh a friendly smile when the rebel offered him a bottle of something sweet and fermented and not at all objectionable. It was not some exclusive Air Command access code that would allow Captain Whiteside to reach other operators. It was the simple fact that she had the necessary security clearance to access their planes' processors. And now also, through the new ANI, anyone currently linked to them.

Rakh seemed to have forgotten that nearly every piece of hardware owned by the Shri-Lan had been built through Union contracts. Nova's signal would not only destroy the Union pilots, but the rebel fleet as well.

And then, Lok thought to himself, the balance would be restored. The three-hundred year old Union fragmented, the Shri-Lan reduced to nothing, other minor rebel groups made powerless, and then the Arawaj would take their rightful place as the rightful rulers of this sector, the way Pe Khoja had intended.

He had been so close! Not so very long ago, Tharron, once a powerful rebel leader, had relied on Pe Khoja's abilities to consolidate the rebel factions, turn their operations profitable, and present a united and very powerful opposition to the Union's rule of Trans-Targon. Pe Khoja had been Tharron's most highly-placed adjutant and only a single assassination away from taking the leader's place. Until, that is, Tharron's single-minded obsessions had destroyed it all. His inept sons had taken over and shunted the Caspian Arawaj faction aside with sheer fire power. The fragile alliance of rebel blocs had splintered.

But now this woman, Whiteside, the one who had played a part in Pe Khoja's end, would be the key to finishing the work. Sao Lok felt a peculiar, nearly spiritual sense of rightness, of pre-destination when he thought about her role in his plans. In time she would come around. He had seen it in her eyes when he proposed to her the possibilities he envisioned. She heard him. She wanted to understand him despite the relentless brainwashing she had endured from an early age. It would take time to undo all that, but after the destruction of the Union fleet and of the Shri-Lan there would be plenty of time. Once she truly understood the wisdom of putting an end to the Commonwealth oppression, she would use her knowledge of what remained of the Union to make the victory complete.

Sao Lok was unaware of the distant smile that played over his long face when he thought about the power he would wield with her at his side. Was it possible, he pondered, that she might even join his clan? Not as a breeder, of course, but nevertheless tied to him in ways that would ensure his position as the head of the Arawaj. She was as strong and fearless as any Caspian female and would be a powerful force within the new leadership of Trans-Targon.

Of course, he thought, she was only Human and like all of them guided by irrational motivations and emotions that had long puzzled Caspians. She could well continue to cling to her stubborn loyalties to her Union, her Delphian mate and the half-breed they had made. Unfortunate and disappointing, he thought with a mental shrug, but not all would be lost. If she failed to appreciate the magnificence of his plans for her, she would still annihilate the fleet and he would then hand her over to Pe Khoja's clan as agreed. It would earn him the gratitude of that group, if nothing else.

"Drink up, Arawaj," Rakh intruded upon Lok's private thoughts. "The girl is yours. Do what you want with her. If she doesn't kill us all trying to jump us out of here."

* * *

"Let's see if we can get this motherless bucket of bolts home, Shan Jovan," Nova said in her best Air Command pilot voice when she and Jovan had settled into the pilot couches on the bridge.

There was only one rebel on the bridge to watch over them, along with another pilot and navigator who would assist them once they made the jump. So far, they had managed to delay while Nova occasionally opened the keyhole only to let it collapse again, traded some pointless and entirely made-up jargon about Delphian mental disciplines and, for the most part, simply spent their time resting, eyes closed, as they pretended to explore the void beyond the keyhole.

They began each session with a short khamal lasting only long enough for Nova to cast about for Tychon's presence, feeling him somewhere out there, but not yet near Dannakor. The pain this caused Jovan was intense and, as much as she ached to do so, Nova avoided speaking to Tychon. Still, knowing that he was coming closer, no doubt at the head of the entire Vanguard wing, helped her remain positive and focused.

The door behind them opened and Rakh entered the bridge, followed by Lok. He put a booted foot on the edge of Nova's couch and propped his folded arms on his knee as he bent forward. "So how are our little co-pilots on this fine day," he said brightly.

Nova glanced at Jovan who also seemed puzzled by Rakh's demeanor. The rebel captain seemed almost cheerful. "Could use a cup of tea, to be honest," she said. She felt Sao Lok hover near her shoulder.

Rakh smiled and waved his hand carelessly at the guard slouching nearby. "You heard the Captain," he said. "See if you can find her and her Delphian friend some tea."

The surprised Terran moved to the door.

"Sweet tea. None of that Centauri crap!" Nova yelled after him. She frowned up at Rakh. "What do you want, Rakh? We're a little busy here."

He nodded into Lok's direction. "We've had a chat and decided that you're taking us to Gramor."

"Gramor! Which one?"

"Gramor Bejo."

"Why there? It's nothing but rocks. We're going back to Dannakor, I thought."

"Don't be absurd. By now that sub-sector is going to be choked with Air Command patrols. I'm sure they're wanting you back. Do you really think I'm going to jump into the middle of that?"

"I could maybe jump us out early. But Gramor! This isn't some commuter transport you can just stop to drop off passengers. I'm not even sure I know how to find the Gramor system."

"You better." Rakh's oddly amiable expression returned to its previous glower. Nova was almost glad. At least that one she could read. "Don't play with me, Whiteside. If we find ourselves anywhere near an Air Command ship every last one of you is going to die before we get boarded."

"We've been mapping for Dannakor," Jovan interrupted. "Now we'll need more time."

Rakh glanced at the navigator who shook her head. "Once she's through she'll know where she's going," she said.

"I said don't play with me," Rakh snapped and grasped the front of Jovan's shirt to lift him out of his couch. "So far you haven't had much pain, Delphi, seeing how much more polite you are than your pal here. But if you want pain we can get that for you."

"You'll find that Delphians are a lot more durable than

you think," Jovan replied calmly.

"Why are you baiting him?" Nova said to Jovan. She gestured at the navigator. "They're not stupid."

"I suppose," he said. "At least not for a bunch of Centauri."

Rakh raised his fist to strike Jovan.

"Stop that," Lok said. "He's doing that on purpose. He's stalling, trying to get you to incapacitate him."

Rakh shoved Jovan abruptly back into his couch. The youth raised his hands to straighten the long strands of his tousled hair and Nova was sure she had seen a grin on his face.

"Is that what you're doing?" Rakh looked from Jovan to Nova. "Stalling? Hoping someone's going to come through that breach and rescue you?"

"I might only be a Level One but even us chartjumpers know that isn't possible. They won't know where we exited." She glared at Jovan. "Leave him be. He's just a kid. We're all getting jumpy here."

Rakh leaned down and jabbed his finger between her eyes. "The only jumping here is what you're about to show us, Whiteside. You're out of time. If you don't make an attempt in the next few hours you will find out what pain is, both of you." He straightened up. "And don't worry. It won't incapacitate either of you. We know what we're doing, for a bunch of Centauri." He turned to take two cups from the rebel that had returned to the bridge. Grinning, he handed one to Lok and emptied the other with a few deep gulps. "Fine idea. I should have tea more often. Now get busy. I'll expect to hear the call for entry prep before shift's end."

Lok waited until the Shri-Lan had left the bridge before he handed his tea cup to Nova. She wanted to refuse but then her parched throat won the internal argument. She sipped some of it and then held the cup out to Jovan. He shook his head.

The Caspian barely glanced at the youth. "I am going to

offer Rakh to hold the others for him on Gramor," he said in a low voice. He said nothing more but his expression invited her to draw her own conclusions. She raised an eyebrow in question and he smiled encouragingly. If Rakh left the other captives behind when he rejoined his rebel fleet it would be far easier to liberate the hostages.

If only she knew what he and Rakh had schemed! No Arawaj went out of their way to cooperate with the Shri-Lan yet some sort of alliance had sprung up between them that went beyond merely being stuck out here together. Or was it possible that Sao Lok was sincere? Was he merely humoring the Centauri to get them back to Trans-Targon? Did he really have some grand scheme to end the wars?

She nodded. "Thanks for the tea."

"I will try to get you something to eat before you make the jump. It will no doubt be a difficult undertaking."

Nova exhaled audibly when he had left the bridge. Sao Lok confused her and, in his presence, she balanced on some internal fulcrum swinging from deep suspicion to actually wanting to like the Caspian.

She nodded to Jovan. He complied by reaching out to touch the interface at her temple. She closed her eyes.

What was that about? she sent moodily. *Leave the rebels to me.*
Because you're so good at getting beaten up? How's that arm?
Don't remind me.
How much time do we need?

She allowed him to draw her into a deeper khamal and began to look for Tychon's mute presence. Distance had no meaning when, aided by Jovan's powerful mind, it came to feeling his presence, but she was able to tell that he was physically closer now. She bit her lip to keep a smile off her face when she felt Tychon's touch.

They've jumped to Dannakor, she conveyed to Jovan. *Only a few hours out now. They'll be at the keyhole soon.*

He's not well, Jovan replied, feeling Tychon almost as clearly as Nova did.

Was a long jump from where they came from. He's so tired.

Never too tired for you, Greenie, came a distant reply. Tychon added a mental question about their wellbeing.

No worries, she replied. *The kid's a handful. Is that what we have to look forward to? Remind me to ask your mother about dealing with Delphian adolescents.*

Tychon sent a smile when they both perceived Jovan's indignation.

They want us to jump to Gramor Bejo.

Why?

I have no idea. Nova waited when Tychon's concentration wavered.

His attention was back on them a few moments later. *There is a new Arawaj base there. I thought you're on a Shri-Lan ship.*

We are. But the captain and one of the Arawaj rebels here are hatching something. Made some sort of deal.

Any idea what they might be planning?

Just a feeling. The Arawaj tried to talk me into joining them. He also let it slip that some of his people are looking for revenge. For Pe Khoja. I guess he had a bigger following than we thought.

Again, a pause. Then: *I'd say! He had a clan numbering over a hundred, including five mates, three of them female. And at least a dozen adult offspring by them.*

And all of them angry with us. Lovely.

We'll send a message to Air Command to direct their search for you to Gramor. It'll take a while. Gramor is at the ass-end of the sector.

Major! Did you just say ass-end? Who is there with you?

Let your friend there rest. I need to rest, too. Trying to dig you out of that hole is going to take all we have. And get the kid some food. He's starving.

And not admitting to it. They have us on some pretty short rations here. I hope you've got the galley stocked up. I could eat my own cooking right about now.

Let's hope it doesn't come to that.

Nova smiled as he faded from their thoughts.

Are you all right? she sent to Jovan.

Getting used to the headache. He's right. Let me rest a few hours and then let's do this. He did not break their khamal but simply drifted into a sleep-like state. Nova also settled into her couch and, in her Human way, used the training she had received from Tychon to quiet her mind and let meditation supply her brain with the rest and energy that her starved body could not.

Hours passed as they dreamed quietly. She was aware of some restless movements as their guards traded places, Rakh came by to rant something she ignored, below them something massive sounded in the engine rooms, followed by a short disturbance in the ship's already unstable gravity fields. Finally, something that felt as assuring as if Tychon had placed his hand on her shoulder reminded her of the task ahead. She reached out in a similar way to Jovan.

He opened his eyes and stared at nothing for a moment. "It's time," he said.

"It is." She turned to their rebel guard that had looked up from whatever he was watching on a screen when she had spoken. "Water. Now. And some food. It had better be edible if you ever want to see Trans-Targon again."

"Are we actually going to jump?" the navigator in front of them said. She looked up at the ship's main view screen that displayed exactly nothing.

"Going to try," Nova replied. "I don't suggest you plan any reunion parties just yet."

The Feydan, a large, capable-looking woman whose brown skin was intricately tattooed, moodily checked controls that by now were probably as ready for sub space entry as they had ever been. "This isn't what I signed up for," she said, as if to herself.

"What did you sign up for?" Jovan said. "Murdering soldiers? Destroying unprotected settlements? Watching your rebel friends rape and torture civilians?"

"Jovie..." Nova cautioned.

"Let her answer me. What is so important that you need to blow up a skyranch or hijack a transport of nothing but migrants?"

"Freedom from your Centauri overlords," the woman

spat. "They don't belong here. Nor do her people. I don't understand why you treat them like brothers. They will take your planet, too, if you let them."

"Now you did it," Nova sighed.

"I think we've managed to keep them at a distance," Jovan replied, ignoring Nova. "Perhaps if your people hadn't been so quick to invite them to your shores, eager for their toys and trinkets, they would not have made themselves at home there."

"With guns and base stations in orbit!"

"That are also used to protect people. Your people, Feydan. In case you've forgotten that the rebel is as much of a threat to Feyd as it is to Delphi." He held up a long-fingered hand. "And, although I would not call them brothers, you cannot deny that they belong to us. The evidence is in your blood as much as it is in the mirror." He gestured to Nova, whose people were almost indistinguishable from Feydans.

Nova rolled her eyes, relieved when their guard returned to interrupt the debate by tossing a few bags of rations and water at them. Rakh was only a few steps behind him. "Glad to see you," she said and tore into her share. "I mean that. Truly."

They ate ravenously and never had lukewarm water tasted so wonderful.

"All right, all right, all right," Rakh said, nearly wringing his hands with excitement. "Jump us!"

"Give us a moment," Nova said. She connected her interface to the rebel ship's processor and nodded to the navigator. The system came online and recognized her mental control of the helm. A warning went out to the rest of the ship to prepare for a rough ride. "You can't rush these things."

"How would you know? You've not done this before."

"Probably a good reason not to rush this! Now quiet, everyone." Nova looked over to Jovan who did nothing to disguise the fear and worry on his angular face. She reached for him and was surprised when he took her hand.

Trust Tychon, she sent. *This jump is nothing for him.*

When he's the one doing the jumping, Jovan replied but then caught himself. *I'm sorry. I know you can do this together.*

We, she corrected him.

What happens after? When we get there? They'll kill us all.

The Shri-Lan don't kill Delphians. You're worth a lot. Your family will make sure you are returned to Delphi.

He stared into the middle distance. *I have no family. The enclave is all there is. And they don't pay ransom like some of the clans have.*

Then Tychon will! I promise you. They won't give us up without a fight.

He gave her a hesitant smile. *You have much faith in your people.*

I better.

"What is holding this up?" Rakh snapped.

Ready?

Let's do this.

She relaxed into her couch and cast her thoughts into the vast void that separated them from Trans-Targon. By now she was so used to Jovan's silent assistance that she felt Tychon's presence almost at once.

Ty, she sent.

He hushed her wordlessly, knowing that they would need all of their energy for the navigation they were about to undertake.

I just wanted... If I don't make it, I mean. Cyann... I don't know...

She felt both Tychon and Jovan working to calm her thoughts, their touch on her mind soothing and reassuring.

I'm scared.

No, you're not, Tychon sent. *You are Captain Nova Whiteside, V7, daughter of Ironballs Whiteside and you can do this.*

Ironballs? Jovan interjected.

Ty, I told Jovan you'd look after him if I don't make it. Promise me you look after them both, she added, meaning Cyann.

I promise, he replied immediately as if he saw little point in having to even consider such an unlikely situation. He sent an abstraction that appeared in her mind like his hand reaching out to them and she took it. *I'm not worried. You can do this. Let me pull you through. Do not engage the ANI for the jump, no matter what.*

She turned her mind to the keyhole and carefully nudged the tiny breach in space to open it. The processors came alive, churning data and immense calculations to comprehend the anomaly and what they were asked to do with it. Nova directed the ship's energy into the void.

Tychon took control of the processors, using Jovan's abilities along with his own to find an exit near the Gramor system. She felt the strain he endured in maintaining this control, and the pain that both Delphians suffered as their brains fought the unnatural link to both Human and machine.

Warning signals erupted on the controls in front of them as Nova accelerated the ship toward the newly created jumpsite.

"What's happening?" Rakh shouted.

"I don't know," the navigator tapped her controls. "It's because there are two of them, I guess." She rerouted some power to give Nova more to work with. "Processor thinks it's being hacked from outside the system."

"Ditch the firewall, then."

"Done." She cursed. "Life support compromised. Evacuating lower deck. Long range sensors gone. Port shield minimal. All weapons offline."

"She tricked us!"

Found it, Tychon sent. *See it? Good. Punch it!*

Nova shot the ship forward and into the frightful nothing that connected the two points in space. For a too-long moment there was nothing. The ship's unnerving shimmy ceased, all sound stopped, and even the couch on which she lay had lost its meaning for her body. Only the thought of her hand clasping Tychon's remained with her as the cruiser hurled through the breach and then burst back into real space.

Sound returned. Lights. Excited voices babbling something she did not understand. Pain in her head.

Nova looked over to Jovan. "Jovie?" The Delphian lay limply on his bench, his face bloodless, eyes closed. The hand she had held had dropped to the side. "Jovan!" she cried. She pushed herself up from her seat. Darkness descended and she felt herself falling and then there was nothing.

EIGHT

"Tychon!"

"Is he dead?"

"Why do you have to say stuff like that, Acie?"

"Well, he kinda looks dead."

"He's not dead!"

"Let him rest a while."

Tychon groaned and waved his hand weakly as if that would make them all shut up. Surprisingly, it did. He lay exhausted and with a pounding headache in the *Dutchman*'s pilot couch and wished he were still unconscious.

Nova? he sent and winced at the new stab of pain in his head.

There was no reply.

He tried to sit up but quickly gave up on the attempt. The others were hovering around him and Seth reached out to help. The cockpit spun crazily for a moment and then settled back down. "I can't feel Nova anymore," he said. "Or the Delphian."

"Did it work? Did they jump?" Vincent said. He handed Tychon a cup of water. "Do you want something for the pain?"

"It worked. They jumped." Tychon said. "No pain killers now. We need to go after them."

"Can you take two jumps like that?" Acie said. "That's a big strain on your neocortex. You could damage yourself."

"We know where they are," Vincent said. "So maybe you should rest for a little while."

"I have to know if they're all right."

"That won't do you any good if you burn yourself out," Seth said. "Did you take out their sensors?"

Tychon nodded. "Did we hear back from Carras?"

"Yes, finally. He's got Air Command convinced that we've tracked them to Gramor. They're sending a couple of Eagles ahead of an attack unit. Won't be there for a while, though. Not a lot of keyholes connecting to that sub-sector directly."

"No more than this one. It'll still take the rebel ship a while to get to Gramor from where I put them. Without their sensors we can jump after them and follow at a distance. It'll give me time to recover."

"You can't jump now!" Vincent said.

Seth turned when a squawk from the com console alerted them of an approaching ship. "Your friends," he said to Tychon. He reached around Acie to answer their request. "Ahoy there!"

"Identify."

"You first."

Tychon sighed.

"This is the UC *Niedra*, AC. You are in Dannakor air space," came the reply. "We have an emergency situation and this area is under investigation by Union Air Command. Move away or state your intent in this area."

"Oh," Seth said. "Sorry about that. We'll be on our way."

"What is your heading?"

Seth shut the com down. "Am I lying or do you want to see if we can get them to back us up?"

Tychon shook his head. "We can't risk that Rakh hasn't managed to repair the long range sensors. If they see an Air

Command ship they'll get desperate."

"They're not going to let us hang around this keyhole much longer."

"Then you better get plugged in." Tychon reclined on his couch and re-engaged his interface. "You two hang on to something," he said to Acie and Vincent who quickly headed back into the main cabin.

Seth linked to the *Dutchman*'s navigational system and moved the ship toward the breach. An urgent tone from the com panel reminded them that the Union ship was still awaiting an answer. Seth shut it down and shifted his attention on the keyhole. It would be up to him to stabilize the out-of-control *Dutchman* when the breach spewed them back into normal space.

"When we get there," Tychon said, "collapse the keyhole at once so they can't follow. I'm going to have to rest for a few hours. Nothing to worry about. Don't rush to Gramor."

"Got it," Seth replied. A Union battle cruiser had left Dannakor's orbit and was coming their way. "How likely are they to fire on a private ship?"

"Let's not find out," Tychon said. "I'm sure they're in no mood to play with us."

"All right. But if you can't get it up I'm going to tell them you're aboard. I doubt they'll shoot at you."

"How about you don't worry about what I can get up, Kada."

They watched the keyhole widen, soon present enough to allow the *Dutchman* to slip inside. "Going negative," Seth said and closed his eyes, all of his attention on his processors.

Tychon let himself drop into a deep khamal. There was no pain now that he did not also have to link to Nova's Human brain but he was aware that he was overtaxing himself as well as the *Dutchman*'s systems. He reached into the now-open breach and felt his way back to the exit point to Gramor Bejo. When he punched through the *Dutchman* responded without a shudder and he let himself drift away.

* * *

Seth looked up from the reader in his hands when a small sound from the cockpit alerted him of their approach to Gramor, hours after they had left that inquisitive Union cruiser behind. Carefully, he shifted Acie who had curled up beside him on the lounger, and padded into the cockpit, stretching his long body as he went.

He studied the sleeping Delphian for a moment. Tychon had not shifted in his eerie rest in the hours that had passed since the traverse to this sector. Not so much as a snore, even. Did Delphians snore? Maybe Nova knew.

He bent over the navigational controls and calculated an orbit entry before returning to the cabin. Acie was sitting up now, looking owlishly around the dimmed cabin. "Are were there?"

Seth nodded and opened some of the supply bins that lined the cabin wall to select clothes and weapons.

"Are you sure this is a good idea?" she said.

"Of course it is. I thought of it, didn't I?"

"He won't like it," she said with a nod to the cockpit.

"He is asleep."

They heard Vincent rummaging around the crew cabin where he had retreated for some rest a few hours ago. He came into the main cabin as Seth exchanged his bright red pullover for a plain gray shirt. Like Acie, he had his doubts about Seth's intent.

"Don't start on me, Old Man," Seth said. "There is no way we're going to get past anyone down there walking around with a blue-haired officer. I'm just going to scout a bit and then come back to the ship."

"I have confidence in your abilities," Vincent said. He went into the galley. "Tea, Acie?"

"Ooh yes!" she slipped from the lounger and went to sit on the stool by the tiny counter. "Lots of sweet in it, please." She turned back to Seth who was adjusting the scanner setting on his wrist array. "Don't bother with that. The place is practically made of crystal. Oscillating like mad. That sort of resonance is going to cause all sorts of interference. You'll be lucky if you don't drop us on our heads trying to land down there." She smiled at Vincent when he found a package of dried berries in the food bins.

"What's shaking the crystal to cause that much trouble?"

"The hydrothermals. Tremendous pressure below the crust."

Seth stole a sip of her tea and grimaced when he tasted it. "What'll work down there?"

"Your nose," she said. "If you start smelling something fruity, get out of there. Critters in the swamp. They'll have you for dinner."

"What kind of critter smells fruity?"

She slid off her stool and picked up one of the data tablets she had studied earlier. She held it level while a hologram hovered above the surface. "Those."

Seth looked at the projection and whistled. "What do they eat when there aren't any Centauri around?"

Vincent took Acie's tablet and gently tapped her on the head with it. "Funny girl. Those critters are microscopic. There is nothing larger than a grub left down there. Unless you're counting Arawaj. Are you sure they are going to welcome you? And I don't mean the critters."

"Sure," Seth shrugged. He tested a short-barreled pistol and holstered it. A few percussion charges went into his thigh pocket. "I've dealt with the Arawaj more than the Shri-Lan. They'll let me land, don't worry."

"It's leaving again that I'm worried about."

Seth went into the cockpit and opened a com channel. "Bejo operator, come in," he said. "Requesting contact, anyone."

There was some delay before they received a reply. "Who's hailing?"

"Bejo, this is the *Dutchman*, private transport. Burned out some coolant coming through that last jump. Hoping you can spare some."

"Hold, *Dutchman*."

Seth whistled tunelessly. None of this seemed to bother Tychon, whose calm face remained immobile. His people did not wake easily and Delphian field agents often relied on proximity alarms to alert them of danger. On the other hand, Seth thought, they were guaranteed a good night's sleep just about anywhere.

"Sethran Kada, is that you?" someone shouted through the cabin speakers, the voice unmistakably Human.

Seth grinned. "Aye, that'll be me."

"Told you!" the voice faded as he seemed to be shouting at someone else. "Damn *Dutchman*! It's me, Jammer. Welcome to Porcupine! Come on down! There's really just one place to land unless you want to end up in the Deeps. The place has been hopping with strange things going on."

"What strange things?"

"Your ears only, if you don't mind. Got anything fun to trade? I'm going nuts with all these Caspians around. Fucking furbutts have no sense of fun."

"I might. Couple of vials of Rocket Juice, if you want. Off Pelion."

"You got a deal. See you when you get down here."

Seth closed the channel and entered the necessary coordinates for landing into his navigator. "And you doubted me," he said to Vincent and Acie. "I'm welcome everywhere."

"Uh huh, except for Aram, Callas and Feron, if I recall."

"That thing on Callas was not my fault. What's porcupine?"

Acie consulted her tablet and then raised an eyebrow. "Pointy-looking Terran mammal." She showed an image to Seth and Vincent. "Not microscopic."

"Prepare for landing." Seth carefully lowered the crash guard over Tychon's seat before he directed the *Dutchman* to the surface. The entry was smooth and, although they were jarred a little in their restraints, it was not enough to wake the Delphian.

Seth took them over a ragged landscape of deep canyons

from which turrets and peaks reached up like splinters. Jammer's description of the place as 'porcupine' was as apt as any. Some of the crystals seemed to lean at dangerous angles as if the rock strata that once surrounded the veins had simply eroded away, leaving only the spikes. There were no valleys, no open spaces, and no seas to make landing any craft possible. Only occasionally a more substantial mountain rose high above the formations. Mist filled the wider gaps and at times seeped skyward before the wind took it away.

"Lots of quartz holding all that up, along with some granite," Acie reported from memory. "Minimal vegetation. You'll have enough oxygen, though. No wildlife or sentient native population any longer. It's habitable down there, if terribly boring. Your friend seems to suffer from that."

"Not my friend. The guy is the worst piece of scum you can imagine. But he likes me, so that's in our favor." Seth nosed the plane down when they approached a plateau of sorts rising high above the crags. From a distance, it looked like part of a mountain top had been carved away to create a landing platform. Long ago, archeological expeditions had created a base here to study an ancient civilization that had either died out or moved on. Part of the peak had been left standing to shelter a derelict huddle of sheds serving the small airfield.

"Look!" Vincent said. "A battle cruiser. Must be the one that Nova was on."

"I wonder if they're still all on board." Seth landed near a few other ships huddling in the lee of the cliff. "Looks like they're getting ready to leave again."

Vincent pointed at the *Dutchman*'s main screen. "What's that? Smoke?"

"Steam. Hydrothermals," Acie said. "Venting everywhere here. They use them for heat and power source."

"Are you sure it's water? Should I take a respirator?" Seth said.

"No, it's just water. Very hot water. It'll be very humid down below. I hope you don't mind fungus."

Seth powered the *Dutchman* down and came to his feet. "Guess I won't need my mittens. You two stay here. Act like crew if someone hails you." He furrowed his brow thoughtfully. "You, Vincent, are a trader I'm taking to Pelion. Tychon's the pilot, dealing with his space bends. You can be my bellywarmer, Acie."

She scowled. "Is that the best you can come up with?"

"If I tell them what you really are they'll steal you. You're far too valuable."

She pouted. "Nice try, Kada."

Seth pulled a small case from one of his bins. "Does this still look good to you?"

She removed one of the vials and used a medical scanner to examine the contents. "Why do you have so much dope on board? You can get arrested for this."

"It's not illegal here."

"Nothing is illegal here!"

"So why are you worried?" Seth gave her another bottle. "What'll happen if you add some of that?"

She scanned it and frowned. "You'd be really really stoned. And babbling like a baby." She looked over to Vincent. "Thiopental. It'll have the Human telling him anything he wants."

"Well, mix us some of that, Doc," Seth grinned. He tapped the data unit on his forearm. "I'm going to leave this open so you can listen in. It'll shut down if someone else intercepts the signal. Start monitoring for those Eagles. They're not going to be welcome here."

Seth left the *Dutchman* as soon as Acie had finished mixing the drug and admonished him about using the correct dosage. A short walk across the windswept landing area brought him to a sheltered entrance near the base of the cliff. Small shards of quartz, some ground to powder, crunched under his boots and he squinted when the fine, windborne grit rasped over his face. He wondered how the Caspians, generally barefooted, fared on this abrasive surface. A Human rebel met him when he ducked into the base building.

"Nice place you have," Seth said, shaking sand from his hair. In here, away from the high winds, the humidity produced by the planet's thermal vents enveloped him like warm shower.

"What do you want here, Kada?" the Human said. Like some of the Caspian Arawaj rebels, he wore only a pair of knee-length breeches although he had opted to protect his feet with boots rather than callus.

"Do I know you?"

"Stories have you working with the Union. That you're actually one of them."

"So *they* think."

"Want to know what I think?"

"No." Seth moved around the man and then quickly grasped his elbow in a painful lock when the Human reached for his gun. "What did I just tell you?"

The rebel grunted, feeling his arm close to the breaking point.

"Where is Jammer?"

"Up those steps, to the front."

Seth released the man without bothering to disarm him and without another look back. The gamble paid off but he breathed a sigh of relief when he turned a corner and started to climb the uneven steps hewn into the rock. The stairs leveled out at times to form short ramps; in other places tall risers required him to heave himself upward to the next as if they were intended for giants. The steps changed direction, apparently following the natural tunnels and hollows caved out of the stone by wind, steam and time. Light slanted into the space from ahead of him and he followed the sound of voices into a larger hall.

"Seth, you dog!" he was greeted.

The Human called Jammer by everyone but his mother waved grandly when Seth stepped into the room. There was another Human here, looking less friendly than Jammer but a lot less interested as well. He was facing a long control board, little more than field equipment, an interface plugged into his work. Both men were stripped down to sleeveless shirts and stained trousers and without visible weapons.

Seth came to where Jammer lounged casually on air bag furniture and dropped into one of them. "How'd you end up in this dump?" he asked, looking around. The room showed signs of having been enlarged with conventional tools and three large window openings were covered by sheets of plastics. None of them fit very tightly and some of the grit drifted over the stone floor where it turned to mud. He armed sweat from his forehead. "They say it's not the heat, it's the humidity."

"What is?"

"Never mind. Didn't expect to find Arawaj here. Lucky for me. For a while I was worried about a Union base."

"On this rock? Nothing here unless you're a prospector, maybe. We're not here for long, I tell you that. We're bugging out soon, or so we been promised." He leaned closer to Seth. "Got my Juice?"

Seth drew back to avoid the man's pungent aroma. Was bathing not an option on a planet practically overflowing with hot water? He fished the vials from a pocket and tossed them to Jammer. "The finest, just so you're grateful." He had no idea about the quality of the drug, never having bothered with the stuff himself. It had been expensive. "Cost you four tubes."

"Four! Fuck you, Centauri." Jammer quickly pulled his hands away when it appeared that Seth was about to take the vials back. "Fine, fine. Whatever. Nobody gonna notice them gone anyway." He leaned far to his left and slapped the young rebel at the com console. "Get down to Te Lar and have them take four tubes to the *Dutchman*, with our compliments."

The rebel removed his interface connection. "She'll probably insist that I shove them up my ass. Or do it for me."

Seth quickly withdrew another vial from his pocket.

"Here. With *my* compliments." He said and handed over a bottle without the extra component that Acie had measured into it.

The rebel took it. "Got crew aboard?"

"Navigator, a smuggler going somewhere and a Bellac with my name all over her." Seth raised a finger in warning. "So keep your hands off that."

"Fine, fine, fine. Go already," Jammer said, fondling his own supply of Juice. "Nobody gonna touch her."

Seth sat back with the air of a man whose business transactions were completed. "So what's going on here? Why are you hiding out in this sponge?" He watched Jammer expertly fill a small applicator with his newly acquired drug and administer it to himself.

The rebel leaned back in his chair and closed his eyes with a long, hissing breath. "Damn fine." He exhaled shakily. "That's got a kick to it."

Seth waited a moment before speaking. "Jammer? You were saying?"

"Huh? Oh. We had to get out of Caspia for a bit. Some of them aren't too happy with what's been happening. There's even talk about allowing Commonwealth settlements on Caspia, if you can believe that! So folks don't want rebels around, making them look bad. Arawaj decided to move some projects off-planet."

"What kind of project?" Seth asked, hoping that the drug was beginning to take effect on the Human. The other rebel would not be gone for long and there was little time to draw the information he needed from Jammer.

"You won't believe it. Damn Caspians came up with a way to take out most of the Union fleet."

Seth raised an eyebrow. "What? From here? Going to throw rocks?"

Jammer laughed. "No, man, they came up with a program for one of the pilots they caught on Dannakor. Red-haired thing. Rude as hell. Damn fine ass."

Seth bit his lip, having nearly asked if she was all right.

"What kind of program?"

"She's got some new interface. They got it to work so that as soon as she tries to use it to send a message from here it'll blow out everyone's brains. Everyone that can hear her, anyway. Don't know how it works but the Caspians are really excited about it."

Seth whistled appreciatively and managed to keep a smile on his face. "Sounds like Arawaj is finally ready to show some muscle."

"Got that right. We're kinda tired of letting the Shri-Lan have all the fun. Although they're in on this, too."

"How's that," Seth asked, trying to sound disinterested.

Jammer winked conspiratorially. "I'm not supposed to know about it, but there's nothing to do here at night but listen to others talk. They don't know I understand the Caspian jabber. I been around them long enough. Shri-Lan's going to start a brawl somewhere. Blow the shit out of some civilian places. That'll stir everyone up. It'll guarantee the whole damn Air Command is in the air and linked to their processors."

"Downright devious," Seth grinned. "They're going to hit Targon?"

"No idea. Probably something more remote. Doesn't matter. They're going to keep everyone guessing and then: Blam! Some place is going to get sacked, bagged and looted while our fine Air Command is chasing ghosts elsewhere. You should join in. Lots of pillage to be had, if you know what I mean."

Seth turned to look over to the com console, in part to keep from driving his fist into Jammer's gleeful visage. "Is that the program in there?"

"Nah. That's not even a long range. I think they keep it up on the cliff." Jammer pointed at the ceiling.

"The girl, too?"

"No. They sent the lot to the *Abiah*."

"What's the *Abiah*?" Seth asked, knowing he was pushing the man too fast. Was he hearing steps coming up the stone corridor?

"The main Arawaj base here, down in the Deeps. Shri-Lan decided to leave the Azon crowd with us for safe keeping. I think their captain, uh, Rakh, wants to figure out who's going to give him the biggest piece for the beaker-heads. So he made a deal with Sao Lok to keep them all here."

"A true Shri-Lan," Seth said. "What sort of base could you manage in a place like this? Those canyons look barely passable. Caves?"

"No. Not really. Don't let this place fool you. There's a whole town of sorts carved right into a mountain. Been there for a thousand years. Can't really see it from the air, can't land on them, can't find it on scanners until you get right close. Can only get there by boat or skimmer, if you go slow." It took a few attempts before he had heaved his bulk up and out of his seat. "Look over there."

Seth joined him by one of the plastic-covered openings. The barren, craggy landscape stretched to the horizon, broken only by swaths of mist and the occasional, needle-sharp rock spire. But taller, well-separated mountains rose like lonely sentinels above the canyons to form buttes with almost vertical cliff faces. "Those are habitats?"

"Not all of them, but a lot. Old, though. No one left now. Guess this place used to be more fun than it is now."

"And they've sent the captives to one of those?"

"Yeah. Why are you asking me all these questions, Kada?" Jammer lurched to the com console when his attention was required by someone on the airfield below. He exchanged some obscenity-studded conversation with them and then watched, along with Seth, as the Shri-Lan battle cruiser lifted off in a massive cloud of glittering dust. "Fucking good riddance," he slurred.

"Where are they off to?"

"Going to take the jumpsite to Pelion. It's the only charted gate in this entire sub-sector. A Shri-Lan wing is waiting there for them. Then the fun will begin."

"You really don't like them much, eh?"

"What's to like? They're despicable enough to give the rest of us a bad name."

Jammer laughed as if he had said something utterly hilarious. But his laughter died in his throat when a Caspian entered, followed by several more of his kind. Some of them wore only short kilts to display whatever pattern on their bodies was prized most among them. Seth recognized the dark patches of the highlands and the stripes of the northern regions. Some, like the man at the front of the group, bore sinuous whorls against a paler background.

Sao Lok's yellow eyes focused on Seth. "Visitor, Jammer?" he said.

"Yeah, dropped by for some supplies."

"The timing of this is... inconvenient."

"I know that man," a female behind him said. "Small time pirate working out of Magra Torley. He was with us on Pelion for a while. Let's not waste time with this!"

Sao Lok nodded. "Get on that thing," he snapped at Jammer and pointed at the com panel. "The Human pilot has escaped on the way to the *Abiah*. Get a crew together."

"Didn't think you'd be the hostage-taking sort, Arawaj," Seth said.

"Maybe it's best that you be on your way, Centauri," Lok said. "We are busy here."

Seth shrugged. "I can help you corral your runaway, if you want." He gestured in the direction of the *Dutchman* parked below.

"She's in the Deeps. Your plane won't do much good in there." He paused to consider. "We can use the help, though. There aren't nearly enough of us to cover that area. If you want to actually *earn* those coolant tubes, Pirate, get yourself a sled and join the search." He regarded Jammer as if studying something especially repulsive. "This Human is of limited use now because of you. So you can take his place."

"What am I looking for? What does that pilot look like?"

"Female Human, red hair." Lok tipped his head toward

Seth's sidearm. "Watch yourself around her. She killed two of her guards when she broke loose and the third is badly injured. She is now armed."

Seth nodded and slipped past the Caspians before someone could question his altruistic offer to help round up the prisoner. He rushed down the crooked steps and out onto the airfield. "Did you get all that?" he whispered into his sleeve while running his hand through his hair. He saw a row of air sleds parked at the far side of the cleared space and headed that way.

"Most of it," Vincent replied amid a wave of static crackling in Seth's ear. "I don't dare to send a message out to Air Command. No doubt a packet will be noticed."

"I'm going after Nova. Try to get Tychon on his feet and get him caught up on that interface thing. We're going to have to find Nova or this program before they'll have her use it. See if Acie and Tychon can figure out a way to scan for the transmitter without alerting everyone. It'll have to be up on one of these mountains to get through the noise."

"She's already looking. Nothing seems to be active. They can't just force Nova to use it, can they?"

"They won't have to. She doesn't know about the program! She'll take the first chance she gets to try to contact us. Let's hope I find her before they do. Out."

Seth had reached the pool of air sleds where a few rebels, mostly Caspian, were milling about, seeming uneager to embark upon a search for the escapee.

"Shut up, everyone," a Centauri shouted. "Where's Dai? Dai, there you are. The Human jumped ship near the Three Points marker, so not too far from here. Head out that way and then disperse. You won't pick her up on your scanners until you're falling over her, so take care."

"No tracks?" Seth asked.

"That crossroads is flooded right now. She'd be walking in water for quite a stretch in any direction. Signal if any of you see tracks where the ground is higher. Saddle up. We've got some backup coming from the *Abiah*. Let's get this done before Lok gets any pissier about it."

Seth climbed aboard one of the air sleds. It wobbled precariously until he balanced the thrusters that seemed not at all willing to work in tandem. He followed the others as they, one by one, dropped off the edge of the plateau and into the canyons.

The Centauri rebel had been right. A shallow lake of floodwater stood where larger gaps in the canyon walls formed a three-way intersection of pathways. All around them jagged turrets of glistening rock rose into the air, some at precarious angles, making the landscape appear more like a cave than a canyon. Massive pseudo-stalagmites of smoky crystal blocked their view of the sky and sunlight did not reach the bottom here. Everywhere he looked, thermal vents spewed steam into the air. Thick mats of moss and other growth clung to the rocks wherever a little soil remained. The boulders, water-filled ditches, and spongy ground promised that handling the sleds down here would not be easy.

Seth sat back on his skimmer and thoughtfully combed his hair with the fingers of both hands. The humidity and heat down here had already turned his skin and clothes damp.

"Going to sit around here all day?" A Caspian had pulled up beside his sled. "Maybe if you wait long enough she'll come back on her own."

Seth grinned and waved as the rebel sped off. The uneven whirr of their machines soon faded among the stone pillars. He circled over the swampy ground, looking for tracks. "This isn't right," he murmured. "What are you doing, Nova?"

He looked around the shadow-filled chasm, noting the dead silence now that the others had left. Nova would not have run off into the wilds on a planet about which she knew little and without even rudimentary equipment to help her survive. No, she would circle back and climb up to the landing area, knowing that help was on the way. But would she recognize the *Dutchman*? It had been years since she had last seen his plane and that was several refits and a paint job ago. To her, it would look like just another rebel ship.

He turned his sled. She would try to get back up to the airfield and find a transmitter to get help for herself and the others. She had no other option. And she would use the ANI instead of a packet transit to avoid interception.

Seth backtracked carefully, keeping his eyes on the uneven ground that threatened to throw his thrusters out of alignment. This terrain was no more suitable for hover sleds than it was for aircraft. Using boats certainly seemed the most sensible way to get around.

Something appeared at the periphery of his vision when he swung his sled around a jagged bend. A sharp rapport rang out and then searing pain drove deep into his chest and right arm. He had been shot! Fighting panic, he slowed the skimmer but then his grip on the unstable machine weakened and it slid out from under him. He landed with a splash on saturated ground and then found himself staring into the barrel of a gun.

"Damn, Nova," he groaned, clutching his arm. "Didn't think you'd still be mad at me."

* * *

"What the hell are you doing here!" Nova exclaimed and tucked her gun into the waistband of her trousers. She pushed his shirt up and helped him pull it over his head. Quickly, she wadded it up and pressed it against his pectoral which was bleeding more than his arm. The bullet had torn along his skin but had not entered his body.

"Came to rescue you," he grunted.

She frowned and looked from him to the crashed sled and then around the steam-filled landscape.

"Don't say it, Red."

"Wasn't going to."

"Yes, you were." He looked down at her hand pressing against his wound. "How bad is it?"

"You're lucky that wasn't a laser."

He sat up with more groans and winces and crawled up onto higher ground. "This was hardly necessary," he growled. "At least last time I saw you, you only kicked me in the throat."

"You deserved that. And the last Centauri that flew through here was looking to kill me. Not a lot of friendly ones on this planet. Got any food?"

"No. Sorry," he said. "They're not looking to kill you."

She lifted the blood-soaked shirt to examine his wound. "So what brings you to this place? Don't tell me you're friends with the Arawaj."

"I think 'friends' is a bit of an overstatement. I've done some, uh, business with them now and again. But I'm here with Tychon."

"Tychon! He's here?" She looked around as if expecting him to appear among the craggy cliffs. "With you?"

"Yeah. Still up top. Sleeping."

"Sleeping!" She sat back on her heels, incredulous. "Oh, right. He had to make two jumps. That'll have him cranky for days."

"Three. We came in from Aikhor. Let's get back to the landing site. Get off this rock."

"We have to get the others," she corrected and walked over to where the sled lay with its nose buried in mud. She heaved on it until it moved back and out of the water with a wet gurgle. "We've still got most of the ANI team and the Delphian here somewhere. I really don't want to lose any more. They're worth more without me around, so I'm hoping they'll be all right for a while."

"Let's get back into those rocks over there," Seth said. "They've got everyone out looking for you. Can you move that?"

"You're not hurt that badly, Kada, you big baby."

"Is this lack of sympathy your way of covering up your guilt over shooting me?" He came to his feet and used his uninjured arm to help her drag the sled away from the ditch that ran through the clearing and into a cluster of sharp-edged pillars of stone. She returned to shuffle through the gravel and matted lichens on the ground to obscure the marks they had left behind.

"So how did you end up here?" she said when they had tipped the sled onto its side. She used her hands to scrape mud away from the thruster ports and intake valves. "Gross. What is this slime stuff?"

"Does it smell fruity?"

"Yeah."

"Might want to rinse that off." He sat on a relatively dry boulder to watch her work. "Kind of a long story. How I got here, I mean. Not the slime. But basically, your CO thinks you're playing with the Shri-Lan now, which almost got Tychon fired and so Carras thought I might be able to help out. Turns out he was right and so here we are."

She looked up. "What do you mean with Tychon almost getting fired?"

"Relieved of duty till they can sort this out. Stripped of his stripes, so to speak."

"So it's just you here? No Air Command support? No Eagles? We have nine more people stuck on this planet!"

"The entire fleet is on alert. But not because of you. Shri-Lan is planning some sort of attack. So a bunch of hostages probably aren't a priority right now."

"I don't suppose," she said, shaking mud off her fingers.

"But you turned out to be one hot little item, Red. Seems that thing in your head is capable of a whole lot of damage if used the wrong way."

"What? The ANI?"

"Yeah. The Arawaj have a program that'll turn you into a walking kill switch if you use the ANI for long range com. Gives everyone who's plugged in an instant embolism or something."

She froze, her unseeing eyes still on her fingers. So that was Sao Lok's big secret. Use her to destroy her own people to end the wars. She felt a peculiar stab of disappointment.

Perhaps, even for just a moment or two, she had thought that, just maybe, Sao Lok really did have a peaceful solution to all of this. Instead, she had once again misjudged a Caspian. Would she ever come to understand their way of thinking?

"That Sao Lok is more devious than I thought," she said. "Well, not much damage I can do while I'm stuck out here in this swamp, is there?" She touched the sled's starter panel. The machine whined a bit but remained on the ground. She tried kicking it but that didn't seem to motivate the vehicle, either, and so she tipped it the other way hoping to drain more liquid out of the intakes.

Seth tapped his own neural implant. "Can't you just pull it off?"

She shook her head. "Not this model. I'd rather not try it, anyway, way out here, without a medi-kit. Who knows what's crawling around out here. The last thing I want is a gaping hole in my..." She glanced at his bleeding arm. "Oh. Sorry."

"Thank you, I was looking for something else to worry about." He came to his feet to crouch beside her. "If you've got water in there you might as well give up."

"No, I don't think so. This piece is bent and is keeping the—" she looked up when both of them heard the low hum of skimmer. She pulled him up and they scrambled into a narrow space among the boulders to hide from the approaching vehicle. He hissed in pain when she flattened herself against him.

The skimmer stopped. Nova and Seth exchanged a worried glance when they heard a splash and then the sound of someone coming closer.

Nova tried to calm her breathing, too aware that she was pressed tightly against Seth's powerful body, which he didn't seem to mind at all. Their bodies were slick with sweat and the oppressive humidity, their clothes damp to the skin. When had he placed his hand on her waist? It felt comforting and familiar. She looked up into his face and found his warmly glowing eyes gaze back at her. Had it been only five years since he left her on that rebel platform? She pulled away a little as if in deference to his injured chest. He tipped his head back against the rock and she was reminded that he was, indeed, in a great deal of pain.

She drew her gun from her waistband. Seth shook his head and reached for his own pistol, a small laser weapon, which he exchanged for hers. Not as effective in this mist but absolutely silent. She nodded and looked around the edge of the rock that hid them.

A Caspian was standing over the broken sled. She watched him bend to feel the charger compartment, checking for heat. He straightened and looked around himself, then slowly backed away, perhaps realizing that he was exposed in a dead-end alcove among these rocks. He had no scanner that she could see and the communicator at his wrist would be useless here. His furred chest expanded, ready to expel the earsplitting cry that Caspians used in battle to draw attention. She aimed quickly and the tracer of her gun lit up the space between them, diffused only slightly by the mist, to find its target. His cry died in his throat when he did.

"You've still got that dead-on aim, Red," Seth said behind her.

"I practice. Looks like we got us a working vehicle."

They stepped out of the circle of rocks. The rebel's sled was still running, hovering nearly silently above the ground.

Seth looked back into the direction where he had left the rebel posse at the three-way split in the rocks. "I was told you were being taken to one of those mountain things. Of course, being down here is really not a good way of figuring out where that might be. Do you know in which direction that is?"

"Well," she said as she climbed aboard the sled and swung her leg over its seat. "I really have no idea."

"And you thought that getting lost down here is a good way to find them?"

"I wasn't lost. I was coming back to wait for Tychon."

"Let's stay away from this channel. Seems to be the way they navigate down here. We'll pick our way through those stalagmite things further back. It'll be slow but safer. Back to the landing field to regroup with Tychon and get me patched up. Then we'll figure something out."

"Is Ty okay? After that jump? Must have been painful."

"He's just beat, I think." He walked back to the dead Caspian to relieve him of his gun. There was nothing else useful to be found there.

She hesitated a moment. "So what do you think of him? Tychon, I mean."

Seth returned to her. "Seems all right. Kind of emotional for a Delphian."

"They all are, believe it or not. You should meet his mother." She lowered the sled a little to help him get on board. He was holding his injured arm with his other hand and she assumed it pained him more than he was willing to admit. "I guess he wasn't too pleased to find out about us, was he?"

"He's all right with it." The sled tilted a little as Seth settled behind her.

"*All right?* He's not jealous?"

"No, I don't think so."

She frowned and then turned halfway around to look at him, again tipping the sled precariously. "Really?" she said, taken aback. "Not even a tiny bit?"

Seth laughed. "Maybe he hides it well. Does that make you feel better?"

She turned around again. "Not really," she grumbled and nudged the sled forward. "Cold-blooded, stone-faced Delphian is taking me for granted!"

"Look out!"

She also saw them now. Four of the Arawaj, each on a sled, had rounded the bend ahead of them. She whipped the skimmer about and sped away, keeping the vehicle over the water channel. Its liquid surface was less effective than solid ground for the sled but still far more accommodating than trying to skim over the composition of rocks and swamp along the edges. The hunters did the same and she had to keep the sled low on the water to keep up any sort of speed with the extra weight her skimmer carried. She heard their shrill screams echo through the canyons, calling to others to join the chase.

Laser fire zipped past them as the hunters tried to force them to give up. Nova was well aware that Seth presented a far less valuable target and it was just a matter of time before he was hit. He returned their fire as best as he could without losing his balance. She slowed the skimmer, turned a corner and then switched direction again, risking dangerous speeds in their desperate attempt to put more distance between them and the rebels.

"Two down, but two more just joined," Seth called to her. He readied a percussion charge and lobbed it at a relatively dry spot at the foot of a crystal column. It exploded with an insignificant popping sound but the base of the spire fragmented into a deadly hail of shards, forcing their pursuers to slow down until the last of the rock had crashed to the ground. "They just keep coming with all that screeching they're doing."

The turns became tighter and the spaces between the rock turrets darker and more narrow, often choked with long strings of mosses and whatever else was able to grow down here. A sharp beam of light tore along Nova's leg to burn a streak along her trousers.

Then something punched into the rear of the sled to skew it to the right where it slammed into a rock, bounced back to almost find its direction again and then tipped on its side, dumping both Nova and Seth into the shallow channel before crashing into the rocks.

Nova scrambled after Seth into the lee of some boulders to fire at the rebels that were coming up fast behind them. There were at least six there now, also off their sleds and advancing.

"You're over your heads," one of the rebels, a burly

Centauri, called out. "We just want the woman. Give up now and you won't get hurt. Much."

Seth's response was a volley of projectiles in their direction. Two of them ducked into the cover of an almost horizontal slab of crystal and he aimed carefully. His projectile weapon splintered the outcropping and it crashed down onto the rebels. "We might have a problem, Red," he said.

She looked around. Narrow channels snaked through the rock spires and thick mist hovered among them to their right. Possibly, a good place to hide for a while. "How far do you think we can get on foot? Four of them are Caspians. They'll have a hard time walking in this muck."

"Can't think of anything better," he said and then ducked when shots strafed over their heads.

Nova fired a barrage back at the rebels. "Okay, this way."

Both of them turned to rush into the murk behind them when two Humans stepped out of the gloom, weapons in hand. "Wrong way," one of them said.

Nova cursed when they were disarmed and hauled back to the open area where the others waited, now seven in total. Seth was pushed to his knees while Nova struggled with her captors. "No!" she cried when a rebel held her gun to Seth's head.

Then the gun was gone. So was the rebel's hand. She stared stupidly at the stump of what remained of her arm before bellowing in pain and rage. The others turned. A hooded figure had appeared from the mist among the stone pillars and shot another rebel. Someone ran at him from the side and he simply reached out with long arms and snapped the man's neck. His hood fell back to show that, instead of another Centauri, their strident calls had drawn the attention of an extremely angry Delphian.

Nova twisted in her captor's grip and the Human, too surprised to react, felt her knee punch into his groin. He gave up his weapon to his peril. She shot him and then turned to the one recently missing a hand and shot her, too. Seth had slumped to the ground and she tossed him her gun before pulling a long knife from the dead rebel's belt.

The large Centauri rebel had engaged Tychon in hand-to-hand combat, the two well matched. A Caspian took aim at Tychon but hesitated when he realized that his shot at the Delphian was no more open than Seth's aim at Tychon's opponent. Nova settled his quandary by burying her knife in his neck. When an opening appeared, she handed the blade off to Tychon who whirled and thrust it upward into the Centauri's body. The rebel staggered backward before falling into the shallow water, at the feet of the last of the rebels. The Caspian's fury over the lost battle focused on Nova and she charged with a shrill battle cry that seemed to vibrate through the crystal spires. Nova bent to catch the taller woman in midriff to let her momentum hurl her over her back. She tumbled into the water and Nova followed to put her knee onto the Caspian's shoulders, keeping her head under water. The panicked woman nearly dislodged Nova but Seth lobbed his gun back to her to quickly dispatch the rebel.

For a moment the silence was broken only by loud gasps for air. Nova turned as she rose to see Tychon move toward her. She flung herself into his arms and felt them wrap around her so tightly that she barely breathed.

"Gods, Nova. You're all right," he said. "You're all right!" He cupped her face in his hands and kissed her cheek, her forehead, her mouth, again and again. "Taking that jump! On a rebel ship! I thought I'd lose you for sure this time."

She buried her face against his chest, feeling suddenly safe and comforted, even standing in muddy water nearly to her knees on this hostile planet. "You said you weren't worried."

"I was scared out of my mind." He lifted her up and carried her like a child to higher ground where he sat down to cradle her in his embrace. She clung to him, reveling in his warmth, his pleasant scent, the sound of his soothing voice.

"You're hurt," he said, examining the scorch mark along her leg. Her skin was singed but not badly injured. He winced when he saw the fading bruise on her cheek.

"I'm all right." She reached up to brush away the worried line between his brows. "You're here. You came for me. How did you find us down here?"

"I'd find you in the dark," he said.

"Umm, hello?" Seth made himself heard. He slouched against a rock and tiredly raised his hand. "Not to make too fine a point of it, but I'm the one that got shot."

Tychon looked up as if only now aware of Seth's presence. He released Nova and stood up to help Seth regain his feet. "That was close," he said, meaning the long scrape across Seth's chest.

"She's a good shot," Seth said, tipping his head into Nova's direction.

Tychon turned back to her. "You shot him? I thought you two were on good terms."

Seth grinned. "She holds a grudge."

They looted what guns they needed from the fallen rebels and then mounted sleds to carefully thread their way back to the main channel. Once they had put some distance between themselves and the carnage they had left behind, Tychon turned them into a passage leading away from the water. The ground rose steadily until they found an open area among the rocks covered in a layer of dry lichen.

Nova looked up to search the fragment of sky visible above the stone walls. "Will we have to spend the night out here?"

"That'll be a long night," Seth said. "Sunset's not even for another week or so, Targon time."

Tychon untied a parcel from the back of his sled and opened it. He handed Nova a package of rations. "You mentioned that you were hungry?"

She tore into the bag. "I was hungry two days ago. Now I'm just starving."

"Turns out it's a good idea to pack up a bit of a kit before heading into unknown territory." He threw a sardonic glance in Seth's direction as he crouched to pull her waterlogged boots off and then, with a resigned sigh, helped Seth with his as well. There was a small radiator in his kit that would dry their clothes at least somewhat in short order.

Nova peered into the kit bag and pulled out a package of medical supplies. "Good concept."

"Acie figured someone is bound to get hurt out here."

"Acie!" Nova exclaimed. "I was so worried about her after Dannakor! You brought her along to this place? What were you thinking? Is Vincent with her?"

"Yes," Tychon said. "Everyone's here except for any sort of backup. We're on our own. Again."

"What do you mean?"

"The Shri-Lan blasted the relays at the jumpsites when they left. Nothing useful left within reach. No way to send a packet to warn Air Command about that damnable thing." Tychon pointed at her interface.

"And no way for the Union ships to know what's waiting for them if they jump to this sector." Nova unrolled the bundle of supplies and avoided his eyes. "You might as well say 'I told you so', Ty. You warned me that this was a bad idea. So get it over with."

"Have I ever said that to you?"

"Has she given you reason?" Seth asked.

"You have no idea," Tychon sighed.

"She never listens to good advice, does she?"

Nova recognized the amusement in Tychon's eyes although his expression remained neutral. She wagged a finger at Seth. "Don't you two even think about ganging up on me!"

Tychon picked up a water purifier. "Get the Centauri patched up and let's sort out a way to get home." He left them to return to the channel.

Nova turned on a portable decontamination wand to carefully treat Seth's wounds and then poured a liquid disinfectant on them just to be sure.

"Sorry," she said when he winced.

"Cold-blooded?" Seth said and nodded in the direction

that Tychon had gone. "Stone-faced? Nova, I've never seen a Delphian as jacked up over a woman as he is."

She smiled slowly, her eyes on her task.

"And you! Vanguard warrior going all melty. What a sight!"

"I didn't go melty! You want some painkiller?"

"No, I'm tough."

"You're afraid of needles."

"It's not fear. It's an aversion."

"Sure it is. I meant topical, anyway." Nova applied a pain-relieving gel to a piece of dressing and taped it over his wound.

"I'm happy for you," he said with a somber note in his voice. "He seems right for you."

"It's a good life, Seth. Sometimes when I'm on Delphi I almost feel like a civilian. I didn't think I'd like it. But once we had Cyann everything changed. Hey, you should come and see her!"

He smiled wistfully. "I'm happy for you, Nova, but also a bit envious. Envious of Tychon for having you all to himself, I guess, but also of you. Your life. Let's not make dinner plans."

She searched his solemn expression that for once lacked the spark of mischief that accompanied everything else he said and did. She wondered if, for all his bravado and adventures, he was lonely. "You don't have to do this," she said. "You can find peace, too."

He grinned, becoming Seth again. "Nah, I'd be bored. So let's just agree that, after I once again save your spectacular backside from the rebel clutches, we'll head off in different directions."

She laughed and waved her arm in a sweeping gesture to encompass their current location. "So far I'm not seeing an awful lot of saving on your part, Kada."

"I choose my time wisely."

"I'll try not to shoot you next time." She poked around the supply parcel. "Look, a dry shirt for you." She looked up when Tychon returned with a bag of cleaned water. She showed him the comb she had found. "Is that to satisfy your vanity or mine?"

He smiled. "Acie packed all this up. She's a sweet thing. We're going to take her back to Delphi with us. She needs to cool down after Dannakor. They're not going to give her anything interesting to do if we take her onto a base, considering her past. Maybe Anders can use her talents. Somewhere far away."

"She'd like that." Nova hesitated before going on. "While on the subject... That Delphian that helped me on the rebel ship. Jovan. He could use a hand up."

"What do you mean? He's a Shantir, isn't he?"

"I'm not convinced that's what he wants to be. He's an orphan. The enclave is all he knows. I don't know if he's meant for that. He's not so sure, either."

"He's got a good head for it," Tychon said, somewhat grudgingly.

"He can use that for anything."

Tychon shook his head. "We don't even know if he's dead or alive right now. Or if any of them are. What do you know about the rebels here?"

She sipped some of the water he had fetched. "They're taking the others to one of those mountains. There are habitats carved into them. I think the main waterway leads to the one the Arawaj are using. There must be markers or something to help them find their way through this maze."

"How many rebels are there?"

"No idea. Mostly Caspian."

"Armaments? Defense systems? Surveillance?"

She shook her head. "They weren't sharing any of that. I'm guessing that there is a good power source for Lok's little experiments."

"Lok got thrown out of Caspia," Seth supplied. "Likely, they're using the *Abiah* place as living quarters for now. Would take a long time for them to be found here."

Tychon nodded. "Nova and I will try to find the place. If

we can climb up on some of these rocks we should be able to get a direction. You go back to get stitched up. We'll assume that there is a transmitter up there, but there may be others. Find them. See if you can take them out without anyone noticing. Acie might be able to hack into their systems. Let's not start a brawl while the hostages are unaccounted for. Then get out of here and see if you can signal whoever Air Command is sending. With the relay gone you'll have to open the jumpsite yourself before you can send a packet through."

"Yessir," Seth grinned.

Tychon looked startled for a moment. "Sorry." He pointed a thumb at Nova. "I'm used to ordering my crew around."

"You don't want to wait till Air Command gets here?" Seth said.

"No," Nova said. "Some of those civilians are in very bad shape. If we can scout out their location and Arawaj numbers we can plan a proper extraction without wasting more time."

"I am also wondering if Air Command will send anyone at all," Tychon said. "Considering what's going on elsewhere. Our priority is the hostages and that program. It'll be up to you to convince them to give us some backup here."

"And who better," Seth sighed. "I'm one of Air Command's favorite rebels."

NINE

Nova had never felt as small and insignificant as she did when standing near the *Abiah*'s towering entrance. There were no doors; or if there had been they would have been made with unimaginable mechanisms to move something as large as this opening would require. As eroded as the landscape around them, the entrance was a long vertical cleft in the side of the mountain and only a longer look revealed so much more.

She craned her neck to see the remnants of endless stories of windows, ledges that might have been balconies or walkways now fallen away, and recesses of rooms whose external walls had crumbled. The hands of thousands and as many years would have been needed to carve this mountain into a city.

They had approached the *Abiah* from the shelter of the canyons where the stone turrets reached like a petrified forest nearly to its feet. Although they had spent the past few hours taking a circuitous route aboard their sleds to avoid the roving gangs of rebels, no one waited here to challenge them, nothing disturbed the silence of the dead swamps. There were no boats moored at the lake that washed around the far side of the mountain and they saw no air cars or sleds. And yet hundreds of pinpoints of light gleamed in the recesses above them like so many windows. Something beyond the entrance hummed steadily, hinting at some sort of power source or engine. Nova guessed that the planet's geothermal activity created more than enough energy to provide for light and heat. And the transmitter.

"Are they all out looking for me?" she whispered. "I don't even see any sentries."

"They think you're alone. There is no one on this planet but Arawaj, as far as they know. And Kada's peculiar crew." He nodded toward the entrance. "Stay to the left."

She moved ahead of him, her eyes still taking in the age-worn carvings, feeling like some ill-equipped spelunker at the mouth of a stupendously immense cave. The misty light from outside faded as they entered a vast chamber and she slowed to give Tychon a moment to adjust to the gloom. They moved along the stone wall, following a flattened walkway that gradually angled upward.

A lake had settled inside the entrance over time, reflecting some light from above. The water was clear and lifeless and fallen crystal on the bottom sparkled like lost treasure. Tychon looked up, like her astonished by the massive crystals that studded the ceiling here. They seemed illuminated from within, lighting their way upward.

"This is—" Nova stopped abruptly when her whispered words were picked up and echoed around the space like a soft hiss, seemingly returning again and again until they finally faded away. She turned to Tychon who had stopped in his tracks. She tapped her neural interface but he shook his head. Using a khamal now to communicate could easily debilitate him for whatever lay ahead. He gestured for her to continue.

They climbed upward along the perimeter of the chamber. Their path narrowed and they soon had to cling close to the wall, their eyes on the treacherous ground. The embedded crystal reflected glints of light as did the moisture seeping from thousands of pores in the stone, lending movement to the glittering walls as they passed. Like the crumbled landscape around the *Abiah*, the place was in a state of decay dating back for millennia.

Nova nearly cried out in surprise when her foot slipped on a loose shard of crystal. Tychon's grip pressed her against the wall until she recovered. When she looked up at him he exhaled sharply, a question on his face. She nodded her assurance that she was ready to continue.

Cooler air met them after climbing a few minutes further and soon they found openings cut into the rock, leading deeper into the mountain. They stepped off the narrow ledge and into a passage. Here, too, a light source seemed to exude directly from the crystal in the walls.

"I've never seen anything like this," she murmured, reaching up to touch the smoky material. "How can you carve out an entire mountain and still work around the crystal veins like this?"

He crouched to look at the ground. "See that?"

She followed the finger he had extended. The floor of the corridor was strewn with dust and gravel and glittering bits of crystal. Clearly, she saw footprints there, made by those of her kind. The sort that wore shoes. "There," she pointed at one made by a larger foot, this one bare and three-toed. "Caspian."

He nodded. "We're not alone, that is certain."

"These are recent." Some of the tracks were ground into debris through which thin runnels of water seeped, not yet for long enough to distort them.

They continued upward, guns in hand, moving slowly, listening to sounds of movement. There were no voices; only the constant hum, now somewhere below them, accompanied their carefully placed footfalls.

Then they did hear movement. Something was coming toward them from above. They withdrew into a shadowed alcove and waited, barely daring to breathe. Whoever was coming their way carried a light with them and the passage grew brighter. Nova saw the walls more clearly now and gasped when the outlines of time-blurred carvings came into view.

Tychon had felt her sharp intake of breath and followed her gaze to the stone portraits. Whatever had lived here, creating this fortress which was perhaps only one of many on this planet, had not been of their species. These beings, as limited by gravity as they were, had four legs ending in short pincers and as many arms, it seemed. Between those appendages they carried a round torso ending in a tail or perhaps another limb curled under their body. Their heads had either been worn from the carvings by time and water or were perhaps just part of their bodies. This wasn't the first time that Nova was faced by a reminder that her similarity to Tychon, and to the Centauri, the Feydans and even the Caspians could not be mere coincidence.

She was drawn from her observation by the sound of hurried feet approaching. They drew back further when the light reached them and three Caspians moved past at a quick pace and without speaking. The rebels took their light with them down a secondary corridor and the eerie carvings disappeared into the perpetual gloom.

Nova reached out and touched the wall. "Spider people," she whispered.

Tychon, who had never seen a spider until Nova had shown him a picture of one not that long ago, raised an eyebrow. "I'm sure they'd appreciate the comparison." He nudged her to follow the three rebels.

They moved onward, now encountering sets of steps hewn into the stone. Each riser was higher than their knees, offering a hint at the size of the *Abiah*'s ancient builders. Among these stone stairs, dwarfed by high ceilings lost in shadow, Nova again felt like an insect crawling around someone's home. Tychon stopped at every turn to scrape a small marker into the rock with a piece of crystal.

The anguished shriek of a Human in pain echoed through the hallways and was then abruptly cut off. Tychon swung the kit bag from his shoulder and placed it on the ground before they moved toward the sound. There were more voices now; a Caspian laughed, another swore. Nova nodded when Tychon pointed at her gun and then a vein of crystal, clearer and purer than the sooty columns outside the *Abiah*. Neither knew its composition; a reflected beam from their laser could be as deadly as a ricochet off the stone walls from a ballistic weapon.

The next turn opened into a long corridor and revealed the shapes of the Caspians crouched near the end. Too far to approach stealthily, too exposed to reach at a run. Tychon stepped back to let Nova move ahead of him. She used the wall to steady herself, her vision and aim keener than Tychon's in the dimly-lit passage. Her tracer flashed in rapid bursts, finding its targets until all three bodies were on the ground and unmoving.

"Got them," she said.

They approached cautiously, looking for the Human whose cry had brought them here, and found a deep trench at the end of the passage beyond the bodies of the rebels. Tychon took one of their torches, adjusted its range and dropped it into the hole.

"Hey, Leon," Nova said brightly. She was greeted by ghostly faces staring up at her in mute astonishment.

"Thank the Gods!" someone exclaimed. "Get us out, please!"

Tychon let himself drop over the edge of the pit. "Remain quiet. Please stand up, Elder Sister. Assist her, please."

Slowly, the survivors of Dannakor responded to Tychon's calm instructions until they were all on their feet and ready to be boosted, one by one, out of the hole and up to Nova. They freed the fittest first to help pull up those needing more help. Soon, seven tired, dirty and weakened civilians sat on the ground beside the hole, as far from the dead Caspians as possible.

"Should be nine, I think," Nova said.

Tychon crouched over one of the technicians who had not stirred when the others had left the trench. He sighed. "Eight now." He stepped back to the far side of the pit and took a running leap at the edge to haul himself upward and out.

"You can't just leave her down there!"

Tychon bent to put his hand on Doctor Unwin's shoulder. "We'll return. Please keep your voices low. We are not out of danger."

Nova looked around. "Where is Jovan?"

"He went for help."

Tychon muttered something under his breath when he went to fetch the kit bag. They distributed what food and water was left along with the medical supplies. "We're going back to the main corridor," he said. "You will walk quietly between Captain Whiteside and myself. Step carefully on the loose stone." He raised a hand when one of the technicians began to speak. "This isn't an interactive discussion," he continued without changing his tranquil tone. "You will hide where we put you, without speaking, without moving, until we return. You will not try to leave this place on your own. No matter what happens. No matter what you hear." He glanced at Nova. "We do not need any more heroes getting lost in here."

The others nodded half-heartedly.

"Do you know where the Delphian went?" Tychon asked.

Unwin nodded. "Some of the rebels were torturing him. He didn't care much about what they said and then one of them cut his arm to see if it's true that Delphians feel no pain. I told them to stop. I told them it wasn't true. But Jovan didn't seem to care about that, either. Then they told us that Captain Whiteside had been captured and killed. That nobody was coming for us. So we got him out of the hole and he left. The rest of us didn't have the strength to follow him."

"Where did he think he was going?"

"The Caspians talked about a control room above us somewhere. And a transmitter. That's how they know that there aren't any Union ships coming for us. Jovan told me he had a copy of the ANI and wondered if it were possible to still use it to reach Air Command. I showed him how."

"What!" Nova gasped. "When? How?"

Unwin shrugged tiredly. "He's Delphian. His brain can activate the unit as if it was tapped into the neocortex itself. Just like he was able to reach you by touching your ANI, Captain." He looked over to Tychon. "We had hoped that this development would entice more of your people to accept the device, Major. It is another reason we invited Shantir Tuain to join us on Dannakor. For you it would be medically entirely unintrusive."

Nova stared wide-eyed at Tychon. If Jovan found the transmitter, time was no longer on their side.

"I am less enthused about your devices by the moment," Tychon said. "We need to move right now. Everyone please get up and come with us. Quietly. Not a word."

Their progress through the winding passages of the habitat tested Nova's patience as much as her faith in Tychon's ability to keep everyone calm and together. She was reminded to have more confidence in both of these things when, after endless minutes, he turned away from what seemed to be a main artery through a smaller network of rooms and tunnels until the space opened up again around them. Here too, the walls were embellished with graceful carvings as high up as they could see into the shadowed vault above. The extraordinary crystal light source lit their way when Tychon herded their charges into a small alcove.

"This will have to do. We'll leave you with this gun. You can see the entrance from here. Shoot anyone you don't recognize coming down this way."

"This isn't much better than that hole you brought us out of," Doctor Unwin complained.

"Here you have a chance," Tychon said before Nova could snap something at the man. "If we are discovered or if

201

Air Command gets here, you will be the first to suffer for it. At least down here you won't be found as quickly. Now, again, stay here, stay together and don't make a sound. We'll return when we've found Jovan."

Nova hurried ahead of Tychon back through the passages, relieved that they were able to move more quickly now. She touched each of Tychon's scratched markers as they passed them as if for good luck. When they found the main corridor they turned and again headed uphill, hoping for the way to the top of the mountain.

Tychon called a halt when the passage split after what seemed an endless climb. Both ways looked equally well travelled, one slightly wider than the other. The walls here curved inward above their heads to meet in a graceful arch. Patterned friezes decorated both sides, still recognizable for their craftsmanship after all this time.

"This is what I get for lazing around Delphi for weeks at a time," Nova huffed, feeling the strain of the climb in the backs of her legs. "Which way?"

"No idea. I don't even feel any air moving through here." He twisted his shoulders as if to rid himself of some uneasy burden hovering there. "This is too easy. Where is everyone?"

"Probably outside looking for me." Nova pointed to her left. "We go this way."

"Why?"

She touched the wall above his head. "Wires. New ones."

He peered into the gloom and saw the gray conduits snaking over the wall, as foreign and out of place here as both of them felt. They followed the cables, their senses alert to sound and movement in the dark, now moving steeply uphill in a passage that grew more narrow with each turn.

"We must be close to the top by now," Nova said when they paused again. She untied her hair to catch it up into a thick knot.

"Shh," Tychon put his hand on her arm. After a moment he tipped his chin into the direction they were heading.

"Voices up there."

They warily approached a sharp bend. The light was brighter here and seemed more like daylight. When Nova peered carefully around the corner she saw that they had, indeed, reached a high point of the edifice. Here, the stone had been carved into soaring pillars that met high over their heads. Slabs of crystal that distorted the view of the broken landscape filled the spaces between them. Some of the crystal had cracked over time and a breeze moved through the space, chilling her at once. Outside, beyond the crystal windows, a flat outcropping of rock might have served as a viewing platform before much of it had crumbled away.

This was where the power cables had led from whatever was humming far below them. They snaked to a control panel positioned awkwardly on broken blocks of stone and from there to the apex of the chamber. The serenity of the ancient structure only underscored the temporary, makeshift arrangement.

Nova grasped all this in seconds. What really drew her attention was Jovan standing in the middle of the room, a gun held in both hands and aimed at Sao Lok.

"You're not going to shoot me, boy," Lok said. "I've watched you for days. It's not in you."

"Step away from that board," Jovan said. His voice was strained although tightly controlled. The clothes that had done so well to compliment his graceful body were stained and torn. There was a deep scrape along his arm and his hair was carelessly gathered at his nape with a strip of cloth. "I won't tell you again."

A smile appeared on Lok's narrow face when he saw Nova step into the arched doorway. He raised his hands. "All right. Don't shoot," he said to Jovan without the slightest hint of fear in his voice. "I'll have to activate the transmitter. Then you can use it."

"Stop!" Nova called out. "Don't touch that, Jovan."

The young Delphian froze but did not look at her. "We need to warn Air Command!"

"Give the interface to me," Tychon said.

Jovan turned at the sound of Tychon's voice. "Shan Tychon!" he gasped.

Nova stepped around him and raised her gun to Sao Lok.

He smiled at her, wrinkling his nose in the process. It looked nearly sincere. "I had every confidence you'd find one of my transmitters, Captain. But I'm amazed that Major Tychon has managed to track you to Gramor. You are indeed resourceful."

Jovan lowered his gun and reached into a pocket to withdraw the small disk. He took a step toward Tychon and then, as if afraid to approach any closer, held his hand out to him. Tychon took the interface and dropped it to the ground where he blasted it with his pistol.

Sao Lok gave a tittering laugh. "Thank you, Major," he said.

"You find something funny here, Arawaj?"

"That interface you destroyed had only limited access. It would have sent my program to a few fighter pilots, shuttles, cargo transports perhaps. A waste of my efforts but better than nothing at all. But you do not disappoint and here you are." His yellow eyes lit on Nova's temple. "Now you have no choice but to use Captain Whiteside's unit."

"I have no intention of using it, Lok," Nova said. "I know what it does. Is this what you had in mind when you asked me to join you? Did you really think I would help you destroy the fleet?"

"I'm an idealist. But you yourself said that you would give your life if that meant peace for everyone else. Is that not also true of your fellow Union soldiers? Your pilots and agents? Would they not also want these wars to end even if their lives paid the price?"

"I can't speak for them."

"What if I told you that your signal will also reach just about any Union-built ship in the rebel fleet? By now I am guessing that most of their craft are also in the air."

Nova frowned. "Your program can do that?"

"Indeed. This will mean the end of the Shri-Lan. Just imagine! I can see that you're tempted by that possibility."

"You don't know me at all," she said.

The gentle and reasonable expression on Sao Lok's face changed to show them someone who has reached the end of his willingness to be either gentle or reasonable. "Then I suppose it was wise of me to add a little more incentive to the plan for you, thanks to our Shri-Lan friends." He looked over to Jovan. "Tell them, boy."

"Delphi," Jovan said. His voice shook with anger and fear. "They are going to hit Delphi. Within hours."

Nova felt the blood drain from her extremities and staggered backward when her legs threatened to give out. She could not possibly have heard those words just now. She turned, thinking that she might faint, to see Tychon equally stunned by this revelation. "Is this true?" she whispered.

"It is," Lok said. "It took very little to convince Rakh to start testing their new toy on Delphi. Obviously, they're not going to get much further than that."

"So you know that the ANI is useless for keyholing? That the jump there will likely kill Betl? And you didn't tell Rakh?"

"Of course not. He'd have his people choose a more strategic target. Please understand me, Captain. I truly wanted you to see the rightness of what I'm trying to do. For all of us. And for a moment I thought I had you convinced. You thought about it, I know." He shook his head, apparently saddened by his failure to sway her. "I may be an idealist but one must plan for all possible outcomes. And so Delphi will be what motivates you to make the right choice."

Tychon strode across the room and pushed the Caspian against a crystal wall already veined with long cracks, a dangerous snarl on his bloodless lips. "Disable that program."

"That isn't going to happen, Major. And I, unlike your noble Union agents, it seems, am willing to die for my cause."

Tychon looked angry enough to push the Caspian

through the hazy window. But he let him go with the barest shove. None of them here had the skills to amend the program, undoubtedly coded to Lok's touch.

Nova shook her head, trying to understand. "This can't be happening. We have to end this!" She moved to the control board.

Tychon grasped her arm. "Wait."

"What's there to think about?" she cried, trying to shake him off. "My baby is on Delphi!"

He pulled her close to prevent her from reaching the board. She struggled briefly before slumping in his arms.

"That's so touching," Sao Lok marveled. He swept his hand dramatically toward the control panel. "How many Delphians are there? A fragile population of perhaps three million. You can save them by giving up a few thousand Air Command lives and resetting the balance of power in this sector. That's not such a poor trade, is it?" He tilted his head to smile at Nova. "Imagine: instant peace among the stars! How does it feel to have such power, Captain?"

She lunged at him, prevented from attacking by Tychon's grip on her arms. "I am going to tear your face off, Lok."

He waved his six-fingered hand, dismissing her threat. "We all die, Captain. Are you going to let your child die while you live a little longer?" His eyes shifted to Tychon. "And are you going to allow the Shri-Lan to destroy your people? They will target the Valley and the city first. There is nothing your pitiful Union base on Delphi can do once the Shri-Lan keyhole into their air space. How typical of Delphi arrogance to think that we cannot touch you. It was just a matter of time. Today's lesson will be painful."

Nova looked up at Tychon when he slowly released her arms. She had never seen him so completely out of his depth, so utterly doubtful. His people had never, as a race, taken up arms against anyone. Delphi was perpetually at peace, perpetually neutral, trading its plentiful resources to ensure the Union's protection against the Union's enemies. The population, concentrated in just one area of the planet, might never recover from an all-out rebel attack. She felt his apprehension and rage like heat radiating from him.

But what would happen to them if the Union as well as the rebel fleets were gutted of their pilots and operators? It would take years to replace them all. And who would rise to power then, and where would that leave Delphi? Where would it leave the other planets that had come to rely on the Commonwealth for peace and prosperity?

And what about her own daughter?

Being Delphian and being Tychon meant that he had never compelled her to yield to his wants and he would not do so now. This was no longer an Air Command operation and he was not her superior officer now. She wanted to shake him, to demand that he, just this once, tell her what to do.

She looked around the room looking for some answer written among the ancient carvings in the stone. Her eyes lingered on the inactive control panel for a moment and then followed the cables up to the apex of the dome.

"Why are you doing this, Lok?" she said tonelessly as she walked to the control panel. She hesitated before activating the transmitter and chose the coordinates for the jumpsite leading away from Gramor. All of them heard a mechanical buzz when the transmitter above them adjusted to the planet's current angle. She returned to Tychon's side with a meaningful look upward. His brows twitched as he tried to discern her intent. "Stop this madness," she added.

"Madness? It's brilliant! I only meant for you to cause a little damage before your people complete the ANI which will undoubtedly prevent innovations such as mine. But when the Shri-Lan joined the party I realized the true potential for a decisive strike against the Union. How could I resist turning this into the greatest battle that never took place?"

"Enough of this," a harsh voice cut through the silence that followed Lok's words.

Five Caspians moved into the crystal dome, guns in hand.

Out of habit and training, Nova stepped away from Tychon to spread out their target.

"Leave this to me, Vir Khoja," Lok said to the woman who had spoken. Her luxuriantly gleaming hide bore the stripes of Caspia's northern region, the dominant sector of their planet.

Nova heard Tychon stifle a groan.

Khoja ignored Lok's objection. "Send your signal, Human," she said in heavily accented Union mainvoice. "End this. We have other business."

Nova shook her head. They needed more time! "There has to be another way."

The Caspian looked to the younger Delphian standing silently nearby, utterly shaken and confused by these events. "This is what your Union brought you, Delphi. And this Union agent is going to let your planet be destroyed, along with her own young, just so that the mighty Air Command does not suffer defeat. This is what you ally yourself with!"

Jovan swallowed. "What other business?"

"We did not kill your mate," Tychon said. "Although I don't suppose it makes any difference now, does it?"

"None." Her cold smile did not touch her eyes. "Watching you destroy your own clan would satisfy us completely, but that is not why we are here. We want to see the end of Centauri dominance of your Union and that goal is in sight now. You will launch that program at your fleet, save your planet and then face our retribution for Pe Khoja's loss."

"Pe Khoja was a murdering psychopath!" Nova hissed. "He deserved what he got!"

"By your measure, Human. His mates, his children, did not deserve it." She nodded to the control board. "Have you made your choice, then?"

All of them started when an ear-piercing shriek rang through the countless passages of the *Abiah*. It echoed eerily, seeming to multiply as it rang through the mountain's crystal veins, taken up by another shriek before it finally died down.

Excited shouts reached them in the language of Caspia.

"A plane approaches eastwards. Not one that belongs to our people."

Nova, as the least surprised of all of them, immediately aimed her weapon at Vir Khoja and fired. Tychon was not far behind and shot another of the Caspians before flinging himself behind some of the stone blocks scattered throughout the space. Nova whirled to take out a third and then moved to Lok.

But the Caspian had already rushed to where Jovan still stood. He snatched the gun from the youth's hand and jammed it under his jaw. "Back," he hissed at his hostage. "In there!" He forced Jovan toward one of the side passages.

"Jovan!" Nova cried. She ducked a projectile that shot past her to shatter a massive pane of crystal. Razor shards rained down on her and smashed into smaller bits on the ground. She felt blood trickling where one scraped along her cheek. Tychon shot two of Khoja's followers and the rest were driven back into the shelter of the corridor.

More battle cries rose from the depths of the *Abiah* as the rebels were alerted to the crisis in the dome. Distantly, answering calls rose from the crystal canyons.

Another shriek stabbed her ears, this one much closer. Nova turned to see Jovan's hands clasped around Sao Lok's head as if he meant to crush it. His expression was utterly devoid of emotion while something ghastly was taking place in the Caspian's brain. After a long, terrible moment, Jovan dropped the lifeless body.

Nova rushed over to him. "What did you do? What was that?"

Tychon picked up a piece of broken stone column and heaved it at another of the crystal panes. It shattered to open the way onto the crumbled platform ringing the dome. He stepped outside to search the horizon, apparently not troubled by what had just happened.

"You said your people couldn't do that!" Nova shouted to him. She turned back to Jovan who stood over Sao Lok's body with terror and awe written on his face. He looked at his hands and slowly balled them into fists.

Tychon came back inside and grasped the youth's arm. "He's a Shantir, Nova." He aimed past her to take down a Centauri rebel that had appeared at the opening to the passage. Those that followed held back now, unwilling to enter the open space between the entrance and their quarry. "Come on!"

Still mystified by what had just happened, Nova ran past them and out onto the platform. A cruiser swooped into view from the other side of the mountain. "Is that the *Dutchman*?" She fired her laser into the air to draw his attention, wagering the rest of their otherwise very short lives that this was Seth and not another rebel plane. He came about and directed a volley of his own at the top of the dome. Something impacted up there and then they heard a loud crash as a construct of twisted metal, formerly a transmitter, crashed through the crystal roof to shatter on the floor.

Tychon motioned for Seth to hover near the platform outside the dome.

"You're not serious!" Nova shouted over the noise of the plane. The *Dutchman*'s airlock door slid aside to reveal Vincent, waving frantically.

"Just don't look down," Tychon advised. He pulled Jovan forward. "Can you do this?"

Vincent had spotted some of the rebels now inside the dome and laid some covering fire, using bright tracers to keep the laser going to the correct target.

"Jovan!" Tychon grasped the youth's collar as if to shake him. "Come on!"

Jovan blinked, startled out of whatever had claimed his attention.

Nova stepped closer to the edge of the platform when a piece of it crumbled under her feet. She threw herself back just before it fell away and tumbled into the depths below. "Damn plane used to have a ramp. Where is the ramp?"

"Careful," Vincent shouted. "The ledge is paper-thin. You'll have to jump!"

Nova dared not to ponder this proposition for any length of time. She glanced quickly at Tychon and then back at the ship hovering beside the platform. Vincent raised his arms. She ran. She jumped. Her shin collided painfully with the edge of the door and then she was inside, helped by Vincent's strong hands. Acie was behind him and dragged Nova farther into the hold.

"Ty!" Nova shouted and turned back.

Tychon nudged Jovan ahead. More agile than she would have thought, he leaped at the opening and landed on both feet just inside the portal. He tumbled aside at once to make room for Tychon in the small space.

Tychon turned when one of the pillars supporting the dome's roof collapsed behind him, bringing down more shards of crystal. Nova joined Vincent in firing at some of the rebels, holding them back to give Tychon more time. She knew that Seth's view of the platform was limited to a few camera angles when he moved the ship further along the platform, away from the now heavily damaged area. The ship briefly made contact with the edge and, feeling that, he pulled away before more pieces broke off.

"Now," Vincent yelled. "Jump!"

Tychon did, just as one of the rebels stepped out onto the platform and took aim. A bullet tore into his thigh as he leaped and Nova screamed when he missed and only one foot landed on the bottom frame of the *Dutchman*'s gate. Flailing, he managed to grasp an intake valve and now clung to the ship's exterior beside the door. A laser impacted only a handspan from his extended arms and Vincent answered. The rebel tumbled off the platform and into the Deeps.

"Seth!" Acie yelled into the ship's interior. "Turn the plane! But don't go anywhere."

Seth responded by rotating the plane to offer only its hull to the enemy's fire. Now there was nothing below Tychon but the distant and jagged crystal spires. Nova looked outside to see that his leg was bleeding profusely. She refused to look down. "He's not going to make it till we can land somewhere."

Jovan pulled her back. "Hang on to me," he said, shouting against the wind whistling through the cargo space. Nova grasped his arm while Vincent hooked his hand into Jovan's waist band. Acie clung to Vincent's vest, more out of fear than any ability to keep the large Human from being pulled outside along with the rest of them.

Jovan leaned far out of the gate and reached out to Tychon who wasted no time in worrying about the likely outcome of the offer. Their hands locked around each other's wrist and then he released the valve to swing into the ship, crashing all of them to the floor.

Nova rolled over to him. "Are you okay?" she asked breathlessly.

Tychon gaped at her for a moment before laughing, even as he grimaced in pain. "Go," he said. "Hurry."

She scrambled to her feet once she saw that Acie had pressed her hand firmly over the spurting wound on Tychon's leg.

"All aboard?" Seth asked when she leaped into the cockpit.

"Did any of the Air Command ships arrive yet?"

"Not a single one. Busy, I guess. So I thought I'd start smashing transmitters. I want to point out that it's a whole lot easier to find a transmitter when it's actually turned on."

"That's what I thought. Do I still have command level access to this plane?"

"Just like you left it."

Nova connected her ANI to the *Dutchman*, likely the only transmitter on this planet not tainted by Lok's kill switch program. She leaned on the com console as if pressing her hands against the smooth surface could improve the connection. Without the packet relays destroyed by Rakh on his way to Pelion, the only way to reach anyone outside this sub-sector was to use the ANI as it had been designed.

"There it is," she whispered when the *Dutchman* located the jumpsite. There was no need to widen the breach by very much. Carefully, she directed the processors to probe the void. She tried a few of the mapped terminals until the ship made contact. "I think I've got it," she said. "There's a ship out there! We've got us an Air Command ship!" As in the lab on Dannakor, she requested and was instantly granted access to link her systems to the distant carrier. From there, the ANI used the communications system to interface with the ship's operator.

"Hear me," she said. "Don't be alarmed. You will not be able to reply," she spoke aloud to keep her thoughts organized and to let the others hear her message. "Contact Air Command immediately, closed band, top priority. The Shi-Lan attack is on Delphi. I repeat: Imminent enemy incursion directed at Delphi, likely from Pelion." She repeated the message to make sure that whomever she had just utterly frightened by this apparently telepathic message hadn't fallen off their chair. To many of her fellow pilots, the ANI concept was still only a distant possibility. "Secondly, requesting a hostage extraction on Gramor Bejo. Hostages are in danger, so spare us a spanner and get here immediately." She hesitated a moment and then winked at Seth. "And then send this message to Targon: Captain Nova Whiteside reporting for duty. Eventually." Nova dropped her link to the ship and collapsed into the *Dutchman*'s co-pilot bench.

Seth turned to look at his passengers as they staggered into the main cabin, taking in Jovan's torn and filthy clothing, Nova's bloodied face and tangled mass of hair, Tychon's bleeding bullet wound. "So where are the others?"

EPILOGUE

"You're not hiding, are you?" Nova said softly when she finally found Tychon reclining in one of the rooms overlooking the verdant fields of his clan's estate. His faraway eyes told her that he was deeply immersed in a khamal, likely one used by Delphians to heal their bodies, and she stroked his cheek until he blinked slowly. He shifted his arm when she laid down beside him, carefully avoiding his injured leg. "Weren't you going to join us?"

"It's so peaceful here," he said.

She had to agree. Two of the walls of this room were made entirely of windows, now flung open to allow Delphi's cool breezes to waft through the room, bringing with them the smell of the fields and trees outside. Gauzy curtains moved hypnotically, creating a play of shadows over the tiled floor. It was Nova's favorite retreat, a soft and feminine space in her often hard-edged world and she had not expected to find him here.

"I just talked to Acie and Anders. He said to come by tomorrow, before they leave for Shaddallam."

Tychon's lips curved in a smile. "What's going on with those two?"

Nova grinned back at him. "What do you think?"

"And Vincent is allowing that? Anders is... well, you

know. Anders."

Nova reached up to push a long strand of his hair behind his ear. "She's got Vincent around her little finger. As long as she's happy, so is he."

Tychon nodded contemplatively. "She's safer with Anders than risking her neck with the likes of Sethran Kada."

"He saved all of our necks," she reminded him. "That was a bad spot we were in."

"Yes, it was. Let me know if there are any more scruffy ex-boyfriends that are useful."

She poked his chest. "Not jealous, are you?" she teased.

He turned to her and slipped his hand under her blouse. She purred happily when he leaned over to kiss her. "You're here, aren't you?" he said. "With me."

She returned his kiss but stopped him when his fingers strayed to the waistband of the sheer skirt she wore over her tights. "We're busy this afternoon, remember?"

He sighed. "I was hoping to make you forget that."

"Come on, get up." She helped him swing his legs over the edge of the lounger and put his feet on the floor. "Carras is already here. He's waiting in the garden."

Tychon grumbled when she handed him the cane he was using for now. Acie had removed the bullet from his thigh even before they had returned home but the damage was extensive and would take time to heal. The rebel attack on Delphi had already been averted when they arrived but several squadrons of planes were still deployed, nearly hostile when Seth's response to their inquiries was not to their liking. Eventually, the *Dutchman* was allowed to land and medics stood by the airfield to whisk them away to the base hospital.

By the time they were released from there Seth had already left without revealing a destination to anyone, no doubt to avoid lengthy farewells and, Nova suspected, the even longer debrief the rest of them had to undergo before Air Command had their notes organized. Nova had not expected him to announce his intentions but Acie had been in tears over his sudden departure. Anders, immediately enamored by the quirky and sweet-natured Bellac, had managed to divert her attention, much to Vincent's relief.

Colonel Carras was relaxing in the shaded arbor of the compound's inner courtyard when they joined him there, chatting amiably with an aunt and one of the staff members. They excused themselves to leave the three alone over a platter of Delphian delicacies and pitchers of water flavored by local fruit and herbs.

"How's the leg, Ty?" Carras said, pouring for Nova when she held out her cup.

"Mending," he replied.

"It would mend faster in the enclave."

Tychon looked up sharply. "You're here for the boy, Tal," he reminded the Colonel, not unkindly.

"So I am. How are things here on Delphi?"

"Tense," Nova said. "I think the Clan Council has learned a lesson, although they're not likely to admit it. There will be a great deal of hand-wringing and debating before they'll allow an expansion of the base. Phera will rant and carry on and then they'll concede to the traffic monitors. I imagine that no plane will be allowed to land here unless it's on the base. It's doubtful that they'll permit more relays but Ty figures they'll spring for the additional satellites in orbit."

"Anders has been busy!" Carras said.

Tychon nodded. "He knows how to work on both sides of the fence."

"Any chance of Delphi actually joining the Common-wealth?"

"Not even a little."

"Hmm, yes, well." Carras picked a sprig of fruit from the platter. "Perhaps that's for the best. What's going to happen with the ANI? I see Nova has gone back to yesterday's model."

"It's been set back by years. I think they've realized that it's too much of a good thing," Tychon said with a lopsided grin. "Too many vulnerabilities that come with it. Too easily exploited."

Nova sipped her water. "The day will come when we master those keyholes," she said. "But maybe we'll take some time to boost our defenses. It'll change everything." She glanced at Tychon. "Tuain knew that. All of the Shantirs know that."

"From what I've heard," Tychon continued. "None of the ANI developers are interested in continuing on the project. Especially not those that lived through Gramor Bejo."

"How many survived?"

"Eight of the ones that ended up on Rakh's ship," Nova sighed. "Out of dozens we took away from Dannakor." It was only a small consolation to her that Rakh's cruiser, with all hands aboard, had been destroyed by the Vanguard squadron the moment it emerged over Delphi. Spanners at every keyhole in Union territory had opened a passage to Delphi when Nova's message had reached Targon and hundreds of Air Command ships had arrived within hours. A defensive net in Delphi's air space, focused over the Chaliss'ya valley, ensured that few of the enemy craft made it anywhere near the surface. The Shri-Lan sustained quick and devastating losses before calling off the incursion. Nova gazed past the pretty arbor to the snow-peaked mountains at the edge of the valley, looking as constant and protective as they always had. Nothing ever seemed to disturb the peace here and few of Delphi's civilians were even aware of what had occurred.

"The Arawaj got tossed out of Gramor," Tychon added. "There weren't many left, so it didn't take long for the other hostages to be found. The archeologists can return now, I suppose. It's a remarkable place."

One of the staff members came into the courtyard to announce their visitor. Behind him followed Jovan, looking shyly around the well-kept estate. His steps faltered when he saw them gathered in the shade. Tychon had spent the trip back to Delphi deep in a pain-blocking khamal, oblivious to them all, and Jovan had still not overcome his awe of the officer.

"Jovie!" Nova called to him. "Come join us."

A flush of color filled his cheeks, quickly hidden by his hair when he bent to sit down. She was glad that he had not dressed in the Shantir novice's robe, nor the trendy garb he had when they first met over Dannakor. He was dressed simply in well-cut trousers and a long vest over his blouse. "I'm please to see you, Elder Sister."

"Welcome, Jovan," Tychon said. "We want you to meet Colonel Carras."

Jovan turned to the retired Colonel. "I'm grateful that you came to see me," he said.

"I came to take you with me," Carras corrected genially. "I've secured a place for you at one of our flight academies. For a Delphian, thirty-two is not too late to begin. It's on Magra but there are always transports travelling to there, so you really won't be too far from home."

Jovan stared, speechless.

"It's not Air Command and you won't be asked to join the military. But you will learn aviation and you can study whatever they don't teach you at the enclave. Languages, exo-sciences, politics. We are always glad to have another Delphian among us."

Even Tychon smiled when he saw the undisguised joy on the youth's face. "It is up to you to decide if you wish to return to the Shantir enclave," he said. "They have no objections to letting you go."

Jovan looked into Nova's beaming face. "This is very generous of you. All of you."

She put her hand on his. "I'm still alive because of you, Jovie. A lot of people are. You are capable of so much; it's time for you to find out what you can do."

He shook his head. "I don't know. I was just scared the whole time."

"That's a good way to be, son," Carras said. "It tends to

keep you alive."

Tychon studied Jovan carefully. "Are you recovered? It was harrowing for all of us."

Jovan nodded but his eyes were on his hands. Taught to be a healer and a mental adept, he had used his gifts to kill; surely a tremendous shock for the young initiate. "The Shantirs have declared me well." He hesitated before meeting Tychon's eyes. "They send a message, Elder Brother. They are asking you to come to the enclave. To receive healing, nothing more."

Tychon glanced at Nova's hopeful and curious face. "I see that Nova has found yet another ally in her schemes."

Jovan stood his ground. "Will you accept?"

"I have a message for the Shantirs," Tychon said.

Nova winced, waiting for whatever cutting remark he was about to convey.

"We'll make a deal," Tychon said. "If the Shantirs will go to the Council and voice their support of Nova's rightful place on Delphi as my wife and accept our daughter as Delphian I may consider a visit." He looked around the astonished faces. "With Cyann."

Nova jumped up and wrapped her arms around his neck, not sure if she was happier because of his willingness to make amends with the Shantirs of Delphi or his somewhat peculiar marriage proposal. It didn't matter. "I so love you, Ty!" she said and kissed him noisily.

He hummed and pretended pain in his leg to return her to her seat. "Yes, well, we'll see how they do," he said with a glance at the other two men. He focused on Jovan. "Mind this, though: I will have no talk about my son."

Jovan leaned forward, about to voice some opinion when he saw Nova's nearly imperceptible gesture of caution. He sat back again. "I am certain my brothers will respect your wishes, Shan Tychon."

Carras pushed his chair back from the table. "And so young Jovan and I will make our way to the enclave. A few things to organize and you're on your way to Magra, Jovan.

What wonderful excitement lies in store for you!"

"Wait," Nova said. "I want Jovie to meet Cyann!" She hurried into the breezeway to the garden and called for Pryca to bring the girl. The nurse was already prepared for this and emerged with a well-rested and fed baby. Cyann babbled happily and lifted her hands toward her mother. Nova took her into her arms and returned to the garden.

"Here she is," she announced. "Doesn't she look just like Tychon?"

"She does not!" Tychon declared at once. "Thankfully."

Jovan looked up, uncomfortable with having a two-year old thrust at him but bravely accepted the child when Nova sat her on his lap. "She is sweet," he said dutifully, admiring the pretty little face and the fluff of blue curls. She laughed up at him and he was struck by the deep blue of her eyes. His smile faded. "Gods," he whispered, barely forming the word.

"What is it?" Tychon said at once.

Jovan could not take his eyes away from the child. "She..." he began. "There is..."

"Jovie?" Nova said, startled by the expression on his face.

The youth raised his hand and then stopped it to look at Tychon, a question on his face. After a thoughtful moment, Tychon nodded. Jovan cupped the baby's head in his hand and closed his eyes.

"Ty..." Nova said nervously.

He took her hand and said nothing.

Cyann stopped wriggling and looked up at Jovan's face. He opened his eyes again. Another moment passed while they regarded each other silently. "They were right," he murmured. He seemed utterly unaware of any of them.

"About what?" Nova said.

Jovan blinked, startled from his thoughts. "She's Delphian, in all ways that matter. I pledge my liege, Shan Tychon."

Nova looked from one Delphian to the other. "Pledge my liege? What does that mean? Why do we need liege pledging?"

Tychon tilted his head. "So it will be, then," he said. He turned to Nova. "As my affinity is to Phera, so this boy has asked to join our house."

She looked to Jovan, astonished. "What? Why?"

"The reasons are his own. But it is a life-long commitment that will not be broken."

Nova looked from Jovan to the child on his lap, aware that she had missed something very important. Something very Delphian that she might never understand. But over these past few weeks she had come to know Jovan in ways people rarely saw each other. Her trust in him was absolute and her faith in his future unshakable. If nothing else, she thought, perhaps this was one small way for Tychon to regain the son he had lost.

But for a moment she had seen something else in Jovan's eyes. When he had touched Cyann's mind he had found something there that astonished him. Something important enough for him to pledge his life to her clan. She glanced at Tychon, her mate, and wondered if he had seen that, too.

"She will be a beauty, I'm sure," Jovan said. "With a brain to match, just like her mother."

Cyann grabbed his nose with a gleeful squeal, startling him.

"That maddening curiosity she also gets from her mother," Tychon said.

Chris Reher

ABOUT THE AUTHOR

Chris Reher is a first generation Canadian currently and out of necessity residing on planet Earth (which, in the general and interplanetary scheme of things, could *really* use a catchier name. Imagine heading past Proxima Centauri and someone asks you whence you came and you tell them "dirt". All theological implications aside, that just won't do.)

When not finding ways to defy the laws of physics or torture her subjects or entice them with inter-species hanky-panky, she designs web sites or writes about designing web sites. She enjoys long walks on the beach or, given the local beach shortage, writes about beaches far beyond Proxima Centauri.

www.chrisreher.com

Also by Chris Reher

The Catalyst

Only Human

Delphi Promised

The Gods of Chenoweth